Minx

'Perhaps confinement and punishment excite me in ways whose mysteries I do not know,' said Amy to her maid. 'It's a shame there is no man at hand to give it to me. Where are they when you need them? Never available, that I know. Never available with their hearts and never available with their cocks.'

She was thinking of the elusive Ralph when she said this, for it had not, in truth, been her experience to suffer many unavailable men. Men had always wanted to ravage Amy Pringle. However, as a consummate minx it was her prerogative to turn her head the other way – to pretend that she did not see them clamouring with need, passion and devotion.

Minx

MEGAN BLYTHE

BLACK
lace

Black Lace novels contain sexual fantasies.
In real life, make sure you practise safe sex.

First published in 2001 by
Black Lace
Thames Wharf Studios,
Rainville Road, London W6 9HA

Typeset by SetSystems Ltd, Saffron Walden, Essex
Printed and bound by Mackays of Chatham PLC

ISBN 0 352 33638 2

Chapter One

The household of Lancaster Hall had long prepared for the arrival of Miss Amy Pringle. The arrangements made to meet her approval and to prepare for her comfort had been extensive, expensive and extravagant. The Earl of Hacclesfield had ordered the freshest flowers to be brought in from the greenhouses and they had been arranged in exuberant showers of foliage in the halls and corridors. The orchards had sacrificed apples and pears. His last three apricots, a composite of three perfect and rare fruits, were designated to pride of place in a glass bowl in the bedroom of the lady herself.

The 'blue' room was a luxurious boudoir on the second floor. Refurbished and redecorated for the comfort of Miss Pringle, it now boasted blue damask walls, heavy velvet curtains of cream and gold, a four-poster bed wrought in carved wood picked out with gold leaf, and some treasured polished wood cabinets on which the newest Wedgewood china had been placed. The ceiling was a fresco of saints and angels flying in a rococo motif of swirling clouds and floating grapes. It

1

had taken the artist Upton Lovell a year to complete this saga of excessive pageantry and it had cost Lord Hacclesfield what is commonly known as a 'pretty penny'.

There was a comfortable day bed, made from the wrought iron that was becoming *à la mode*, and a harpsichord on which Lord Hacclesfield hoped that Miss Pringle would practise the music that she was said to enjoy and which was so appropriate to a young lady of her social standing. Young ladies, in his view, were simple enough. Their only purpose in life was to display their accomplishments in order to obtain a position of marriage. Accomplishments were the thing; little arty talents that could please a man and make him feel calm. If a pleasant singing voice was accompanied by a demure presence and obliging manner, no squire could ask for more. Lord Hacclesfield's mind's eye enjoyed the thought of innocent Miss Pringle's shining locks bent over her instrument as she picked out the melodies of Henry Purcell with delicate feminine fingers whose graceful pallor demonstrated the exquisite emblem of noble excellence and whose very daintiness made a man feel like a man.

The harpsichord was not the most important asset won by the visitor who stayed in the 'blue' room. The advantage of the 'blue' was not so much in the luxury of its rich furbishings as the view from the windows. The room was known to provide one of the best aspects in the house. Its vistas were even more spectacular than those enjoyed by the chambers of Lord Hacclesfield's sons, Ralph and Bubb. Indeed, Bubb enjoyed a rather poor show, over the servants' quarters, to be exact, where his daily scenarios showed several washing lines, the doings of those employed to place garments on the washing lines, and the arrivals of lowly tradespeople whose business it was to deliver

2

candles or cotton or to offer their services in the skills of knife sharpening or bird plucking or tincture making.

Bubb never complained, but there it was. Everybody else looked over roses or mazes or lily ponds. He saw butchers and gardeners. The views presented by the 'blue' room alerted no mundane agitation. The windows stretched almost from floor to ceiling so they bathed the chamber with the full glory of the morning light and afforded a magnificent view to the empire that was Lord Hacclesfield's huge estate.

This spectacle revealed itself in a panorama of landscaped lawns, tended mazes, grottoes and follies which stretched to stables and water meadows, outhouses and farmhouses, tenants' buildings and then beyond to the endless tapestry of greens and browns that made the Derbyshire landscape.

The person who looked out of this window would know one certain truth: every tree, cottage, flower-bed and stream – everything as far as the eye could see – was owned by the third Earl of Hacclesfield. The motivations that compelled Lord Hacclesfield to make immaculate presentations to herald the arrival of Miss Amy Pringle were not vulgar in their intent. He was not filled with the need for ostentation (heaven forbid!). Or even to impress. He certainly did not need to impress Miss Amy Pringle – the Hacclesfield family tree stretched back to 1310 while the money of her family had arrived very recently from a line of distilleries. Her late father's title (such as it was) was relatively new, having been created by George III, and its prestige was undermined by the fact that that particular royalty had taken to talking to trees as if they were the King of Prussia.

The Earl of Hacclesfield was imbued with a basic pride in his position and in the responsibilities that

3

ineluctably arrived with old money. The Hacclesfield family was the richest in Yorkshire and Derbyshire and their properties ran well into the borders of both counties. No other host was so well equipped to provide entertainment and luxury. An invitation to Lancaster Hall was a much coveted thing, desired by all walks of life. Balls, soirées, card games, musical evenings, theatrical events – all were talked about for weeks. Lord Hacclesfield wished to keep it that way. The prestige of a family was important: to promote the glamour of one's own cause was to ensure confidence and sustain credit.

In regard to Miss Pringle herself, Lord Hacclesfield's intent was not to impress so much as impose. The redoubtable peer wanted to ensure that Miss Pringle moved in an environment built to his own construct and composed entirely of his own device whose effect would be to encourage her to appreciate the opportunities that she was being given.

He also wished to communicate the faultless taste that was inherent to the family mien, to advertise their breeding and to imbue a sense of the inimitable dignity that arrives with class. He intended to provide a goal to which the young woman could aspire, and encourage the natural gratitude that must arise in the heart of anyone on whom glamorous civilities and generous gifts are bestowed.

In other words, the third Earl of Hacclesfield wanted to keep Miss Amy Pringle in her place. The arrangement made to marry Miss Pringle to Lord Hacclesfield's son, Viscount (Ralph) Fitzroy, was the result of a finely balanced business decision that benefited both parties with rewards that were beautiful in their unarguable logic.

Lord Hacclesfield saw Miss Pringle's nuptial fee as an indispensable addition to a fortune whose founda-

4

tion, though stable, did not allow him to make the entrepreneurial business investments that he longed to pursue in India and Africa. He did not wish to destabilise the legacy left to him by his progenitors, but he did want to gamble. Miss Pringle's dowry – a sum of £20,000 – was a stake that could be used to make daring investments in foreign lands, lands which were making other men rich, and which could make him richer.

Miss Pringle's dowry, then, was much the same as the pile of chips that a player takes to a gaming table. It had been acquired purely to provide recreation for Lord Hacclesfield as his twilight years drew in and the task of the running of the estate slipped slowly into the hands of his sons.

The proposed marital liaison had come about as a result of a sad tragedy that had blighted Lancaster Hall with the shroud of death. Ralph Fitzroy had been happily married for two years to Lady Miranda (*née* Keeble), whose family owned the lands that ran alongside the borders of the Hacclesfield estate. The match had been one of love as well as mutual advantage, but Lady Miranda had been carried away by smallpox at the age of 25, leaving her widowed husband without a son and with a weight of grief that still burdened him. Lady Miranda had been loved by all. Her loss had been a dreadful blow that still left a space in all domestic activities. Something was missing and everyone felt it.

Ralph still stared at the place that she had once filled, opposite him, at the dining table. He had grown thin and gaunt and the family were worried about him. Lord Hacclesfield's decision to re-enter the marriage market was motivated as much by concern for Ralph's mental health as it was by the attraction of remuneration.

The benefits to Miss Pringle, meanwhile, were so obvious that it is almost an insult to the intelligence of the reader to offer up a detailed outline. In brief, though, the situation was as follows.

Her marriage to Lord Fitzroy would provide her with a title, a requisite that she did not currently possess: she would become chatelaine of Lancaster Hall and her children would be part of a dynasty that counted a prime minister, a herald extraordinary and several pursuivants amongst its number.

It was also a dynasty that had engendered several individuals of a more louche disposition: Highworth Chalgrove, for instance, a notorious bounder and ravager of women; the poet Hinton, voyeur, flagellant and catamite; Lady St Aubyn, (Arabella) an adventuress who enjoyed being tied down to the billiard table and violated by any members of the gilded aristocracy who happened to be staying at the hall.

Lady Arabella's pursuits had turned her into a legend. Poems had been written describing her deviant requests and, locked in the family vault, there was a series of pornographic illustrations that lovingly detailed the rose-lipped opening of her ever-spread legs and showed scenes of wanton postures where she not only fingered her own backside but allowed that same passage to be penetrated by several peers. These graphics displayed the queue of dandies standing behind Lady Arabella's brazenly offered derrière, and also depicted the family butler, Stave, holding a silver tray on which pats of farm-churned butter were offered to each man in order to further increase the smooth pleasure of his enjoyment.

Another series of lithographs (which had once been secretly distributed, to the horror of Lady Arabella's husband but to the further prestige of her reputation) showed Lady Arabella demonstrating a joyful inclination to sadism. Three naked youths were tied to the fireplace in the great hall. Their breeches had been pulled down to their ankles, showing six shapely calves. Their bare buttocks faced towards the incorrigible lady as she whipped them one after the other with the lash used to drive the horses forward when she was running about the countryside in her coach. It was a sharp stinging thing, and the artist had accurately drawn the slim scars that were left behind on the white skin of the mortified men.

Lord Hacclesfield (who was quite closely related to Lady Arabella, through his mother's side of the family) chose not to remind himself of these facts when he stomped up and down the sweeping staircase of his great hall, where the faces of his debauched forefathers stared down from innumerable gilt frames.

Below stairs, in the servants' hall, the preparations to receive Miss Amy Pringle took a different timbre in that they were conducted in an atmosphere of genuine exuberance. The arrival of Miss Pringle heralded a wedding, a wedding meant a party, and a party meant ale, wine and food, even to the lower orders who made up Lord Hacclesfield's dependants.

The women, especially the younger maids, were in states of excitation, carried away by the ardent fervour that such an event entailed. The young men, affected by this, found themselves wanting to possess them. Members stiffened painfully in tight breeches as the youths riled each other by revealing their desires.

John Somerley, an under-gardener, told Tollard, the boot polisher, how he was going to throw Lady Hacclesfield's maid-in-waiting, Fanny Mutterton (a girl with many airs), face down over Mrs Turville's kitchen table. Her skirts were going to be lifted up and young

John was going to relieve himself in the gorgeous warm crevices of creamy flesh and white thighs.

Tollard replied that he wanted to pull Milly Morden's fresh linen blouse from her shoulders, muzzle her breasts and bite the red nipples with nipping teeth. He would nibble and lick her into a seizure of pain, pleasure and supplication. Then, said Tollard (a cheeky lad of 20), he was going to put his right hand full up Milly's snatch, into her insides, and he was going to manipulate them until she screamed and creamed and begged him on her knees to allow his cock into her mouth.

That was Tollard's plan and, if any observer had noticed the flirtatious spirit of this mentioned maidservant, they would have opined that he was destined to have some luck in achieving it. Milly's nether regions were a furnace of frustrated need. Her own hands often went down to her fanny to provide relief and Tollard had once caught her doing so, legs akimbo, skirts above her head, in the apple store. Fingers rubbing, face flushed, Milly moaning. Tollard had never forgotten this sight and was determined that the next time she needed to find relief she was not going to be alone.

The servants' hall, then, was immersed in an atmosphere of hormonal heat where the maelstrom of desire subsumed the rationale of all as minds became deranged in the prospect of ecstasies whose invisible trigger had been the promised arrival of Miss Amy Pringle.

Discipline in the lower ranks began to break down. As the head butlers and cooks became busier and busier, the younger people began to concentrate on each other rather than their tasks.

The impending hour of Miss Pringle's arrival drew forward. At 12.30 p.m. Lord Hacclesfield's valets turned him into a black coat made from the finest wool whose silver-grey lining was embroidered with his family crest. He emerged from his dressing room like a galleon about to engage in war. Nothing would impede his progress. Nothing ever had.

He busied himself with the last-minute details and astute inspections that were the rigours of grand hospitality.

He did not believe that any employee of any rank could be trusted to fulfil their obligations to the perfection that he desired. Lord Hacclesfield was a man who would run his fingers along the polished mahogany of an inlaid bookcase to check for dust. He would check the back of cabriole legs to ensure extreme sheen. He would sniff white cotton linen to ensure that the smell of stringent airing emanated from it. He would personally see that every pane of glass and item of solid silver cutlery had received due attention.

His low opinion of his servants was confirmed when he noticed that a white smear of polish remained on the brass of the fire grate in the hall. Not a man to vent spleen in the ordinary symptoms of reddened features and vocal bellow, the peer's fury arrived in the form of cold and cruel *froideur*.

He was 48. Tall (six foot one inch), dark and imposing, with flashing black eyes and high cheekbones, his severe jaw had not dissolved into the jowls that usually arrive with middle age. Lord Hacclesfield was a man who instilled fear and respect in roughly equal quantities.

He demanded the immediate presence of Milly Morden and she arrived, neat in the clean uniform of a maid ready to join the line of servants who were to go and greet Miss Pringle outside the mansion. Her appearance was smart enough, with an ironed apron

9

and polished lace-up shoes, but her heart was beating and she was discomposed with anxiety.

Milly Morden knew she was in serious trouble. Maidservants were only summoned by the lord when they had failed to perform to the high standard of his expectations.

Her employer barely bothered to describe the nature of her mistake. He merely pointed perfunctorily to the offending grate, flipped her over his knee, pulled up her dark skirt, trussed up the plain white cotton petticoat, and with her body folded over his leg, he thrashed her shivering naked buttocks with his riding crop. He did not have the time to instruct her, only to beat her. This, he assumed, would be enough to discourage any further interruption in the smooth running of his important reception.

Milly Morden's face almost brushed the earl's polished black riding boots; she could smell the musk of his body and the leather of the boots as his blows seared through her trembling skin. Lord Hacclesfield whipped Milly long and hard, striping her behind again and again, lost in the calm cold rage of the truly terrifying master. Some are firm but gentle; some are cruel but kind. Lord Hacclesfield was implacable.

Soon the great hall echoed with the wailings and misery of the beaten lass as the pain burned her bum and she resolved never ever to think of the attentions of Tollard when she should have been focusing on her job.

Pushing the lazy girl away from him, Lord Hacclesfield barked at his butler Headley.

'That should have been your job, Headley,' he snapped. 'I do not wish to have to discipline maids when I have more important concerns, do you understand?'

'Yes, my lord.'

'Don't let it happen again.'

'No, sir,' said the butler, resolving to give Milly Morden a caning that evening for getting him into trouble.

'That girl won't sit down for a week,' he promised himself.

Lord Hacclesfield had inherited his estate from his father, the second earl, when he was 23. He was accustomed to unquestioning obedience from all who attended him. He bade, everyone obeyed. This had always been the law of his life. He ran his lands and holdings as a principality where most inhabitants were dependent on him for their livelihoods. He believed in his power to instruct and his right to do so; he was of better birth and better bred than most people and these genealogical gifts brought rights and responsibilities.

If his satisfaction was not complete, the person who offended would, at the very least, feel the sharp sting of his tongue. If they were lucky. They were as likely to feel the sting of his whip on their thigh or his palm on their buttock.

Cooks were punished for poor pastry; serving girls would be spanked for poor service. Posterior parts were tender. He knew it. They knew it. Consequently he ran a household where every component tended towards efficiency and where members worked hard to perform their master's wishes with assiduity.

Milly Morden had been warned about the frightful fury of her employer's displeasure but as a relatively new arrival to the servants' hall, she had never experienced it before. Humiliated and dejected, she wiped a tear from her eye as she withdrew to an attic dormitory to study her pink skin and allow the air to circulate around her backside. The chill cooled the burning inflammation but her smarting buttocks rubbed painfully against the crude cotton of her blue skirt.

11

Fanny Mutterton appeared at the door.

'For goodness' sake, Milly Morden!' she snapped. 'Miss Amy Pringle is due any minute and you're up lookin' at yerself. Mr Headley's goin' mad! They're all waitin' for you! What in cripes sake's the matter?'

'Oh, Fanny, the master thrashed my poor bum with his crop,' snivelled Milly.

'Serves you right for mooning about that stupid Tollard and not getting on with your work. I knew it would get you into trouble. Still, I know how you feel. The sting'll soon go. He gave me what for only last week, some dust or something under a bed. Bent me over a foot-stool and gave it me hard on my bare bum with a ruler from the schoolroom. Couldn't sit down for days. But you'll get it again if you don't come on NOW!'

Milly followed Fanny to the entrance hall of the mansion where the entire staff were assembled outside in a neat row of hierarchical order, from head house-maids to second laundrymaids, from coachmen to sawyers.

Headley marched up and down the ranks, checking uniforms, ensuring cleanliness, making sure that all were correctly positioned in the place of their rank.

'Stop your twitching, Morden, for goodness' sake,' he instructed Milly, who was fidgeting as the cotton of her garment chafed her smacked red cheeks.

'The master whipped my bottom, sir, Mr Headley,' she whined.

'It serves you right, young woman. I would have pulled your skirt above your head myself if I had seen the state of that brass. What were you thinking?'

Milly sniffed.

'If you sniff again, Morden, I will repeat his lord-ship's action on your posterior,' Headley threatened. 'I

12

will do it harder and longer and you will suffer from my chastisement for a week. Now hush your face.'

The minutes passed slowly, heavy with expectation and excitement. The shards of the May morning sun played on the magnificent Palladian facade, highlighting the crevices of the Corinthian pillars and causing reflections to play across hundreds of dark window panes.

Finally the crunch of hooves on gravel could be heard at the bottom of the drive. Four shining horses galloped forward, dragging their coach behind them, a liveried driver calling to them. All eyes turned. The coach shot towards them, big now, and loud.

'Here she comes,' said Lord Hacclesfield. 'Everyone ready, please.'

'Stand up straight!' Headley hissed at Milly. 'Do up your button, Tollard, for christ's sake.'

'Here she comes.'

The Earl of Hacclesfield stood at the front of his assembled household. He prepared himself to demonstrate the myriad delicacies of protocol. He expected to help a tired young woman out of her carriage with a strong, polite hand. His duties were to ensure that she was availed of her parasol, that she did not trip on the steps that led from carriage to gravel and to aid her prettily to his portal.

This plan for decorum was not to be.

The coach had come to a halt in front of him. The four horses were stamping, steaming and snorting, but otherwise there was silence. The door of the coach remained shut. No demure lady, well outfitted in a travelling suit, in a hat, or in anything else, materialised. No face, pretty or otherwise, appeared at the window.

Lord Hacclesfield leaned forward, ready to take a step. Perhaps the little precious, exhausted by her journey, had grown wan, even weak.

13

He took another tiny step, expecting with every second to see the affianced appear, all tripping grace and polite affectation. He expected to feel tiny white fingers flutter on the top of his own firm knuckles, searching for his support. He expected to see a polite blue eye shyly downcast, overcome by the sheer nobility of his presence and the power of his grandeur. He expected to see a young woman overcome with shyness, excitement and respect.

At least a minute had now gone by. The door remained closed.

'Perhaps she has fainted,' somebody suggested.

Lord Hacclesfield was gesticulating to Headley to open the door when the window slapped down and a loud voice echoed from within.

'Hulloo!'

Lord Hacclesfield thought, at first, that some kind of accident had occurred and that the traveller within the vehicle was hurt. No woman in the experience of his years had ever made a sound like this for any cause, let alone in the manner of a greeting. He took a couple of steps backwards, unnerved, wondering what was going to happen next as he studied the situation much as he would study the path of a fox that he was pursing in order to gauge what decision it was going to make.

He looked at his wife to see if she had noticed this bizarre turn of events, but Lady Hacclesfield had not. Lady Hacclesfield's mind (for want of a better word) was floating in a place of its own, a place that Lord Hacclesfield had long ago given up trying to understand.

Once beautiful, his wife now reclined in a sensual indolence whose perimeters were defined by comforting glasses of laudanum and a group of servants who waited on her hand and foot. Lady Hacclesfield had long ago drawn back from any duties involved in running the estate or from any tiring opinions that could be offered with regard to family activity. She left everything to her husband, her sons and the head servants.

She stood smiling at her husband and at the carriage. She had not heard the 'hulloo' from within and, even if she had, her thoughts about it were likely to be one of acceptance rather than any intelligent analysis.

Lord Hacclesfield sighed. He should have disciplined Aurelia when he first married her but he had allowed her to do as she pleased. The result was this. A spoiled woman addicted to luxury who was of no help to him in the business of his life and property.

She had come to him, a dowry of £15,000, an heir-apparent in her family tree, all finery and wealth. She had been the belle of the county, acknowledged as such and famous for it. And, though charming on the piano and efficient in the art of cross-stitching, her most accomplished skills were revealed in the intimacy of the bedroom where her achievements were borne of natural talent. At 21, Aurelia (*née* Lady Darwell) had been possessed of a fine round white body made of smooth faultless flesh and blessed with a soft, scented malleability that had driven her husband wild with pleasure and desire.

They had, consequently, enjoyed three years of marital bliss, and bliss, in Lord Hacclesfield's opinion, was the right word.

His wife's mouth alone had been enough to provide happiness and satisfaction. He could still sometimes feel her fine wet soft lips kissing the end of his prick – drawing his juices to the end, maddening him with stiffened need, licking, sucking, teasing until he either ejaculated himself into the soft crevices of her décolletage or yanked her legs apart and thrust himself into her, pumping her until she moaned.

15

The tightness of her warm cunt! The sight of her on all fours on his bed, cotton nightdress pulled up to reveal the white orbs of her buttocks, the fur of her minge, the crevices of her exciting womanhood, all displayed for him and him alone. He would often stand in front of her, enjoying the hardness of his prick as he looked at her on the bed, face down in her pillows, backside raised, ready to receive him.

Sometimes he had slowly removed her clothes, garment by garment – frock, bodice, corset, pantalettes. He would discard them, throw them to one side, and encourage her to lie on a rug by the fire, so that he could merely watch her and hunger after the silky finish of her skin, the protuberances that ripened in all the right places. He would watch her, stiff as hell and wanting her, but making himself linger, so that when he did finally partake of the delight of the event, he was a thirsty man who had made himself wait for the last glass of vintage wine available in the cellar. He had, by self-control, availed himself of the headiest and most poignant sensual pleasure.

Those early days of marriage had been the best of his life. Happy in the bedroom, he had allowed his wife to engage herself in her own devices.

When she was wayward, or failed to fulfil the basic wifely duties, he had never taken his crop to her, as he should have done. If she irritated him with the signs of early slovenliness, and he reprimanded her, she would simply drop to her knees, insinuate her fingers into the buttons of his breeches, draw out his prick and place it softly into her mouth.

A glowing red helmet and the overwhelming desire to fuck prevented reprimand; indeed, it prohibited any sensible discourse. He would simply take her wherever they were – on the stone floor of the dining hall, on the

16

shiny damask of the chaise-longue, over a desk in the schoolroom.

Thus she pleased him, so he allowed her to do as she pleased.

He should have whipped her well and good in the early days, as a man must teach a young animal before they pick up the unsocial tricks that stay with them for the rest of their lives and render them eternally displeasing as a companion.

He should have tied his wife by the wrists to a post of their four-poster bed, pulled up her lacy linens so that they were knotted above her waist. He should have made her feel the vulnerability of an innocent flesh that had never been trained with a hard hand, and he should have whipped her until the tears ran down her face.

This, combined with the harshest of words and the strictest of lectures, would have been effective. It would have changed the course of the marriage. But he had made the mistake of allowing her to divert him from the philosophy that was not only his stringent belief but also his métier.

Now he was burdened by a lazy madam. She was (he told himself furiously) an old dog who could be taught no new tricks.

Suddenly the door of the carriage snapped back off its hinges with a loud crack and, at last, at last, the future lady of the house of Hacclesfield appeared.

Though momentarily relieved that nothing untoward had happened to the person inside the coach, Lord Hacclesfield's senses were no further comforted by the sight of the person who leapt out of it much as a racehorse leaps out of its box.

Not only did this young woman spring out of the carriage unaided by the arm of any man or servant, but, when she arrived on the gravel in front of him,

17

there was no sign of any of the symptoms that befit a person whose goals should be to advertise their personal charm and graceful propriety.

The honey-blonde hair was dishevelled. Having long ago fallen out of its coils, it wisped around her forehead in an untidy array. There was no parasol and, even worse, no bonnet. The colletage! The colletage was just short of unbelievable. A brown velvet travelling coat was unbuttoned to reveal a cream silk dress. Fitted with the high waistline of the Empire mode, it pressed two ripe white breasts up and these breasts could be visibly seen due to the fact that the panel of the upper part of the dress was a rectangular patch of lacy gauze.

For all intents and purposes, the upper part of this woman was naked. Nothing was left to the imagination. The lacy part was almost translucent.

Lord Hacclesfield could hardly stop himself actually gawping. He had never seen a pink nipple so entirely exposed. He had hardly witnessed such a thing in the bedroom, let alone outside his house in front of 45 servants.

And this was not all.

Miss Amy Pringle was now addressing him before he had greeted her. She was initiating the intercourse!

Lord Hacclesfield did not know that Miss Amy Pringle had a long history of initiating intercourse and had no intention of changing this particular habit. In these seconds of reception, he was bathing in relative innocence. In these blessed seconds the horrors of Miss Pringle's demeanour could be explained by the trauma of a long journey.

'Lord Hacclesfield,' she said jauntily, staring up into his grim face with an expression that could only be described as both happy and amused.

The stern peer bowed stiffly.

18

'Welcome to the Lancaster Hall, Miss Pringle,' he growled, attempting to stare her down with the expression that he reserved for the worst of his servants. He could control everyone from the lowliest menial to the most arrogant country squire with one flash of his black eyes. Such was the power of this stare that one undermaid, a potato peeler, had actually fainted. Other underlings who experienced this silent glare could feel the tingle on their backsides even before they had been punished.

This look did not necessarily arrive with a whipping, but it certainly accompanied the threat of such a thing. A maid who received this look was a maid who had better look about herself if she wished to keep her clothes on her person and retain her dignity.

The implications of these resonances were lost on Miss Pringle.

A painful flush started to creep into Lord Hacclesfield's neck.

He was beginning to lose control.

Miss Pringle giggled.

Lord Hacclesfield looked down at her face. He did not think he had ever seen a girl so defiant or so provocative. Her blue eyes, circled with long dark eyelashes, flashed with challenge; her mouth was pursed into a permanent pout which occasionally dissolved into a teasing grin; her skin, though faultless, was refreshed by a brazen bloom of health that, in his opinion, would have been better replaced by the pallor of neurasthenia.

Miss Pringle, undaunted by the steely glare of her older and better, merely looked him straight in the eye and grinned like a person who has been getting away with it all her life and plans to get away with it for a great deal longer.

Lord Hacclesfield nearly slapped the pert hussy

there and then, but, gathering up the dignity that had made hundreds of Hacclesfields great, he led her slowly down the parade of people that had lined up to greet her.

He explained the absence of Ralph and Bubb.

'I am afraid my sons are detained in the course of the duties of the estate. We tried to rearrange the appointment but it could not be done. They both send their heartiest apologies and will be at dinner tonight.'

Miss Amy nodded, as if listening, but her eyes were staring boldly into the face of Tollard who, as boldly, was staring back.

Lord Hacclesfield, sensing flirtatious outrage, pushed her in the small of the back so that she was forced to move forward, away from the lascivious attention of Tollard and towards Milly Morden, who, as her bottom was still burning with the pain of humiliation, was possessed of some dignity and politesse.

'Milly Morden will be your personal maid,' said Lord Hacclesfield.

Milly Morden curtsied.

'You will be expected in the drawing room at six. A gala dinner is to be held in honour of your arrival.'

The stern peer bowed stiffly and withdrew, leaving Headley the butler and Milly Morden to show Amy Pringle to the 'blue' room.

Amy Pringle cast her belongings in a mêlée of velvet and silk over the various commodes, cabinets and velveteen chaises-longue dotted around her room. There were four leather trunks in all, all embossed with her initials and all locked down with brass locks. One was devoted to her library. Miss Pringle's reading was wide and varied and it was one of the primary reasons that wherever she went in life, trouble seemed to follow.

She had read works by Defoe and Fielding, Rousseau and Shelley; she had read incendiary suggestions by rebellious Whigs and postlapsarian theories by free-thinking scientists. She had read pamphlets by Paine (that denounced the monarchy as useless) and she had read the lewd ponderings of Monk Lewis.

Her head was filled with ideas, a dangerous thing in the year of 1790. Ideas were considered to be explosive commodities – they should be contained and controlled and they should only be present in the minds of those born with the abilities to manage them. Royalties, for instance, and peers destined to run the realm.

Amy had emerged from a background whose inherent lack of convention was (fortunately) unbeknown to Lord Hacclesfield. Her father, the distiller, had appeared to be respectable in the eyes of the world. He had upgraded himself with some fortuitous connections to the royal family that arose as a result of duties administered rather than the lucky social connections brought by birth right. He was, in fact, a voracious libertarian who had fallen in with the ideas of the French revolution, who agreed with the philosophy of Rousseau, and who had been fascinated by intellectual bohemians such as Mary Wollstonecraft.

He had allowed an atmosphere of intellectual investigation to perpetrate his home and, in consequence, the inhabitants were equipped with independent minds.

If Lord Hacclesfield had known these facts he would have been appalled and would have entertained no notion of receiving any member of this family to his home. But he did not know these facts. The Pringle clan, through the vagaries of fate and the decorum that was the facade of manner, provided a seemingly charming exterior whose front presented no danger to those who believed in the necessity of convention with the same adamantine faith that they believed in a God that was both Christian and Conservative.

Everywhere Miss Pringle went, chaos followed. Her behaviour, perverted by confidence, opinion and knowledge, had become most liberal in its proclivities and it was underpinned by a stubborn courage that brooked no fool.

Miss Pringle was blonde. She was petite. In some lights she looked as if butter would not melt in her mouth. But she was a force to be reckoned with. The Hacclesfield family had no idea what they had allowed into their midst.

A second trunk was filled with the rich accoutrements that were her daywear – chemises from Paris, cottons from Ghent, lace from Flanders and batiste from Valencienne. There were merinos and shawls, expensive nankeens and muslins.

Scores of dresses from different fabrics were teamed with tiny spencer jackets tailored to fit and made in contrasting colours. Various boxes revealed flat pumps for wear in the house and leather boots for riding. A chamois leather bag contained dressings for the hair; a small ornate cabinet lined with velvet held a collection of jewellery that included diamonds from her mother's side of the family, pearls bought by her father, a little pin or two left by aunts. It was a respectable array, if not a magnificent one – the pieces of true value would remain with her mother. The adornments beautified her neck and ears with grace rather than grandeur.

Miss Pringle's trousseau seemed to be comprehensive and above criticism until one learned a salient fact whose knowledge came to surprise all who learned of it.

No underwear graced the luxurious items of her

comportment. Most ladies opted, at least, for linen bodices (to protect the bust) or pantalettes or even little coverings of embroidered gauze. They had neatly woven stockingettes and some had even clung to the support of light corselettes.

Miss Pringle, though, had long railed against the discomfort provided by undergarments. She did not need their protection and she did not like their constraint. She liked to feel conscious of her fanny, her groin, the sensitive flesh of her buttocks – all available, all aroused by the soft lawns of her beautifully made dresses.

Her life had been spent doing much as she pleased, when she pleased. The sartorial decision enabled her to lift up her skirts and sit down on the erect member of any stable-lad or gardener or lord or alderman that she chose. A nude minge was a convenient minge; there was much pleasure to be accomplished for those who relinquished the fuss and bother of undergarments.

Milly Morden followed her new mistress around the 'blue' room, attempting to tidy and fold as the various garments were vollied hither and thither and flew around the chamber like bad weather.

Finally she persuaded Miss Pringle to rest herself in front of the looking glass on the dressing table and allow her toilette to be prepared for the gala dinner that was to be held in her honour.

This grand feast was designed to launch her into local society, a society that had talked of little else for many months (being rather bored) and awaited the sight of Ralph Fitzroy's second wife with the curiosity and concern that a patron awaits the unveiling of a portrait that he has paid for, that is destined to hang in public, and which he has not, as yet, either seen or approved.

Milly Morden knew that Miss Pringle's appearance would reflect on her personal skills in regard to looking after ladies of leisure. If the hair and adornments met with the approval of her lord, then she might climb back up the ladder of approval down which she had so recently and painfully fallen.

Her judgement should have told her to be as silent as possible in the face of the storm that was Miss Pringle, but Miss Pringle allowed no such defence in her presence. She needed to find things out; information was power, and Miss Pringle was well aware that she needed power if she was to survive in this new and dangerous terrain.

'What is Ralph Fitzroy like?' Miss Pringle asked.

It was the inevitable question. Miss Pringle was, after all, destined to marry the man, though she had little memory of him apart from some childhood visits where they had ridden together and eaten an apple or two on the lawn.

'I know very little about him, Miss Amy,' said Milly, attempting to train her mistress's wild blonde curls into a vestige of neat coils.

'He is very respected, but he never speaks. I am afraid he changed the night that Lady Miranda died. Sometimes I hear him walk the corridors at dawn, pacing up and down. He never laughs. It's been three years now, but I don't think he has got over that death, Miss Amy, I really don't.'

'Mm,' said Miss Pringle, snorting at the irritating thought that she should have to compete with the shadow of some long-dead girl whose only contribution was to do as she was told and cause no trouble and generally waft about the place inspiring devotion. Lady Miranda, Miss Pringle secretly suspected, had been a bore. She was possessed of no apprehension at the idea of the late Lady Miranda; the woman had no

24

breath, after all. She was a wraith whose only glamour was youthful demise and all the false memories of nostalgia.

'What then of Bubb?'

'Well . . .'

Milly flushed.

'Come on – out with it!'

'Well, er . . .'

'Yes.'

'He is well liked in the servants' hall, miss.'

'You mean he has had sex with everybody.'

Milly Morden nearly dropped the silver-backed hairbrush at the force of this direct approach.

Amy Pringle read the maid's crimson blush as a sign of the affirmative.

'Oh, miss,' Milly tittered. 'He has the biggest knob in the county.'

'Really,' said Miss Pringle, sitting upright on the velvet cushion, her back suddenly erect as interest trickled down from her mind, through her spine and suffused her body. 'Really,' she said again. 'I like a good big dick.'

Milly Morden spent the rest of the session devoting herself to Miss Pringle's toilette, while regaling her with stimulating details as to the exact proportion of the younger Fitzroy's penis and the intensity of the pleasure that it perpetrated.

She told Amy how those lucky enough to experience penetration by this enormous asset could never forget it. Bubb Fitzroy's organ was only slightly smaller than that of the average horse in Lord Hacclesfield's stable. It slithered its way into a girl's excited pink lips, slipped easily into her inner self, and then raged, endless and relentless, through her whole body, unleashing emotions that she never knew she had, causing fits of quivering pleasure that did not even abate when the hard thing exploded and withdrew. She knew of maids whose trembling had lasted for hours afterwards, and who now thought only of receiving this good hard gift again and again.

'Oh,' said Miss Pringle, as she heard all this. 'My fanny is on fire with these tales of Bubb's dick.'

Miss Pringle walked over to the bed, drew back the embroidered white curtains, and lay back on the soft down of the cream coverlet. Hoiking up her skirts, she spread her thighs and pointed a moist red opening in Milly's direction. Crimson lips were swollen; her orifice glistened with need.

'Come,' she ordered. 'Come at once and put your fingers here, Milly.'

Milly walked obediently forward and placed four of her small fingers deep inside her mistress. There was warmth and juice. Her mistress's pelvis started to vibrate and she moaned.

'Finger me. Finger me as if you were Bubb's dick.'

Milly, having had some experience of this on herself, repeated the performance on her mistress's button, which, despite being from a higher order, seemed to be roughly similar in its make-up.

Amy Pringle, with her maid's knowing fingers manipulating her, threw her head back, abandoned all the worries of the vexatious journey, all the pressures of an arranged marriage, and released herself to a grateful climax that rattled in her throat and vibrated her body with satisfying shudders of spent lust. Ah, lust. Amy Pringle understood lust. And she knew it was not love. Still, there was gratitude to acknowledge and protocols to administer – there always were. She knew Milly could be her friend and ally, but she also knew that she, Miss Pringle, must retain the authority of the upper hand.

'You will learn, Milly Morden, that amongst your

duties will be the immediate relief of your mistress when it is requested and as it is requested. Do you understand?'

'Yes, miss.'

Milly applied herself again. Pushing her mistress's pelvis on to the bed with her left hand, she went in with the fingers of her right hand, fiercer this time, rubbing her clit with the palm, delving with stiff digits, reaching up to the stimulating places that she knew, from her own pursuits, agitated and relieved.

Thus she controlled the lush pink of her mistress's wanton pussy and gave it all the appeasement that it needed.

Amy Pringle came for the third and last time.

When she had recomposed herself, she made an assured proclamation.

'We are going to have fun, Milly.'

'Yes, miss.'

Chapter Two

The Earl of Hacclesfield and his wife sat alone in the drawing room. They lived at opposite ends of the house (a distance of some two miles) and rarely saw each other as their lives ran on parallel courses. He, up early, managed the estate; she, up late (if at all) pottered about. He ate downstairs, served formally in the dining hall, usually with his sons in attendance; she tended to have her meals brought to her room. They rarely met, except at formal family events, when an invitation from a neighbour was offered, or to cooperate in some legal or business matter.

Ralph's engagement fell into the last category and Lord Hacclesfield wasted no time in approaching the subject with his wife. He had sent one of his valets with a hand-written note to request her presence half an hour before their guests arrived for dinner at 6 p.m. He wished to discuss the curse that had befallen their house in the form of Miss Amy Pringle.

Lord Hacclesfield was very vexed. He felt as though his evening attire was too tight; the black silk tailcoat clung to his chest and made him feel asphyxiated, and even the cream silk of the shirt itched. The fire was too hot. He moved away from it. The wine was too cold. He snapped at a servant. Then he marched up and down, ploughing a furrow with his leather boots until he expostulated.

'That girl is pert!'

His wife, sitting on the sofa, floated in a soufflé of net and taffeta – an orange and gold affair that obeyed no modes from Paris and was rigged with an unnecessary number of pie-crust ruffles that paid no compliment to her ever-expanding physique.

She fanned herself gently and remained calm, a state of mind that laudanum gently bestowed, though narcosis also brought elements of mental confusion and bouts of amnesia. Lady Hacclesfield had to struggle a little to recall to whom her husband referred and then to create a memory of her likeness in her mind's eye. The elaborate flowers and feathers that wound around the coils of her head shivered like shubbery in a March breeze as her forehead inclined with the effort of thought.

'She seemed a nice little thing to me,' she said vaguely.

She gesticulated to the servant to pour her another glass of wine. It was her third and she did not care if it was cold or hot or made of calves' trotters, so long as it provided the desired effect.

'I am sure Ralph will like her,' she added.

'Ralph will like what I tell him to like,' her husband retorted. 'Take it from me, Aurelia, that girl is trouble. Trouble, trouble, trouble.'

He stared gloomily into the fire. If he had been carrying his whip he would have swiped it but a whip, unfortunately, was not included in a gentleman's formal evening wear.

He entertained a brief pleasurable vision of spanking

29

Miss Pringle's arse with leather-gloved hands, watching the cheeks rise up in red pain and hearing her squeal for mercy. She would be made to do as she was told.

This stimulating reverie dispersed with the arrival of their two sons, Ralph and Bubb. Ralph, tall, dark, aloof, like his father, was Lord Hacclesfield's pride, being conscientious, efficient and responsible. Bubb, though amiable enough, was less of a joy. He had taken after his mother, not only in his plump and blond appearance, but also in his inclination to the priority of pleasure over duty.

They slumped on to the sofa in a most informal manner.

Bubb giggled with his mother. Ralph stretched his long legs out in front of him carelessly.

'I hear Miss Amy Pringle has finally arrived,' he said.

'And that she is beautiful,' Bubb added.

'I'll thank you not to gossip with the servants,' their father barked. He knew that this was the only source from which they had gained this disinformation and he resented the lads accepting the descriptions provided by unreliable menials before hearing the opinion of their elders and betters.

'Does she hunt?' Ralph inquired.

'I do not know if she hunts,' his father replied.

'She certainly looks as if she does,' said Lady Hacclesfield.

Lord Hacclesfield shot a cold glance at his wife. She had delivered this observation as a compliment to the newcomer's spirit and health.

'I hope she does,' said Ralph.

He ran with the hounds at least three times a week; the danger of death excited him, the need to survive rejuvenated him. The pursuit was the only way to forget the painful wraith of his first wife whose unparalleled beauty still lingered in his mind and whose loss still visited him with recurring pain. Hunting had become the point of his existence.

Lord Hacclesfield did not voice the dread of his doubts to his sons. He considered the moment too early to voice his premonitions. He had decided to give Miss Amy Pringle another chance. She was, after all, in their midst at his volition and he had to take responsibility for his decision; her failure would reflect on his judgement and, he feared, on his authority.

Lord Hacclesfield did not like to be wrong and in his opinion he very rarely was. He was hoping that the horrifying first impression caused by Miss Pringle's unproper behaviour was an aberration brought on by the trauma of her journey and her sudden initiation into an environment where all elements were strange to her. He was hoping that a finer side would assert itself, and that, even if it did not, the lady would benefit from moving in a circle where examples could constantly be set.

Ralph, having lost interest in the subject of Amy Pringle, was about to ask his father about the welfare of a recently born foal, when he was interrupted by the arrival of the first of their guests – the Bishop of Bath and Wells and his wife Fancia.

Dignitary and spouse swept into the room like a cortège, accepted glasses of champagne with gracious nods, and settled themselves in to make themselves as pleasant as was possible considering the extreme nastiness of their personalities. The bishop and his wife loathed each other. Indeed, the bishop regularly prayed to the God of his understanding to hold his hand behind his back in order to avoid stabbing his wife to death with a knife.

The ecclesiast was followed by Trenton Dastard, two

dowagers, a squire and an ageing heiress who had been snapped up by the latter.

They collected amiably enough, talking of matters of the country, of the doings of parliament, of some social scandal or other.

Time was drawing on and Lord Hacclesfield's eye was firmly on the Thomas Pace bell-top bracket clock that sat on the mantelpiece. A lovely piece, the backplate was engraved with scrolls and flowers, while the mahogany case was decorated with flame veneers, brass caryatids and scroll feet. It had kept perfect time for ten years and it now told him that the hour was 6.10 p.m. precisely.

Miss Pringle had taken it upon herself to be ten minutes late. While others in the county could ride for miles through all weathers and down muddy tracks in order to fulfil their social obligations, Miss Amy Pringle could not. Miss Amy Pringle had to make a society of his friends (and her betters) wait for her.

The saucy minx was defying him.

Time was the one thing about which Lord Hacclesfield was most strict. Even his wife (with whom he was lenient) knew that; even she managed to appear at designated appointments at the hours he dictated. Everyone knew that he was a busy man, that his minutes were precious and that he had much to do. The hegemony of his household relied on the fact that this importance was faithfully respected. He had been known to order the cook to cane an undergardener for bringing in the strawberries a mere three minutes after the ordered time, and a maid named Maisie suffered a severe smacking when she brought his hot morning water 30 seconds late.

Thirty seconds meant 30 hard slaps on bare skin. His morning ablution was an exquisite ritual whose accuracy initiated the day and set up the process of smooth efficiency. No contradiction could be entertained, no flexibility allowed. If the water was late, the shave was late, if the shave was late, the dressing was late, if the dressing was late, the breakfast was late, and then the appointments shambled into each other and chaos contaminated his life. No. The unfortunate Maisie was severely tanned that day. It was a morning that she was to remember well.

Sometimes 30 seconds felt like 30 hours to the earl. Miss Pringle's tardiness caused the minutes to move forward in a slothful torpor that he found unbearable. She was an affront to his very being.

Another round of champagne was served. The bishop began to become quite drunk and Trenton Dastard was one step away from reciting his own poetry – an always unpopular event as it derived from Lord Rochester's works and was anarchic in its intent. He would inevitably target the bishop's wife to hear it as she was the least suitable person to do so.

Ralph watched this happening and groaned.

Sometimes he did not know why he retained his friendship with Dastard. They had met at Cambridge and cemented a liaison that had somehow never dissolved, despite Dastard's unparalleled liberalism, cavalier inebriation and insane gambling. He was a rum fellow, but fun. Ralph had to admit that. There was always some excitement when Dastard was around.

Bubb made himself amiable between two dowagers, who clacked and clucked and croaked, jingling their jewellery and heaving their cleavages. Bubb liked old women. He liked all women, actually.

The dowagers, like everyone who lived north of Leicester, had heard of Bubb's legendary gristle and they both entertained notions of experiencing it. They weren't that old, they told each other in the carriage on the way to Lancaster Hall, and from what they had heard in the drawing room at Stanton Manor, there was plenty to go round.

Bubb, always willing to please, allowed himself to be swept up in amiable flattery and flirtation.

Lady Hacclesfield told the bishop's wife that Miss Amy Pringle was charming and accomplished and would make a pretty wife for Ralph.

Lord Hacclesfield, hearing this ludicrous parlay, inwardly cursed his wife for her stupidity. He felt ready to explode.

He looked at the carriage clock again: 6.25 p.m. His very fingers itched. If civilisation had not provided him with a reasoned mind, he would have sprinted up the stairs to Amy Pringle's room, dragged her out of it, pulled her by the hair down the stairs, and physically thrown her into this room, where she would have had to repossess herself as best she could.

Finally, at 6.30, even Lady Hacclesfield had begun to notice the tardiness of the hour if only because the bishop's wife kept talking about how hungry she was, and one of the serving maids had waved at Headley in a manner that represented an emergency in the kitchen. Lady Hacclesfield sensed that the dinner was at a delicate stage of its preparation and was minutes away from actually being spoiled.

She fanned herself, drank her ninth glass of wine and hoped for the best.

Finally, finally, at 6.36 p.m., as Lord Hacclesfield was about to have a seizure, the door slowly opened and Miss Pringle made her entrance.

What an entrance it was.

The room, enthralled, dissolved into silence. Every eye focused on her as if entrapped by her invisible charisma.

She was a beauty; no reasonable person could deny

34

this fact. Her hair, dressed skilfully by Milly, was arranged into sweet curls on either side of her head, causing emphasis to her fine brow, to the firm chin and the high cheekbones.

Her skin, smooth and milky, was tastefully enhanced with tiny pearls threaded on thin gold threads that shimmered gently as she walked. She carried a neat embroidered evening bag whose gold chinoiserie matched the patterns of her satin evening slippers.

She floated gracefully across the room as a soft mist of white. Lord Hacclesfield sensed two tiny seconds of relief; the girl, at least, was presentable. It was only when she drew closer that the full enormity of her enterprise presented itself.

Miss Amy Pringle's evening dress was made of the flimsiest of silk chiffonettes. Enrobed in a cloud of translucent film, the effect was not to cover or camouflage her modesty in any way. The weave of the material was such that it provided a clear picture of the body moving underneath it. That is, in most lights, the dress was see-through and Miss Amy Pringle was naked underneath it.

It was possible to see every part of her – the dark hairs of her groin, the cleft of her pelvis, the curve of her breast, the rude red nipples that she had brazenly rouged to enhance the effects. From the back it was possible to clearly view the curve of her spine and the cleft of her buttocks.

She was a naked woman moving in a crowd, a naked woman who knew that she was naked and was enjoying every minute of her base enterprise.

Trenton Dastard leaned in closer from his position on an ottoman to ensure that what he thought he saw was correct. He had seen similar ensembles – on the Greek statues in various museums, for instance, and on the bawds that bedevilled the low-houses in Cheapside – but he had never seen a county drawing room thus enriched.

'That,' he told himself, 'is an entertaining bint.'

Ralph Fitzroy noticed that Miss Pringle's modesty was clearly compromised but thought that it must have been some mistake on her part; that she had dressed without appreciating the transparency of the fabric and was cavorting herself in ignorance.

Lord Hacclesfield nearly dropped his glass.

He was so shocked he wondered if his eyes were working correctly. He had fallen off his horse once, and, feeling dizzy for some time afterwards, had seen a pink deer. Perhaps this was a similar hallucination – a trick of the light initiated by some mental abnormality.

It was not. The truth was that the dress was transparent and Miss Amy Pringle was naked underneath it.

She was exploiting him with mockery and there was nothing he could do. She knew it and he knew it. He could not accuse her of being naked, even if he had dared in front of this assembly. She could deny it. She could enact innocence and he would look like a sordid voyeur.

Lord Hacclesfield knew that he had to establish his authority there and then or all would be lost. The scandal of his submission would spread around the shires like the plague and all the respect that he had earned over the years would dissolve overnight.

He opted for the simplest strategy.

'You are late, madam!' he bellowed.

Miss Amy Pringle dropped to her knees in a neat curtsy that was faultess in its grace and humility. She cast her eyes down and whispered in a voice of meek abjection.

'Please accept my humblest apology, my lord.'

Although unnerved by this sudden and inexplicable concordance, Lord Hacclesfield managed to gesticulate to a servant to lead the gathering to dinner. Ralph Fitzroy presented himself to Miss Pringle, bowed, and offered to guide her to the table.

She took his offered arm and smiled secretly to herself.

The placement of a dinner party is usually arranged by the lady of the house as she is the hostess. Lady Hacclesfield, however, had long ago surrendered all relevant duties in order to partake of a louche regime guided by her own hedonism. Thus Lord Hacclesfield had arranged the positions of each guest with the help of a factotum who had inscribed each card with the initials of every name and arranged them around the long polished table that swept down the middle of the dining hall.

Lord Hacclesfield's plan was not to everybody's taste. Trenton Dastard, who had hoped to be placed next to Miss Pringle, was squeezed between the ageing heiress and the bishop's wife; the bishop, meanwhile, though grateful for a position that prevented sight of his wife (whose aspect inevitably put him off his food), was placed opposite the squire to whom he owed quite a large sum of money.

Amy Pringle was, as appropriate, to the right-hand side of Lord Hacclesfield and to the left of Ralph.

Crab soup went round calmly enough; not too salty, not too cold. Everyone enjoyed it with spoons raised and nodding agreements about the virtuosity of the Lancaster Hall cook – a Mrs Prenderghast who the bishop's wife had been trying to lure away for years, and would have succeeded if the sums of the bribes had been one or two shillings higher.

Lord Hacclesfield sipped a glass of wine and actually began to relax. His wife sat at the end of the table flattering the bishop and making sure everybody's glasses were full. Gentlemen were not difficult to please; flattery and alcoholic beverage were usually enough to keep them satisfied.

All was well until the quail. Trenton, always inclined to ennui, began to grow restless, and who could blame him? He was drowning in a lake of placidity. The bishop's wife and the ageing heiress were both ghastly women, small-minded in their perspective, arrogant in their airs, ignorant, unread and unimaginative. Trenton felt the life drain out of him and he studied Miss Pringle partly for his own recreation and partly to ascertain if she was a partner in crime. She was sitting opposite him. Her face glowed in the candlelight and he could see mischief in her dancing eyes.

Amy was also bored. Lord Hacclesfield could only communicate the direst trivia and Ralph was devoting all his attention to the dowager on his left who had hunted all over England and had an endless fount of mundane anecdotes on equestrian subjects.

Trenton fired the first shot by introducing politics.

Ralph, aware that he was out to cause trouble, slung him an angry glance.

Trenton caught his friend's expression and chose to interpret it as a sign of encouragement.

Addressing Lord Hacclesfield, he asked (with studied innocence smoothing his brow), 'Sir, may I ask you what you think of the French?'

'Oh, for Christ's sake,' Ralph muttered under his breath. He reprimanded himself for allowing Dastard into this midst. Rows were his repartee – his only talent, in fact – and he had lobbed the most incendiary device possible into their midst. It was well known that Lord Hacclesfield hated the French with an intensity that was almost pathological.

Ralph made a slicing motion across his throat with

his hand in an effort to curtail this destructive sally, but Trenton merely smiled and continued to focus his attention on the interesting corner that was filled by the alert figures of Lord Hacclesfield and Miss Amy Pringle.

Pugilism was now in the air.

Lord Hacclesfield's politics were moulded by retention. That is, he supported anything that promoted the status quo, because the status quo was represented by his property – houses in three counties and some of the most valuable farmland in England.

He had been hit on the head during the Gordon Riot of 1780 and this had instilled a personal belief that the constitution of England was doomed to be destroyed by an orgy of sedition. The French Revolution fanned these fears and confirmed his distrust of radicalism. Once inclined to sympathy for the lower orders (though believing that they should learn to accept poverty and suffering as part of the nature of life) he now knew that they were a mass mob conspiring to achieve political dictatorship by violent ends.

'The French have introduced savagery to the civilised world,' said Lord Hacclesfield. 'Robespierre is a symbol of all the vices of men.'

'And what thinks Miss Pringle?'

Lord Hacclesfield was taken aback. He had never heard a lady's opinion being asked before, let alone an opinion referring to European politics. But he remained calm, sensing that Trenton Dastard was teasing her in order to stimulate the company with evidence of the lady's discomfiture, or even to avail himself of the opportunity to advantage her with some information and thus to provide service and refresh himself with the knowledge of a good deed done.

Lord Hacclesfield did not like the poet much – he had known his father and dissolute activities ran in that family like bad blood – but he assumed that, as a man, he would stick with his kind and sustain the dignity of his gender.

He could not have been more wrong. Trenton Dastard, despite being vain, selfish and lazy, was one of those rare men who not only genuinely liked women but was unafraid of them.

The poet smiled encouragingly at Miss Pringle. He had an attractive smile, in a leering kind of way. He wanted her to voice her thoughts.

Thoughts she had, thanks to her dear papa, who had allowed opinionated argument at his dinner table. He had never minded contradiction and enlightenment from his womenfolk.

Her words arrived clearly and lucidly in a defiant articulation that caused beads of sweat to break out on Lord Hacclesfield's brow and stick there like tears of unhappiness.

The bishop's wife actually gawped, as if she had just seen a rat walk across the table.

'War serves no purpose,' Amy said firmly. 'If England wishes to gain access to the ports to the New World it should do so by other means.'

'It is not just about new ports, madam,' said Lord Hacclesfield, laughing in a way that managed to be exquisitely patronising. 'It is about quelling a dictatorship and retaining the lands of our great empire!'

'Miss Pringle sounds as if she is falling in line with reformist thought,' said Trenton, helping his quarry to realise the full performance that her role required in this drama.

'I am unashamed to fall in line with Monsieur Rousseau,' she said, her eyes flashing with dangerous intelligence. 'I think that his *Discourse* was a masterpiece of speculative anthropology. I, like him, believe in the essential goodness of man and that evil only arrived with the evolution of property and society.'

The bishop's wife licked her moustache nervously with a thick pink tongue.

Lord Hacclesfield's body temperature rose.

'Madam,' he snapped nastily, 'I hardly think you are informed to speak of men's subjects. You would do well to keep to needlework and the poor basket and things that befit a young lady –'

'On the contrary,' she interrupted. 'I would warrant that I am as well informed about current affairs as any person at this table. I have read *The Rights of Man* by Mr Thomas Paine and *On Civil Liberty* by Mr Richard Price. I have noted Edmund Burke and know all the works written by both William Pitt the Elder and William Pitt the Younger. Furthermore, I have been to Paris and I have lived amongst the French. My mother, you may or may not be aware, was related to Madame Pompadour.'

The knowledge that this arriviste was not only a cheeky harlot, but that French blood poisoned her veins, caused the food to burn like acid in the pit of Lord Hacclesfield's churning stomach.

Trenton Dastard was now thoroughly enjoying himself. He had not had so much fun since three prostitutes went down on him under a table in an alehouse in Chelsea.

'I do not think it is a lady's place to read books,' the bishop's wife sniffed.

'I do not think it is a lady's place to bathe herself in the laziness of ignorance and prejudice,' Amy Pringle retorted. 'And I do not think prudish piety is a suitable replacement for enlightened discourse.'

The bishop's wife went very red and made a choking noise.

'When I was young,' she managed to croak, after a

41

sip of water was offered to her by a solicitous Trenton, 'when I was young, we spoke only when spoken to and when we were spoken to we considered it a privilege to be noticed by our elders and betters! The only book that should be read by any woman is the Bible, and that, Miss Pringle, *is that*!'

'Hear hear,' said Lord Hacclesfield, resorting to the brusque skills of debate that he had learned during his passing experiences in the House of Lords.

'That's as well as may be!' said Amy Pringle, now venting the full focus of her determination on the bishop's wife, 'but, lest we forget, your youth was a *very, very* long time ago.'

By now the room was silent as each guest listened to these contentions with various reactions.

Ralph was surprised. Miss Pringle's vehemence was unexpected. He had been led to believe that he was to marry a meek lass who understood the expedience of fulfilling her personal cause and would be humble to this process. He watched her much as he would watch an innocent new puppy that had just bitten his finger.

The bishop missed the confrontation due to a mixture of advanced intoxication and deafness, but had he been aware of it, he would have applauded Miss Pringle, as he would have applauded anybody who put his vile wife in her place.

Lady Hacclesfield, judgement clouded as always, vaguely sensed that there was trouble at the end of the table, much as one senses a grey cloud arriving on the horizon. She would not actually run for cover until a servant provided her with an umbrella or other form of protective appliance.

Bubb was strangely aroused by the show. He did not know why, he only knew that the blood was surging into the sinew of his prick and it was rubbing forcefully against the tight constraint of his breeches. He longed for relief.

The dowager sitting next to him noticed the protuberance extending in his lap and that its proportion fell in line with its advertisement.

'This man is hung,' she told herself.

A thin, big-breasted woman of 50 or so, the dowager was a rich woman resplendent in a symphony of lilac and silver that enhanced the white streaks in her dark grey hair. She had been handsome. Some said she still was. The life had not drained out of her, that much was certain.

She sat with her back straight, diamond tiara twinkling over the steel-coloured sea of her hair – an immaculate, immobile arrangement thanks to a mixture of egg white and secret ingredients known only to her maid.

Her diamond necklace rose up and down as the breath of her chest quickened. She smelled the scent of her own excitement and sensuality seeped into her pelvis as a grasping wet need.

She wanted Bubb's thing between her legs; she wanted it hard and she wanted it now.

Slowly, smoothly, she slid her hand beneath the tablecloth and allowed her bejewelled fingers to migrate to Bubb's thigh. From here they rambled casually between the warm passage of his legs and towards the groin itself, a hot place that was now dominated by the huge stress of his dick.

Her fingertips lingered and lay softly on top of the buttons on his fly. They felt the muscle lurch again and swell still further.

Then, with an insidious panache, more subtle than the snake in Genesis, more dexterous than a magician, she unbuttoned his trousers, slid her fingers into the opening and gently closed them around his burning knob.

Bubb groaned, but no-one noticed. All attention was fixed on Miss Amy Pringle and her dreadful confrontations with Lord Hacclesfield.

Bubb's shaft bounded out and into the dowager's hand. Her fingers closed around it as she attempted to ascertain his width; they could not do so. The girth forced them apart, as a fat stomach must force a belt to break its buckle; her slim palm could not contain the monument that was Bubb's lucky birthright. He was huge.

He was so big that the dowager wondered if she would be able to take him. She had not had a man for some years now, not since the death of her dear Jonah, and Jonah's tool could not be compared to the vast squab of boiling flesh that was now filling her hand.

The dowager withdrew her fingers nervously.

Bubb groaned again.

Opposite him Trenton Dastard was trying not to clap his hands and laugh out loud as Amy Pringle continued her attack on the delicate sensibilities of those who were surrounding her.

Lord Hacclesfield was now so angry that he was having genuine difficulty with his breathing.

Eventually, though, his voice arrived, as loud as the howl of a wolf in the midnight hour. He stood up to deliver his command.

'Madam!' he shouted. 'That is enough! Leave the table and wait in my study!'

Amy Pringle thought, at first, that he was speaking to the bishop's wife, who, it seemed to her, was deserving of this expulsion.

She blinked at the irate host in disbelief.

'I said go to my study! At once!'

The young woman flushed, paused as if making a

decision, then, with silent dignity, rose gracefully from her chair and left the table with her head erect.

The door cracked behind her with a snap.

Trenton watched her leave. What a lovely creature she was, so artless and arrogant, the soft white fabric flowing about her body as it lingered in all her curves, the shadows undulating beneath their folds. What he would not give to fondle every part of her living flesh. He could taste the skin on his mouth, smell her hair in his nostrils . . .

'You Judas!' Ralph spat angrily at him. 'What was the point of starting all that?'

Trenton shrugged with the indifference that had made women all over Europe worship his every action.

A flan went round and was eaten in silence. The ladies retired to the drawing room. The bishop and his wife left early.

The men sat in the dining room with port and cigars. Ralph, Bubb and Trenton huddled at one end of the table in a whispered conspiracy of mutual rebuke.

Ralph reprimanded Trenton while Bubb told Ralph that it was his fault for ignoring Miss Pringle at dinner. He knew from long experience that to ignore a lady was to stir up trouble as surely as to step in a badger trap was to have one's ankle snapped in two.

Lord Hacclesfield sat at the other end of the table with the squire.

'The Miss Pringle seems a coltish thing,' said the squire. 'Will she be tamed, do you think, or will you have to send her back to her stable?'

'Good question, Simon. A very good question indeed,' Lord Hacclesfield replied.

'Mind you,' said the squire. 'I have never owned a filly who could not be broken in. They all come around in the end – if you get them young, that is. The ones who need the most mastery make the best rides. That is my experience, anyway. You remember Sally? The grey mare? Impossible when I bought her, impossible! Kicking and shying! She bit the wife, if you please! But the groom took her in hand and now she is as good a mount as you could want. They just need to know who is the master.'

Lord Hacclesfield walked slowly down the corridor to his study where Amy Pringle was waiting. He did not know if she was mad or bad; all he knew was that she was going to submit to his will.

She was sitting – sitting, if you please – on his chair behind his desk. Her demeanour was calm. It was as if she was about to enjoy some pleasurable excursion, so placid was her manner.

'Miss Pringle!' he snapped, marching up to his desk. 'Stand up immediately!'

She rose slowly from her sedentary position and looked him straight in the eye with unabashed defiance.

'Come here, my girl!'

She did not move.

'Miss Pringle, either leave your position behind my desk or take the immediate consequence.'

Now, for the first time, she seemed unsure of herself, and ambled slowly around to where he was standing in front of his desk.

He took his own position behind his desk from where better to deliver his lecture.

'Miss Pringle,' he said, staring down at her with black eyes that were cold and angry and would have caused abject terror to any other person in his vicinity. 'Miss Pringle, I am most displeased with your display.'

'I do not know to what your lordship refers,' she said calmly.

'Miss Pringle, I remind you that you are a guest in

46

my house. This in itself demands a set of protocols that are traditional to the smooth running of polite society. Caustic wit, oral vulgarity and rowdy mischief are not amongst these protocols, and they are particularly not amongst them if that guest is destined to become a part of the family.'

He paused for breath and to collect himself.

Her flashing eyes roved unabashedly around his face and she actually smiled at him.

'Go on,' she said, amused.

Lord Hacclesfield resisted the compulsion to slap her very hard in the face. He felt a strong need to see the tears spring to her eyes and the little lips quiver. He forced himself away from the vision of pleasure that was Miss Pringle begging for his forgiveness, falling at his feet, even, moaning in apology.

He was swept away by the torrent of his words.

'Miss Pringle, you are now out in society; a young lady who is out is bound to obey the demands of her position. She is no longer in, she is no longer a girl who can indulge the carefree abandon that nursery games entail. She is not free, Miss Pringle. She has responsibilities to endure and a destiny to procure. She is a young lady and she must involve herself in all the prettiness that this privilege entails.'

'I do not see why I should be procluded from basic human interaction or be sentenced to idiocy and silence,' she said.

'Then there is much in which you are mistaken,' he said. 'You have, I believe, received some dreadful influences. I know not from whence these came, but they have blemished you and turned you into a vulgarian whose only hope is to be saved by those about you who are blessed with more wisdom, who know better than you, Miss Pringle, and are willing to impart their knowledge.

47

'I will tell you here and now, if your behaviour does not improve, I will direct my lawyers to cancel the prenuptial contracts and alert your mother as to their dissolution. You will, as a result of this scandal, be ostracised from every house in this kingdom. Your prospects, such as they are, will die. You will be condemned to die in the dry dust of spinsterhood – lonely, forgotten and a pariah.'

She seemed, at last, to be listening.

'Miss Pringle, I am going to take it upon myself to ensure that you are moulded to the conformation that will ensure your suitability to enter the house of Hacclesfield as its lady. This is a position of great honour and should not be flouted by cheek or undermined by the ungoverned self-gratification to which you have shown yourself so shamefully prone.

'In the event that you fail to come up to the standard that I require, you will be sent home. You will not marry my son.'

She seemed, at last, at a loss for words.

'Tomorrow morning, Miss Pringle, you will come here, at nine-thirty, and you will be severely punished. You will be severely punished as I see fit and for every sign of the behaviours that I have been unfortunate enough to witness since your arrival. You will also learn the lessons that I order and you will conform to the timetable that I set which will be designed to provide you with the accomplishments that are required of the future Lady Hacclesfield.

'I intend to make a lady of you, and if severe discipline and tough measures are required, then I will see to it that they are implemented.

'Be here at nine-thirty tomorrow, not a second more or less, Miss Pringle, or you will be on the road back to Portsmouth by lunchtime. *Do you understand?'*

Miss Amy Pringle tossed her head, but a pink blemish had appeared on her cheeks and a strange wet was creaming in the depths of her groin. How exciting to meet so challenging a person; she had never in her life been told what to do and when to do it. She had never known the submission of the flesh; it was all so new and eventful.

If Lord Hacclesfield wished to exert himself in this way, then so be it. She would not mind. She did not give a hoot. She was not afraid of him. He was stupid and old and he would not govern her in a hurry!

'I will come as you direct,' she said, and left the room without being told that she could.

Immersed in thoughts about the vagaries that were about to inflict her sensations, she bumped into Trenton Dastard in the corridor.

'I was looking for you,' he said. 'I am afraid I have got you into trouble.'

'Oh,' she said, smiling comfortably, 'I'm not worried. It would take more than that man to cause me anxiety.'

'You should beware of the good earl,' said Trenton. 'There have been many botties reddened in this house.'

'It doesn't worry me,' she repeated.

He looked at her and he believed her. She was free of agitation or fear or any of the maudlin sentiments that her sex inclined to generate. Her breasts moved up and down, slow and taut against the upper panel of her flimsy dress. The cleavage seemed, to him, to be begging him to some adventure; big or small he did not know, but the curves were driving him mad. He wanted to push her up against the wall and kiss her savagely; he wanted to thrust his hand down her décolletage, draw out her nipple and nuzzle it to taut excitement.

He wanted to do things to her.

'Madam,' he said, brushing her cheek with a light finger, 'you have brains and beauty and spirit. You have everything. You are like no woman I have ever seen. I feel that greatness is your destiny.'

He edged his body closer to hers, so close in fact that she could sense his hardness straining against her pelvis and feel it begging for her through the light fabric of her dress, nudging her to notice his need and be merciful.

Mercy was not Miss Amy Pringle's forte; she had had no experience of such a thing, and did not know how to exert it. She was good at riding, she could play lawn tennis, she always won at chess, but mercy? This was an unfamiliar game and she did not know its rules. However, Trenton Dastard emanated a certain promise of cruel lust that she had always enjoyed and, on impulse, she decided to play with him.

This was a man who had long had his way with women. She sensed that Mr Dastard was a conceited fellow, much accustomed to fulfilment – the type who would buy a lady her supper one minute, fuck her the next, then leave her alone in her solitary confusion for weeks on end until she was worked up into a frenzy of need. Mr Dastard was a bastard and, as a result, had probably been worshipped all his life.

But Amy, as always, had a plan.

'You may follow me to my boudoir,' she said.

Trenton Dastard trod behind Miss Pringle as she floated up the stairs towards her bedroom.

His dick was swelling with hard intensity; all he wanted now, all he wanted was to plunge himself into her and bang her until he satisfied himself.

She was maddening.

'God,' he thought in wonder. 'Perhaps I have finally fallen in love.'

Trenton Dastard had never actually been in love, though, as a professional poet, he had often pretended to be.

He had tricked many women into thinking that he was their faithful devotee with his neatly penned words of colourful amour. He knew how to write from the heart but he did not know how to feel from it. He knew how to fuck but he did not know how to empathise. His life was rife with women who would do anything for him, and he was spoiled by choice.

They came to him, sometimes bidden, sometimes unbidden. There was always a snatch to catch, a pussy to prick, a modest eye to stare into with the lascivious intent of one who always has his way. Trenton Dastard was persuasive. He could convince anyone to sleep with him. He had that knack – that mixture of handsome self-confidence and an uncanny knowledge of what women were thinking. These were the tools of his trade. He used them well and to his advantage.

Once the muse had been fucked good and hard he would write lines of satirical epigrams describing the details of her flesh and of her failings. He would denote her blisters and her boils to the commerce of common scrutiny and ensure that the world knew which scar was on which arse in Kensington.

Mr Dastard was a mediocre poet, but he was observant, so the maids who starred in his scurrilous diatribes could be well recognised by their friends and intimates. Trenton Dastard took a perverse joy in the controversy that he caused, the scandals that he broke, and the controversial inches in controversial newspapers that smeared his lovers' names.

Duels were often fought after the publication of his lines, but he did not care. He was a feckless fellow, but, as has been mentioned, he had none of the feeling to which he pretended. But Ralph was right. He was fun. There was always excitement when Trenton Dastard was around.

He entered Amy Pringle's bedroom, his long black

hair streaking down his back (a style he had copied from Shelley on once seeing him across a room in a London salon) and caught himself briefly in one of the pier-gilt mirrors. His brown skin had arrived from a distant Spanish ancestor, supposed to be a pirate, his dark eyes from the same place; they had also coloured his mother, a passionate woman who had died young.

He was not as tall as he would have liked, but he was slim, at least, and his legs were fine. He deserved the adulation that he received.

Amy's maid Milly was waiting in her room to serve her night-time needs. She curtsied respectfully as her mistress entered, and she seemed guileless, but her head was full of knowledge. The word had swept around the servants' hall like an airborne microbe and she was fully availed of the circumstances that had described Miss Pringle's first dinner. She had been sent out, but she had not, as yet, been actually punished. Lord Hacclesfield intended to discipline her, and the poor lady did not know what she was in for.

The servants had been shocked. Their master was a tyrant, but he had never (to their knowledge) smacked a member of his own circle. Milly wondered at the very thought of it; such disgrace and shame. Surely the lady would have to go home, humiliated and humbled? She hoped not. She liked her lady. She even fancied that she loved her.

There was a delicious smell of apricots and roses. A comforting fire had been stoked in the grate; candles flickered in silver holders. Milly had turned down the bed and plumped the lace pillows so that all was ready to achieve her mistress's comfort. A little cotton chemise lay on the cover, ready to be worn for bed.

'This is Mr Dastard,' said Amy. 'Serve him a glass of cordial, please, Milly.'

Milly curtsied again and went to obey the order,

slipping a good glass of liquor into the glass and bringing it on a small silver tray to Trenton, who lay himself on the velvet chaise-longue, lounging languidly in a manner that belied the intense excitement that was agitating his vibrant dick.

Amy leaned down and kissed him lightly on the lips. Her very scent was enough to make a man beg for elopement. The tone of the faultless skin was enough to make a man commit. In the past he would have reeled himself back, knowing the danger of such things, but now all he wanted was her, at any cost.

But it was not to be.

'Mr Dastard,' Amy informed him, 'I am not going to fuck you, but you may watch Milly undress me.'

'Oh, Miss Pringle!' he wailed. 'How you disappoint me! I am bereft. I hardly know what to do with myself. You do not know the torture that you inflict! Shall I beg, shall I prostrate myself, shall I weep?'

'You can if you want to,' she replied, 'but it will do no good.'

'Are you saving yourself?' he asked. 'Are you precious and intact, waiting for the delicious penetration of your husband-to-be?'

He became dizzy at the thought of her virginity. Defloration was more exciting to him than any other that made his wide range of vices.

'Don't be absurd,' she snapped. 'I gave that worthless maidenhead to Lord Cobbold when we were both seventeen. He wanted it, I wanted it. I could have sold it, I guess, but I didn't need the money.'

She further aroused the frenzied poet with a graphic description of the aforementioned 'violation'.

'You ask me how it happened?' she said. 'It was thus. We were at a ball, a grand affair. We had not even been introduced, but he had studied me from the moment of my entrance. I had felt his hot passion seering into me for every moment of the evening and I stared back, immersing myself in his fixated attention, and enjoying it. I knew from the start what he wanted. We did not even speak, but I knew. His eyes would not let me go. But I chose to let him take the lead and I danced as I wished – my card was full with the Lords Browning, Stenning and du Chevalier. They had booked me and there was no room for the strangers that I did not know.

'Finally, as I had finished a waltz with Lord Stenning, I think, Lord Cobbold strode up to me, anger contorting his beautiful dark features. His mouth, twisted with irrational jealousy, his eyes glittering with fury, he grabbed my hand and dragged me off the dance floor and into the garden which, fortunately as it was summer, was balmy with August heat, and private, for most of the guests were still milling in the pleasure of the party.

'Still silent, still leading me hard by the hand, he pulled me into a little gazebo. I did not struggle – it would have seemed hypocritical. I was enjoying myself, and I had never witnessed such intensity of passion – it carried me away. I was innocent, after all, and have always liked new things.

'Lord Cobbold as good as stole my virginity away from me. Still silent, still furious, he pushed me down on the wooden bench and trussed my ball dress up well above my waist. He savagely pulled down my silk petticoats (I wore them in those days, they were handmade in Paris, beautiful things) and, without even bothering to take down his own breeches, he pulled out that big beautiful dick and lunged into me as if it was his very right. There was no pain, perhaps because I have ridden all my life, I do not know, but there was no pain, only the pleasure of sensation as he plunged up into me and banged me until I screamed out with the exuberant knowledge that finally, finally, I had found one of the simple pleasures of human existence.

'Lord Cobbold took my virginity and he gave me my first climax and for that I will always be grateful to him.'

Thinking of the lovely girl ravaged in the gazebo hardened Dastard's muscle to even greater need. It bulged in his pants so that both Milly and her mistress could easily see it abound.

Milly unbuttoned Amy's dress at the back and it slid slowly to the floor as a pool of creamy folds. Neatly stepping out of it, she was now naked. Perfectly proportioned, her breasts were white and round and firm, her waistline dipped in as it should, her arse was nicely rounded with a healthy femininity that was curved.

Dastard watched the show, intense voyeur, wishing all the time that he could have her, that he could push her face down on that chaise-longue, then drag her up on to all fours, so that all he could see was spine and neck and the orbs of her perfect backside. He would have liked to sodomise the saucy thing, teach her that lesson, but it was not to be.

Abstention had been forced upon him by this sorceress. He was made to be a monk in a room full of temptation, sensualised beyond forbearance, hardened to the point of genuine agony, but forced to celibacy. That was his lot.

Milly placed the chemise around Amy and tied the ribbons at the back. Then she served her mistress a glass of cordial and Amy lay on her bed as recumbent as any Venus in any painting made lovingly by all those men who like to stare and reproduce the smooth features of mystifying femininity.

'Please, Miss Pringle,' Trenton Dastard whined. 'Satisfy me. I am going to die.'

He was nearly weeping.

Amy seemed to relent. She nodded arrogantly.

'Milly will remove your clothing, Mr Dastard.'

She motioned to Milly, pointing at the poet's feet.

The maid knelt in front of him and removed his boots, one after the other. Then she peeled his breeches slowly down his thighs and stripped him. The dick sprang up, a hard shaft with glistening tip.

The maid looked at her mistress, awaiting further instruction.

'Lick it, Milly.'

The maid bent down and licked the vermilion tip that now glowed on the top of Trenton Dastard's erection.

He wailed as her tongue triggered every nerve-ending in his body.

Then she took the whole in her lips and rubbed the warmth of her throat up and down on it, as if her mouth was a cunt, soft and moist and tightening at her own volition.

Up and down, saliva and dick, the blood now pulsing unbearably, until all he wanted was one thrust, one final lunge into the soft murk of her white groin, the indulgent welcome acceptance of her thighs, that was all. He was ready to beg for final release. The juice started to bubble on the tip.

'Please,' he moaned. 'Finish me, my love, finish me!'

Even in the frenzy of his insane lust, he could feel Amy's eyes watching him, sense the pleasure of her observation as he writhed in erotomanic humility, detached from love, forbidden from fornication, alone because of some arcane displeasure that he had incurred in the dreadful seat of her soul. If she had such a thing.

'That is enough, Milly. Remove yourself from Mr Dastard now, please.'

Milly did as she was told.

'You may go now, Mr Dastard,' she said.

Mr Dastard fell back into the cushions as if he had been punched in the face. His clothes were scattered, his dick was waving like a weak lighthouse in a storm, his pelvis was convulsing. He was disabled by dissatisfaction.

But there was nothing he could do.

Silently, sulkily, he pulled his breeches back over his burning hard-on and slid his legs into his boots.

'Good night, Mr Dastard,' said Amy.

'Good night, Miss Prick-Teasing Pringle. You are playing a very dangerous game.'

The door closed softly behind him.

'Ooh, miss, you are dreadful,' Milly giggled.

'I know. It is one of my many talents.'

Milly brushed her mistress's hair and completed her toilette with a sense of pleasant apprehension. She knew now that there were thrills to be had and Miss Pringle was going to initiate them.

'Good night, Milly.'

'Good night, Miss Amy.'

The maid left the room and Amy Pringle blew out the candle.

It had been a most satisfactory day.

Chapter Three

*A*my, still half asleep, slowly brought herself into a world that she did not at first recognise; she had awoken thinking that she was in her own home, then she saw the fresh white curtains which fell from the frame of her bed and opened on to her new room. She saw the portraits of the various befrilled royalists who were related to the Hacclesfield family and she saw the chaise-longue where Trenton Dastard had received his due. The scenes of the previous day flowed slowly back into her memory and with them came warm satisfaction. She had found herself in a house full of fuddy duddies and dimwits; they all wanted to make her and mould her. They were doomed to fail.

They were doomed to fail because Miss Amy Pringle was an unusual person. She was not a parochial ingenue. She had travelled extensively and she had lived amongst some of the most debauched royalties of Europe. While many maids of her milieu remained closeted in the security of convention, content to bide their time until a suitable arrangement was made to confirm their conubial future, Amy had spent the early years of her life living near Versailles when the mores of the day were coloured by the libido of King Louis XV, a man who knew no restraint and whose proclivities influenced the behaviour of his court as surely as a stone thrown into a pond sends out a circle of waves.

She allowed herself to drift into reverie; to reflect on how she had become possessed of both an unusual resilience and an exotic perspective.

Amy's 'education' was not an education in the traditional sense of the word. It was an education that befitted all aspirational ladies of the time. The French court in which she had moved was devoted to one thing and one thing only – to please the king and, in particular, to ensure that his sexual appetites were satisfactorily addressed at all times.

Her mother, Ernestina, sunk into dangerously impoverished circumstances after the untimely and premature death of her husband, Amy's father, Hainalt Pringle. Her daughter was on the brink of womanhood and thus required both connections and a dowry if she was to fulfil the full profit of her potential.

Hainalt Pringle had had a useful social prestige bestowed upon him for services rendered to the king in his capacity as Official Sergeant of the Stag (an administrative role pertaining to the royal family's hunting activities), but he had been cut off in the prime of his life and his legacy was such that it forced his wife to entertain a wider breadth of options than would normally have been required by the circumstances.

Ernestina Pringle was an ambitious and independent-minded woman whose own inclinations were the result of prodigious appetites. These were said to have exhausted her husband and been responsible for his early demise, but the fevers that could strike a man down at this time were many, varied and inexplicable.

Blame should not be apportioned to Ernestina. The fatal apoplexy was probably not her fault; suffice it to say that she had to carefully consider her own position as well as that of her daughter and use both her connections and her cunning to implement the means necessary to their survival.

To this end she had cast her eye over the channel to a place where the simple attributes of youth and beauty could propel a woman to unimaginable heights thanks to the tireless energies and unbridled self-indulgence of the man known as the 'Love King'.

History relates that, as a very young man, Louis XV was inclined to a worrying neutrality with regard to matters of the heart. It was thought that this might have been as a reaction to (or silent protest against) the Duc d'Orleans, his uncle, who, while acting as Regent, indulged himself in unbridled pursuits.

His particular joy was to engage in volatile three-somes where one lady would hold down the other so that the duc may enjoy her. This, of course, initiated a fashion, and the court enjoyed a fad where forceful troilism was *de rigueur* and enjoyed as a delicious rite in all the sumptuous apartments of the palace.

No evening was complete unless wine and supper were followed by a voluptuous *ménage à trois* where the marital couple would engage a third party to embroil herself in their needs. Thus Madame la Duchesse de Chateaubriand sat her plump behind down on the stomach of the beautiful Comtesse de Mignon, forcibly spread her legs wide apart, bent over her, placed her face deep between her thighs and licked her to glistening desire while watched by her husband, Monsieur le Comte. His lady, thus physically con-strained and heightened by sisterly ardour, received him warmly when, at last, and as the result of her begging, he inserted himself with ferocious solidity, and lunged until they were both reminded of the early passions of their marriage.

At this stage Louis XV seemed disinterested in these tastes. He avoided orgiastic suppers and committed himself to the merriment of wine and games. His dispassion caused consternation amongst the nobles who circulated in his life – if energy could be expended on drinking and hunting, they asked, why could it not be usefully expended in the boudoir? It was unnatural, was it not, that so lively and handsome a youth should waste his time so when the nubility of the nation was waiting as a happy throng to cause him all the pleasures available to man. And if he could not bring himself to engage in the basic normalities of sexual expression, there was the blood of the royal line to confirm.

The courtiers who milled around in the daily life of the sovereign collected into pressure groups committed to rectifying the matter and dedicated to ordaining their liege into the religion of love.

Seven young women were hand-picked to pique the king's interest.

Seven young women were transported in a fleet of state coaches to Chantilly, where the prince was staying.

Seven young women were ordered to arouse the majesty's ardour and make him a man of the world.

This collection of wild soubrettes were said, at the time, to represent the seven deadly sins. Certainly they were disparate and deviant in their tastes and in their appearances. La Belle Helene, for instance, could befit the sin of Greed, plump as she was, blonde, big breasted and inclined to gorge herself on any sweet-meat that came her way. La Belle Helene liked to eat and fuck in that order. Her favourite pastime, though, was to engage in both pursuits at the same time.

Served a silver palette of delicious chocolate truffles, hand-decorated by the royal chef, she was pleased to place one inside the warm cavern between her legs and allow it to melt there. When the titbit dissolved into a sweet goo dribbling temptingly on her leg, she offered up both morsels, choc and cunt, to the tongue of her friend, Mademoiselle Fleuret, a red-headed miss who nuzzled Helene's delicacies with an enthusiastic enjoyment that culminated in chocolate around her mouth and the noisy climax of the voluptuous Helene.

Antoinette, a dark beauty whom satirists caricatured as Envy, sought to transgress her gender by dressing in manly hunting suits of emerald green velvet tricked out with buttons made of lapis-lazuli. Lean and tall, and manly in her physique, she made it clear that the young prince could have all the illegal pleasures of pure buggery if he so desired. So intent was she to achieve this end that he wandered into a privy chamber one morning to find that she was waiting for him, stark naked, bent over, touching her toes, thighs widespread, back to him, retaining the position with calm grace, so that all he could see were her buttocks spread and the lewd offering of her rectal opening ready for him to take as he pleased.

The ladies committed themselves to their patriotic task with admirable dedication and imagination. They danced close to him, rubbing their warm breasts, whispering dreadful promises of excitation, subsuming him in their scents, their skin, their promises of indescribable transport.

But he remained cold in his regal frugality.

The seven sinful temptresses were forced to return to their various homes, a diaspora of disappointment.

Rumours began to circulate. The ladies of the court believed that their ruler must enjoy the unspoken love of men. Statesmen perceived sinister political motives.

A few cardinals (to whom nobody listened) told each other that, here at last, was a virtuous king, blessed with God-fearing ways that would set a good example to all.

Then the Duc d'Orleans died, leaving the country to be ruled by Louis XV. The duc's mistress, La Duchesse de Faloris, knew where her duty lay and took it upon herself to perform the long-awaited ceremony of defloration.

The initiation took place in the royal bedchamber one sunny morning in April and was witnessed by an audience of *valets de chambres*, ambassadors, and at least three cardinals whose presence was necessary to sanctify it in the eyes of God and to swear to its genuine validity in a ceremony described as the Signing of the Scroll.

Thus the king stepped majestically into the house of pleasure and began to create the atmosphere of intrigue and erotomania that made his reign so enjoyable.

His nuptial obligation was fulfilled in the form of a political arrangement to the dutiful daughter of the former King of Poland, but nuptial obligation was to become a minute aspect of the king's erotic vista.

Queen Marie, exhausted by the dreadful rigours of relentless childbirth, started to decree days of abstention which quickly propelled the priapic energies of her husband to other bedrooms where they became an unassailable force.

To be ravished by anyone is, of course, a benefit, but to be ravished by King Louis XV of France was considered to be a downright privilege.

Wild promiscuity was simple enough. The royal decree was absolute. An order was an order and had to be obeyed without question by all those who moved in the courtly circle at Versailles.

Nobility bought cash and cache, but it also demanded abject aquiescence; the palace was a termite hill where each part of the buzzing heap fulfilled its natural role in the procession of the designated sequences of royal life. The king's will was absolute. It was the only thing that mattered. And it was the only thing that influenced an individual's real destiny. To please the king was to further oneself, and not only oneself, but a good many of one's family and close friends.

Those disadvantaged by prudery or modesty or simple (but unusual) feelings of fidelity towards their husbands had to implement clever plans to circumnavigate royal solicitations without causing offence or risking his wrath. Most, though, were not inhibited by scruple (though failure tended to breed a degree of tight-lipped hypocrisy). The king got what he wanted, when he wanted it.

Valets de chambres would be sent forth to pluck the various duchesses from their places of rest and they would arrive in carefully ordered stages of attractive déshabillé. It was usually night-time, after all, and a lady's toilette was at its least formal – a scant chemise, a silken dressing gown, hair loose. Thus arranged she would submit to the lusts of her master and receive rich remuneration for her favours.

Salaries of sensuality provided independence and luxury to those who knew what they were about. Gaudy apartments, political prestige, even castles and jewels, these were only a few of the benefits to be gained when a lady answered the tap on the door.

Unsurprisingly, then, most ladies made sure that they were ready for such an event and their post-prandial costumes assumed a state that was designed to cause effect in the event of lucky chance.

More than one husband personally escorted his wife

to the door of the royal bedchamber when the nightly knock tapped on the door. Others actually volunteered their spouse's services before they were requested. The debts of a duke can be many and creditors can become downright dangerous when news of a man's gambling losses circulates about the place. A prick to the wife was preferable to a knife in the neck. Sacrifices had to be made.

Marriages were indubitably restored by these processes. Men whose virilities had been undermined by the stress of impending poverty found their health restored by the promise of rewards. Women appreciated the return of their husbands to their beds, inspired by confidence, and vigorous with fresh energies.

The fount of the monarch's boundless sexual energy served to invigorate many people in strange and subtle ways.

The fortunes of Amy Pringle's mother were related to the rise of one Jeanne-Antoinette Poisson, who was to become Madame de Pompadour. Her adept skills not only fulfilled her own professional desires but served to benefit her immediate milieu.

She began life as Madame d'Etoiles, married, it is true, but cognisant of the salient fact that this sacrament should never prohibit the fulfilment of potential.

She set out to attract the attention of the king. Aided by youth and beauty, she accoutred herself in stunning ensembles of the most fashionable styles created in eye-catching colours. As the florid hues of blooms are effective in any garden, so the pinks and royal blues that encased the tempting physique of Madame d'Etoiles lured the king to her natural cause.

Monsieur d'Etoiles was exiled to a well-paid job in Provence and Jeanne-Antoinette ascended to the height to which she aspired.

Madame de Pompadour was one of those women

who understood men. She was untroubled by the dangerous belief (the downfall of so many) that a man would change as a result of the power of his passion. She wasted no time with hopes for fidelity or monogamy or the romance of concentrated focus. They were delusions and particularly misguided when applied to an individual who could have anything or anyone and always had.

Sensibly detaching herself from her own sexual ego, she instinctively catered for the facts of life; lust, though hard and intense and enjoyable, was short-lived. Her days would be numbered if she did not ensure that the king remained engaged and excited. It was not a question of straining herself to remain the centre of the king's attention: this, she knew, was an impossible project. It was a matter of reigning over his proclivities so that she had some control over them.

The king must have the luxury of choice. He must be able to taste many fruits. Madame de Pompadour set about providing those fruits.

Appointing herself 'Surintendent de Plaisirs du Roi', she founded Le Parc aux Cerfs. This was placed in a house on the outskirts of Versailles, a pretty building with extensive gardens and apartments, that was to become an official seraglio – an academy for the training of young ladies predestined to be the king's pleasure.

The aristocratic aspirants received the benefits of lessons taught by the most successful harlot in the free world while Madame de Pompadour received the benefits of official gratitude – both from influential families and from her king.

The population of this strange school was comprised of the daughters of the wealthiest landowners in France; as a son had to attend Eton in England if social progress was to be insured, a French daughter was pushed towards Madame de Pompadour's academy.

There was a long waiting list and the entrance fees were very high. Virgins were preferred: their rarity made them a valuable asset and they could be traded for a very high price in a market manned by rich libertines whose purses were easily opened when this commodity was successfully advertised.

The king himself was known to be particularly enamoured of 'innocence' since it provided a safeguard against the syphilis that ravaged the parts of even the wealthy and the beautiful with vicious but egalitarian zeal. Powerful voluptuaries were not immune from the hideous effects of their choices and the court had seen some dreadful sights as many of their number fell victim to dermatological horror and fleshy degeneration.

Only those in favour with Madame de Pompadour gained access to Le Parc, either as clients, or as students, the latter of whom were the progeny of trusted allies and wealthy connections with whom she wished to retain mutual loyalties. Once they were accepted, and the fees paid, the chosen daughter was guaranteed a presentation to the king. She graduated, as it were, to court. Some pupils, of course, did not please the royalty, but this was a gamble that their families were willing to take.

Thus it was that Ernestina Pringle wrote a pretty letter to her dear cousin couched in the most fetching and flattering terms and enclosing a sum of money large enough to attract her attention but not large enough to constitute vulgarity.

Gracious Cousin,
I implore your kindness in times of familial straits and ask for your favours. My daughter Amy is now of

67

marriageable age and I pray that she might be allowed
a position in your happy house in order that she may
receive the lessons necessary to receive the blessings of
the court of the beloved King of France.
  I remain blindly and passionately devoted to you.
  Ernestina Pringle

So Amy Pringle entered Le Parc aux Cerfs and found
herself amongst a group devoted to a vocation that,
though secular in its sensuality, was devotional in its
specifics.

At first she observed the scenes as an explorer might
regard a hippopotamus in the jungle – watching it with
a mixture of fascinated curiosity and excited by the
strange danger that any rare sighting must ignite in an
adventurous soul. She was never intimidated or
unnerved, but the spectacles that unravelled before her
served not only to formulate the strains of her inner
philosophy but to teach her a wisdom that came to
inform all aspects of her future modus operandi.

The combination of sensual sophistication and the
permission to make use of the tools of femininity were,
perhaps, instinctive to her, but in the lessons learned at
Madame de Pompadour's establishment she found a
material means to express them – the techniques, if
you will, that are required to realise womanly advantages and achieve enriching results.

She already knew how to embrace her own needs
with her fingers and had enjoyed gratifying waves of
self-satisfaction. She knew something of the nature of
climax and release, but she soon came to realise how
simple and ignorant she was in these matters.

The first months of her term at Le Parc were guided
by Madame de Pompadour's deputy, Madame le Fontanelle. A woman of 30 or so, Madame was qualified

for her position by a life that had taught her all the skills required to survive at court.

There were some who claimed that Cerise (which was her name) had attracted the powerful Duc de Vichy when he spotted her out walking in the Galerie des Glaces at Versailles but this was negated by the salient truth that Madame never walked anywhere if she could help it. She had spent most of her life on her back and recumbency was her position of choice. It was more likely that she was presented to the duc by her uncle, a desperate financier who had made some unfortunate choices in his business. The duc had liked what he had seen and paid a large sum of money to buy Cerise. He had not actually done her the honour of marrying her (he had a wife and two children living in Languedoc) but he had installed her in a magnificent chateau and she had reigned supreme for four years until the inevitable occurred and she was replaced by a younger woman.

Cerise le Fontanelle had foreseen this. The life of a *mondaine* is naturally short. The stock must be used when it is at its height and the pension for life must be secured in a short period of time. Cerise's flowering had been exotic and resplendent and she was not bitter. She had never liked the duc much anyway and had resented the tiny proportion of his dick, only bearing it because its size was counteracted by the size of his wealth. Fumbling penetrations were not to her taste (are they to anyone's?). She had cut her losses and retired gracefully to the position kindly offered by her friend and ally Madame de Pompadour.

Madame le Fontanelle greeted Amy with polite ministrations and some private instruction.

She was a tall, slim, elegant person, beautifully dressed (often in the crimson that befitted her name), and walked with grace. As a young woman she had received dancing lessons and was naturally athletic; this exercise had served to benefit her deportment and a natural fluidity of movement stayed with her.

She was not a kind teacher so much as a professional one. She was paid well and she took pride in her work. A job well done ensured continual favour with both the king and with Madame de Pompadour, and Cerise felt that she could not ask for much more out of life.

She was an effective teacher and gained satisfaction from imparting information on impressionable minds whose devotion was not difficult to secure.

Amy met her in her suite, a lush set of private rooms that were her living quarters and which included a well-furnished sitting room luxuriated with soft fabrics, paintings of *fêtes galantes*, and a glowing fire which warmed the room to a comfortable temperature.

'Welcome to Le Parc aux Cerfs, Mademoiselle,' said Madame le Fontanelle, standing up and floating across the room.

'Thank you, Madame,' said Amy.

Madame sat down on a damask sofa but did not ask Amy to do the same. She remained standing like a soldier on parade and her face began to flush, both from the heat from the fire and from the focus of the older woman's eyes that were now fixed on her, drinking in every detail of her person.

'The lessons learned here will be of great use to you,' said the older woman. 'They will aid you in every aspect of your life and teach you all the secrets of true womanhood.'

'Yes, Madame.'

'Now please take off your clothes.'

'My . . . what . . .?'

'Do not ask questions, Mademoiselle. I think you heard me correctly. Your mother did not inform me of any defects affecting your ears. I said take off your clothes. At once, please.'

Amy was wearing a dress that had been especially made for her life in the courtly circles of Paris. It had been the result of many detailed discussions between her mother and a dressmaker in London. It had cost a debilitating sum of money, but it was a perfect combination of modish simplicity and presumptuous trimming. It was the dress of a woman who assumed she was going to travel far in circles of wealth and power. Furthermore, as her mother said, its simplicity meant that it would remain of use when other more frivolous fads had disappeared with time.

The bodice, low cut, revealed her chest to her cleavage and was made of brown velvet; the skirt swept the floor as was the fashion at this time.

The problem was that Amy had had little experience of undressing herself. She had always had a personal maid, and though she had had to leave her behind, she had expected that there would be servants versed in these skills on hand to help a lady with her divestment. There were maids at Le Parc but one was not present in this room. Amy was forced to travel the course alone, and an obstacle course it was, replete with many difficulties.

The bodice, at least, opened at the front thanks to a series of tiny brown velvet bows and these could be unwound, though with unpractised hands it was not easy. She did not know how they worked and spent some minutes fumbling with the first one, yanking and wrenching it to release her from its bondage. The second bow was easier and now her breasts began to pour out as the opening became looser.

She dropped the bodice to the floor. Her torso was naked, her lower body still clothed in brown velvet from the waist down. She could not at first remember how this thing was attached to her body, with what strange bindings or buttons, then recalled that the maid worked from the back and she reached there to find some further ties which, with some determination and dexterity, she finally managed to distentangle. The waistband loosened and the skirt dropped slowly down her legs and fell as a pool to the floor. There, now, was only a simple silk underskirt and stockings; the first undid like the overskirt and also fell easily to the ground. The stockings wound down the legs, though ungracefully, and with some hopping about the room.

These clumsy contortions took twenty minutes or so and were undignified by an ease. Her mental and physical focus had been forced to concentrate on the complex workings of the wardrobe with which she was so unfamiliar. Still, unclothed at last, and naked, she straightened up and stared at her observer with triumph and pride in her eyes.

Madame remained seated regally on her sofa, her back erect, and chin out, her demeanour imbued with the advantage of being fully dressed.

Amy did not mind being naked, particularly. It was quite warm and she did not see that there was anything to be ashamed of, but she was aware that she was being tested and, though she may have failed the test, she was not going to allow Madame to have the benefit of superiority.

Madame le Fontanelle stared with some pleasure at Amy's perfect form. The girl was beautifully proportioned – not too fat, not too thin, a sweet waistline, a flat stomach, delicious peach buttocks, a smooth skin that would stay with her all her life. Some gentlemen might think that she was too boyish; others would like her exactly because this was so. She was fortunate to have plump breasts that supported themselves and gave her a womanly charisma that may have failed her if she had been flat chested.

'Dreadful!' she snapped. 'Dreadful. Dreadful. Dreadful! The object of divestment, Mademoiselle, is not to make a man laugh out loud. The object of divestment is to tease and procure. I will show you.'

Madame le Fontanelle stood up and, with her eyes never leaving Amy's face, slowly began to relieve herself of her rich satin dress. It was a beautiful thing, cut to fit her body and emphasise the slender waist, the low-cut bodice supporting a firm bosom, encasing her form in a sheath the colour of dark blood that was matched by the subtle paint on her lips. The voluminous skirt rustled as she moved. Slowly, smoothly, long tapered fingers moved to the front of the bodice where the opening was fastened with buttons made of tiny rubies. First the top, then the second, then the third, all detached with deliberate purpose, so that the dark cleavage of her breasts eased out of their trapping.

Madame le Fontanelle's skin was a light brown, reflecting her Mediterranean provenance. Her slanted green eyes flashed in a frame of dark eyelashes and her mouth was set in an enigmatic smile.

Amy watched, hypnotised by the darting lights that reflected from the diamonds around the older woman's long neck. Then, magically, the dress dropped to the ground, falling from the shoulder, smoothing down the waist, easing into a pool around the tall body, where it stayed as an ocean of lush red water. Madame le Fontanelle stepped neatly out of it. Now she was naked except for a neat pair of black shoes, adorned with tiny silver buckles, and a pair of thin silk stockings that ended just above the knee. Stepping out of these too, with smooth movement, the clothes were now discarded on the carpet.

Then she sat down on the sofa and slowly rolled the

stockings down her legs, from knee to ankle, caressing her fine calves as she did so, unembarrassed in the grace of her narcissism.

Long, languid, lean, the fine body now melted as brown liquid with the gold velvet of the sofa.

Amy, immersed in this event, delighted in the loveliness of the woman before her. How wonderful to know that a woman's beauty could retain its lines, to be made aware of a future full of feminine enchantment whose mysteries were merely a matter of sensual knowledge. Such long legs, such smooth buttocks, such a neat triangle of black hair between the thighs.

So intriguing was this delicious tableau that she had quite forgotten her own nudity. She wore her skin as a chemise, clothed in her nakedness, and comfortable with it.

Madame le Fontanelle lay as a dark feline sorceress, reposed in unashamed seduction, knowing her powers.

Slowly, still fixing Amy with the mesmerising gaze of her green eyes, she spread her legs apart and revealed the folded crimson recesses between her legs.

'Come here, please,' she said.

Amy could not have done anything but obey. In reality, there was little choice, but even if there had been she would not have taken it. She was transported by the spell, excited by the novelty and propelled by the urge to discover. She did not think; it was as if she had become a doll.

Madame le Fontanelle pointed to her clitoris.

'This,' she said, 'is the centre of a woman's pleasure, as I am sure you are aware. A man often knows little of this place; he often does not care. It is a woman's prerogative – no, her duty – to be familiar with all its secrets, for it can serve her well when the frustrations of reality make themselves apparent in the bedroom. Know this and you know everything. His parts are the subject of another lesson, Mademoiselle, a lesson that you will also be taught, but for now, you will learn about me, and by so doing, learn about yourself.'

Amy knelt down by the sofa and moved Madame le Fontanelle's pelvis towards her.

'Lick me with your tongue.'

She did as she was told, tentatively at first, of course, for this was unfamiliar, and she did not know what she was doing. She only had her own body as her guide, and there was no knowing how others differed.

'A little harder. I like to feel,' said Madame le Fontanelle.

Amy moved her mouth on to the minge with urgency and worked it with her tongue. Madame le Fontanelle threw her head back and breathed out with a pleased gasp. Amy continued to lick her, enjoying tormenting her now, loving the power of giving pleasure, for Madame was now writhing and begging her to go on and on. She was moaning her pleases and Amy knew that to stop would be to torture her. But she did not stop. She wanted to see the finale; to know how far she could go with this simple intimacy.

'Stop now,' said Madame le Fontanelle. 'Go to the chest on the cabinet and bring me my toy.'

Amy went to the cabinet and lifted the lid of an ornate silver chest. Inside there was a velvet purse and inside this a white phallus of smooth ivory whose base was carved silver.

'Lick me some more and then ease this gently into me,' said Madame le Fontanelle.

Amy, on her knees again, licked the swollen labia of her mentor.

'Now! I am coming. For God's sake, now!'

The pelvis was gyrating, the venus was wet with excitement, the internal passage was flooded for reception. Amy gently poked the tip of the dildo into

Madame le Fontanelle's opening, and very slowly eased it in. Then she pushed it up and down until Madame le Fontanelle was transported into some other place, a place where only climax mattered.

Amy pumped her with the dildo.

'Yes, my darling, yes.'

Her body seized, her pelvis thrust up, she gave herself up and collapsed into the velvet, relaxed.

'Good girl,' said Madame le Fontanelle. 'You are going to do very well at Le Parc aux Cerfs.'

Thus the first lesson ended.

The so-called *'maison d'amour'* was inhabited by an unexpected cast whose diversity could be better understood when one knew that it was designed to please a king who had become increasingly perverse as he grew older.

Boredom had set in, as it must when a man can afford anything on the menu. A lobster might appeal at one meal, but lobsters at every table lose their attraction and the gastronome will desire other comestibles. He may even turn to plain fare because he has never eaten it, or he may order monkey's brains served fresh out of the skull simply because he thirsts for new experiences.

The king was always searching for fresh delicacies to excite his appetite. And what delicacies they were.

A dozen or so girls had been picked to cater for his diverse tastes. One or two had been found accidentally by the monarch himself; there was a milliner's daughter called Suzanne who had been found behind a counter in a shop in Paris, and there were three nuns, as Louis XV's eccentricities had taken a religious bent and he believed that to make love to God's wives was to aid one's progress in the afterlife.

Like many debauchees of maturing years, Louis XV

was beginning to feel slightly nervous about his secular exploits and wanted to assuage the unpleasant feelings of insecurity that occasionally shot him bolt upright in the middle of the night. Feeling hot, as if the fires of hell were literally licking his skin, his composure could only be restored by the cool presence of a devout body beside him, a body that could relax his tensions and aid him in prayers for forgiveness.

So the sisters were recruited to minister holy favours and to please the king in all the ways that he liked to be pleased. It was an unconventional combination, but one that seemed to work for the parties involved. The nuns spent their time between Le Parc aux Cerfs, the abbey and the palace. Their duties were not too arduous and their sense of sin was non-existent.

They were doing their duty, after all. The word of the king was the final word. That is what the abbess had told them, anyway; what she had not told them was the size of the generous emolument that it had been her pleasure to receive from the royal purse.

The nuns gave Le Parc aux Cerfs a gravitas that it might not have easily possessed. They also gave Madame de Pompadour an edge over the competition. Houses of pleasure had sprung up all over Versailles, intent on cashing in on the currency that was the king's rampant promiscuity, and the insatiable appetites of his circles. There was also the lucrative tourist trade; Versailles attracted noblemen on Grand Tours and those noblemen, inspired though they doubtless were by visits to Florentine churches, knew that true delight lay in Versailles.

The regular influx of European nobility gave rise to a demand. This demand was catered for by women of lowly stature and commercial concern who founded franchises of bawdy-houses offering a wide choice of pleasure for a wide range of price. You got what you paid for. A low fee bought a cheap strumpet, it was as simple as that – though cheap strumpets were very popular and worked day and night, they represented the bottom end of the market.

Those with money preferred to avail themselves of luxury items. Nevertheless, Madames de Pompadour and Fontanelle had their work cut out for them in their efforts to retain an edge over the competition. Nuns and virgins ensured this. No other local madames could offer nuns and virgins in such replete supplies, or of such a high quality as those available in the royal brothel.

Thus the house emanated a mystique as musky as any civet scent and the heady odour of exclusivity that tends to arrive when an elite is created. The wolves prowled, they snapped at the door, and those with wealth and titles were allowed access. Gentlemen (if that is the correct description) of great renown knew that their disparate tastes could be catered for and were pleased to pay for the recreation.

Amy shared a bedroom (and a bed) with 'La Petite Minette', a moniker which referred, naturally, to her companion's physique which reached a height of just below five foot. Her petite stature belied her personality – though she looked tiny and innocent, she was from Normandy peasant stock and was possessed of a physical strength that (it was said) was the sum of an ox when it came to necessities such as ploughing fields as she had been forced to do as a girl.

All that, though, was well in the past. La Petite Minette was a 'star' pupil and her fame had spread far beyond the boundaries of the city of Paris. Indeed, poems had been written about her in Vienna and Venice, while verses of a less exaltive nature (i.e. rude songs) were sung about her in the galleys of ships sailing to the West Indies.

This celebrity was the result, by and large, of a painting by Boucher who had depicted her naked on her bed engaged in a most informal posture that intrigued everyone who looked at it and enraged the Pope who issued various letters of condemnation and caused a *succès de scandale* upon which La Petite Minette's useful notoriety rested. She sometimes said that she would like to kiss the Pope on the mouth for being so kind to her.

Boucher's image was much copied and printed; La Petite Minette's naked form was reproduced in limited edition folios sold underneath counters and the image had even found its way on to the fans of ladies attending balls in London.

Minette, then, was a pin-up. Everywhere she went people stared and whispered.

She was plump and personable and privileged by a rosebud mouth pressed into the kind of permanent pout that makes men fling themselves off cliffs.

She had been taught how to use that pout to gain results. She may have learned this for herself, with time, but the teachers at Le Parc aux Cerfs hurried the process along.

Minette was a person who knew that one must never show excitement when showered with gifts by wealthy suitors. One must receive all blessings with a raised eyebrow and a polite smile that says, 'Is that all?' The mouth does not emit these actual rude words, but the mien remains calm in the face of real diamonds and gold trinket boxes. A donor must never labour under the impression that he has pleased the object of his desire, for once this occurs he will inevitably fall into complacency, think that he has achieved conquest and, with the pressure off, will arrive with tokens (flowers and so on) rather than the carefully chosen diadems that represent his family heirlooms.

La Petite Minette never allowed any man for one minute to think that he had gained her heart. She was called cold, she was called cruel, but the gifts and men kept coming, to the satisfaction of Madame de Pompadour who kept ten per cent, and to the gratification of Madame le Fontanelle who had taught the protégé many of the devices that she so ingeniously implemented.

She enjoyed the worshipful devotion of several wealthy lovers but the time was drawing near when she would have to make a choice. Highest on the shortlist was the Duc du Rochelles who had presented her at the Opera with admirable panache and gallantry, considering the disopprobium he was suffering from every branch of his immediate family.

Minette's beauty, however, could not be denied and the duc was determined to marry her before the king caught sight of her and all was lost. The evening that he arrived with his late grandmother's diamond tiara was celebrated with champagne.

La Petite Minette, always impressed by celebrity, would enjoy telling Amy tales about the famous men who had visited the house and once detailed the memorable occasion at which Casanova had supped and fucked.

'The Great Lover Himself?' said Amy, who always enjoyed a tale, especially when she and Minette were lying in bed and, in the event of arousal, release could be achieved by warm and friendly fingers.

'The very same,' said Minette, well aware of how the details that she was about to impart would affect her companion.

'Do tell.'

'It was a great day for Le Parc. I have never seen Madame le Fontanelle so nervous. I have never seen such excitement, so many preparations! Monsieur

Casanova had sent letters from Venice describing the exact nature of his requests and Madame le Fontanelle set about obeying them in every detail.

'He paid many, many thousands of livres. Madame would never reveal exactly how many, but I know it was a lot, for the expenses were great.

'There were to be no virgins. Monsieur Casanova does not like to waste time with them. He has had bad experiences, apparently, and though he occasionally enjoyed defloration, it was not his main delight. He prefers married women, for they have had some experience, and they are less likely to cause romantic complications.

'The virgins, once taken, tended to cry and follow him about, and Monsieur Casanova's life was complicated enough as it was – he was a spy, you see.'

'A spy!' said Amy. 'I did not know that.'

'Ah, *oui*, he was an *homme d'espionage*. It was the reason I believe that he had to leave Venice in such a hurry ... anyway, Madame le Fontanelle was directed to avoid virgins, which was simple enough, of course, but it meant that I had to be excluded from the festivities ...'

Minette said this primly, as if virtuous morality had directed this stance when, in fact, it was well known that she was sensibly retaining her hymen in order to sell it to the highest bidder.

'I heard all about it later, of course. And I was able to watch some of the events through a window until I was caught by Madame le Fontanelle, who threatened to tan me in public if I did not go to bed immediately. But I saw most of it and heard about the rest of it later.

'Madame le Fontanelle found four ladies who had long foregone their innocence and all of whom were experienced in the games of love. She also knew that they would enjoy the drama of new adventure, being

81

inquisitive and intelligent and easily bored. Josephetta and Marie-Claire were married; Ines had long been a mistress to the Duc d'Escalier (who contracted her out for the evening) and Simonetta wanted the money to go to London to join her lover.

'They all received specific instructions as to what would be expected of them and the means to best smooth the transaction. They were all professional.

'The preparations! They went on for days. Lanterns were hung in the gardens; the gardener dyed twenty doves mauve and pink; a band was hired to play viol and pipe as *le monsieur* arrived. The whole house was scented with jasmine, every mirror polished, every carpet beaten.

'He was served his supper in *le grande salon*. Les Madames Pompadour and Fontanelle entertained him themselves, and gave him the best wine of the house.

'Then they retired and the four *mesdames* were ushered in by a servant. They were all naked and they were all masked, the colours of each mask matching the colours of their pubic hair, which had been especially dyed for the occasion.

'Simonetta was splendid in white and silver ostrich feathers; Ines had a pink fur mask over her face; Josephetta was a vision in black and gold with high coiffure and pointed shoes. Marie-Claire was a peacock in blue and green.

'They stood in a row before him, all masked, all nude. And he inspected them, as a sergeant major will inspect a row of soldiers, gazing at them with intensity and circling them like a dog.

'Occasionally he would lift a bejewelled hand and stroke their skin with his fingers, a nipple, a shoulder, the skin of the buttock, and each would shiver involuntarily, for of course they were excited. They all

82

wanted him, but they already knew that only two were going to be allowed this privilege.

'Their fannies were warm, but there were to be only two and the two who were chosen would be paid more. Simonetta was particularly nervous as she really needed the money. She knew that her lover was waiting for her and it would not be long before some other hussy filled her place.

'He then bade them all to crouch down on all fours with their buttocks in a row facing him.

'This they all did, so that there was a neat line of bottoms round towards him, their masked faces away from him.

'He knelt behind each one of them – and do you know what he did?'

'I cannot imagine,' said Amy, who could, but who was more interested in hearing the facts.

'He slowly inserted two fingers into each one of them and fingered them in order to assess who was the wettest. Poor Simonetta lost as nervousness had prohibited her, and Ines too fell by the wayside. Josephetta and Marie-Claire were dripping and they were the chosen ones.

'He then bade them all stand up and hold hands and thus he led them to the *première chambre* in order to have his pleasure.

'Simonetta and Ines were forced to watch the proceedings tied up. Josephetta and Marie-Claire, still masked, were bade to lie on the bed, one on her back, one face down.

'Josephetta, who was on her back, was then fingered some more until she was writhing with the want of him. He encased his hard organ in a thin sheath of kid leather, a very fine thing, and one which he had had hand-made. He had a huge supply, and it protected him as well as increasing the pleasure of the ladies.

'He lunged himself into her, bringing her to the heights of pleasure, as Marie-Claire listened to her cries for help and of joy.

'Marie-Claire began to beg him to enter her, yelling out that she would die if he did not. She was face down. He pulled her buttocks towards him and did her that favour. He took her like a dog, and pumped with his delicious throbbing hard leather-covered dick.

These scenes left Amy excited.

'My,' she said.

'You like that?' said Minette, placing her fingers into Amy with skilful wisdom.

'You like that?'

'I like that.'

And Minette with kindly grace brought Amy to the climax that had begun at the idea of the great lover and ended with the real softness of her companion's skin, the passion of her caresses and the hard nubbing of palm on clit.

One day in June, when Amy had lived at Le Parc for three months or so, Madame le Fontanelle called her to her study and announced that she had been picked to entertain the Duc de Lausanne. This was considered to be a privilege. The duc owned vast estates in the north of France; he was related to the king and he was well connected. If Amy pleased him, her success would be assured and her reputation would spread. It was a way to garner a useful kudos that would bring her to the attentions of the most influential people at court.

The Duc de Lausanne taught Amy Pringle things about humankind that she could never have realised in her imagination, fecund though it was.

The duc galloped up to the house on a frothing black stallion with an entourage of four noblemen, all resplendent in dark velvets, all carrying swords, all young and handsome and confident.

Wine was served in the premiere suite, a large salon decked in ultimate luxuries – soft sofas, gold tables, silken wallpapers, ornate sconces from which candles flickered the complimentary light that hide a lady's infirmities and provide a golden glow to her complexion. It was also equipped with a large bed covered in red velvet that had seen the scenes of sensuality that had made Le Parc aux Cerfs famous.

Amy looked her best. Carefully dressed by Madame le Fontanelle, she was gorgeous in a cream silk embellished with gold brocade and ivory lace.

The duc was interested in sodomy, that most Catholic of requisites, and Madame le Fontanelle had decided that it would be to Amy's advantage to learn this skill. It was a necessity, she believed, for all her girls, both of use in regard to birth control, and because it allowed a virgin to remain intact. It was one of the most requested sexual activities amongst her noble clientele. Buggery was a career move.

The Duc de Lausanne was a tall, lean man of 28. His long face was blessed with jagged cheekbones so defined that they made him look almost gaunt. Indeed, some ladies claimed that he looked as if he had been exhumed, so pale and hollow were his features. But, to Amy, he had the fascinating appearance of a Gothic wraith; his blue eyes were piercing, his nose, though long, gave the face character. His blond hair was also long, almost to his neck line, and added to the pallor of his appearance. His mouth, sensual, was set in determination when in repose, but lightened with warmth when he was amused. The duc's smile changed his personality; he turned from an intimidating sullen aristocrat to a charming lover in the fleeting seconds that are fluid emotions, and though he was not often amused, his smile was enough to reassure his lovers that he was human, after all, and there was actually a heart beating in the lean body of this stern man.

He was, at first, a little threatening. He was accustomed to obedience and he was unaccustomed to articulating warmth. Humanity was not often asked of him: he had estates to run, after all, and he had been to battlefields at the behest of the king. He had seen much and he knew to keep his silence if he was to preserve himself.

Amy experienced some of the palpitations that are the anxieties akin to stagefright. These performances were new to her and she was not, at this point, naturally confident. The duc was magnetic, but he was also a stranger, a stranger dressed from head to toe in skin-tight black leather. The breeches were leather, caressing his long thin legs like soft skin; his riding coat was also leather, cinched in at the waist, immaculately tailored to his shoulders and chest. His riding boots were also dark leather. He was a tall blond succubus dressed in black and she had never seen anything like him before.

She was too aware of her own inexperience; too worried by the vagaries of the unknown. She was stepping forward into a dark place where anything could happen and where if she was not pleasing to this important customer, there would be repercussions of detriment. She did not want to fail.

But the duc quickly took control and she, relieved of the tension of making decisions, allowed herself to be carried forth.

'Mademoiselle,' he said. 'You are as lovely as they say you are.'

Amy curtsied and lowered her eyes.

'Thank you, sir.'

His four friends were sitting, long and languid, in the various chairs that dotted around the room, and she was aware that they were all assessing her and awaiting instructions.

'Turn around, please, madam.'

Amy did as she was told, allowing him to survey the back of her neck, the cool white of her shoulders, her waist, and then around to her cleavage and her face.

The duc liked what he saw.

He stepped towards her and stroked her cheek with one finger, the lace of his sleeve lightly touching her skin, his calm blue eyes drinking her in. Vision had long impressed the duc; the power of sight was his pleasure and he knew how to stimulate himself with the fleeting aspects that were a lady's cosmetic flirtations.

'Pierre,' he said quietly. 'Please remove the lady's robe.'

Pierre, a dark man with amused brown eyes and a trail of black hair, slowly raised himself to a standing position and ambled over to the middle of the room where Amy and the duc were standing facing each other.

Slowly, with intent but with none of the comfort of speech, he eased his sword out of its scabbard. It was long and silver and lethal and, at first, Amy suffered the momentary panic of death; for a few seconds her mind actually threw up the possibility that this Pierre, this aide of the unknown the duc, was going to kill her for his master's pleasure; that the fetish of the duc was to see the blood ooze from a woman's chest, that his luxury was to see her slowly fall to her knees so that he could luxuriate in the dark joys of necromancy.

But this terror was tiny and fleeting – the seconds of imaginative impulse thrown up in momentary waking nightmare. Horror was not the order of this day. The duc was not a savage; he was a sophisticate, though he did enjoy the experience of Amy's vulnerability. He knew enough about women to sense that here was a brave maid who could easily turn to true defiance when experience had provided her with confidence, but now, now she was his because she knew nothing. It made him want to protect her, and to want to protect her was to feel the blood surge into the leather-bound groin.

Silence was still the atmosphere – silence and candlelight, and the smell of leather and men who rode and the lemon cologne that Madame le Fontanelle had splashed on Amy's neck in the preparations of her toilette.

Madame le Fontanelle had kissed her.

'You will please,' she said. 'You are special.'

Now the dark Pierre brandished his lethal sword with skill and, standing some distance from Amy, with the accuracy of a talented marksman, he pointed its very tip at her as if he was about to plunge it into her. Amy, determined not to show fear, stared unblinking into the eyes of the duc and he stared back, a half-smile on his lips, the erection now pulsing in his prick.

Pierre slowly brought the sword down from the front of Amy's dress and sliced the bodice with the razor-sharp edge so that it opened, like a peeled orange, allowing her breasts to spill out of it as two orbs buttoned by two hard brown nipples. Slowly he sliced the lethal stainless steel down her front and the dress fell into two pieces.

The cream silk fell, like curtains, on to the floor. It had cost many livres. It was her favourite dress. Now it was in a pool of silk on the floor around her feet and she was naked except for the matching silk shoes and silk stockings gartered with lace just above her knee.

Pierre stepped away and was replaced by two others, actors on cue, who took Amy by each arm and forced her face down over the red velvet bed.

Then, with soft cord, they bound her wrists above her head and arranged her legs so that they were splayed out, spreadeagled.

The pale flesh of her thighs and buttocks were a delicious palette of provocative sensuality; they exorcised all the duc's old demons and replaced them with a host of new ones.

A velvet cushion was placed underneath her stomach so that her buttocks were raised towards the man, allowing him the pleasure of the spectacle of her naked arse, waiting for him, constrained and under his control.

Then someone else came forward – she did not know who, but she was aware that there was a stone flagon in his hand.

'Spanish olive oil,' said the duc. 'The best in the world. It comes from the olive groves of the Spanish king himself . . .'

Alien fingers smothered the warm grease into Amy's backside, rubbing it over her buttocks, down the cleft, and finally insinuating the tip of his finger slowly but with determination, up her back passage and well inside her, manipulating her rectal muscles and whispering encouragement until she was relaxed and ready to allow the nobleman the pleasure for which he was waiting, hard dick in hand, as his minion prepared for his entrance.

Amy, face down, could see little: she could only sense and smell. There was musk and leather and sweet olive oil. She was glad that the goblet of red wine had relaxed her; she was not anxious now, only interested and excited.

She allowed herself to sink into the endless soft red

velvet, to offer up her intimate privacy to the order of the man.

And now he was on her; she could feel the leather of his thighs and then the tough knob, a hard thing easing itself into her back passage, insolently teasing all her unknown areas, finding new routes to the depths of her insides, until her head was dizzy and she howled out the pleasure of this new enjoyment.

He was in her now, all the way, and there was only him and her. She knew that she was being observed by the men in the room, but she did not care. In these moments there was only the duc and his dick and the rampant plunging of hard gratification.

Her bottom wiggled, her pelvis jolted, and she moaned the whimpering supplication – an animal whining that the duc loved. Oh, how he loved it. He withdrew sharply and shot himself over her writhing orbs.

She lay silently on the bed for some minutes, attempting to re-enter reality. Somebody untied her wrists. Two men led her to the bath salon and lowered her into the warm scented water that was awaiting her.

Five of them watched as Amy lay in the iron bath, torpid and dreamy, as Madame le Fontanelle gently soaped and sponged away the oil and the musk.

And then the duc himself lifted her on to her own soft bed where La Petit Minette was waiting for her, warm and naked and ready to stroke her as she fell to sleep.

She never saw the duc again.

Chapter Four

*A*s Amy became engaged in the mores of le Parc aux Cerfs household, she came to learn its ways and to fit in with its intentions. The warm months rolled on. Her breadth of knowledge widened, her sensualties awakened and her libido became enlightened with the full scope of erotic experience.

Some days were devoted to riding, some days brought dancing lessons. On Mondays there was a reading group; on Tuesdays conversations in French. Thursdays were energised by the famous artist Bon Boullibonne, a man whose personal mien was dominated by his *joie de vivre* and his hair which was thick and brown. He regularly ran his fingers through his spectacular locks as if in order to ascertain that they were all still there or, perhaps, to indulge himself in an appreciation of their smooth silky texture. If he was not doing this he was flicking it off his face in a bird-like gesture that served to exhibit the thick beauty of his curls as they briefly rose up in a hairy cloud around his head before settling back down on to his shoulders. Imagine these particulars combined with adamantine

91

self-belief and clear brown eyes and you have Monsieur Boullibonne.

He was not tall, but he was ebullient and he was persuasive, and these gave him presence. He was also possessed of an attractive smile and an easy laugh which, when combined with the shameless flattery that he deployed with convincing panache, served to provide him with a wide circle of female admirers who were pleased to submit to his every whim.

The son of a hat-maker from Perpignon, he had made his way to Paris after learning basic painting techniques in Montpellier and serving an apprenticeship to the portrait painter Marchant.

Marchant, one of the busiest portraitists of his generation, employed several assistants to finish the various details to his paintings. One would devote their days to depicting fruit or flowers, while another would finish the gleam required of a battledress. Bon Boullibonne proved himself to be a master at realising flesh and drapery folds and it was to these ends that he mainly worked.

Marchant taught Boullibonne the importance of accurate decorative detail, but he also taught him the importance of surrendering reality to the commercial priority of flattery – a rule of design that had to be obeyed by anyone who wished to either accrue commissions or make money.

Boullibonne had learned this lesson well and had implemented it to his advantage when commissioned to paint the Duchesse of Montpellier. She was known as La Grande Madame, not only because she was grand in the English sense of the word, but also because she was vast in size. Teetering over the edge of Rubensque into the realm of unmanageable adiposity, La Grande Madame was both tall and wide. Her shoulders were Herculean but it was her breasts that attracted universal comment. They were said to be the largest in France, and possibly Europe. Certainly there were no known contenders for this prime position of mammarian prestige. Her body was dominated by two swollen balloons that billowed out of the middle of her thorax and could only be contained by complex structures made out of leather and whalebone and designed by a peculiar man who worked from an attic in Marseilles.

Boullibonne was fascinated by La Grande Madame. He adored her amplitude – the roundness of her arms, the way that the skin folded over her belly and thighs like reams of smooth pink fabric. And he loved her breasts, the way they bounced and wobbled, the way they were applied to her – cumbrous protuberances destined to cause chaos.

He quickly insinuated himself into her affections, which was not difficult – he was handsome and charming and 23. She was rampant and unrestricted and 43.

His particular pleasure was to submerge his face into the warm pink interior of her cleavage until he was actually short of breath; then, with heart beating and his chest heaving in a desperate bid for air, his groin would surge with turbulent desire and he would suck on her nipples like a baby on a bottle until both he and Madame had encouraged the compulsion to unite in insane fusion.

Sometimes he would lose his dick between the rolling flesh of her thighs, winding himself towards her hidden hole with clever pelvic contortion and the instinct of a blind man – for her legs were undulating matter of flowing skin and the tiny bulb of her mons was well hidden. He preferred to release himself between her breasts as she pushed them on to his twitching shaft, squeezing them on to him as they became moist with her sweat and his juices.

These scenes of soft, corporeal confusion were of

great delight to Bon Boullibonne, but the work itself was more difficult. The portrait of La Grande Madame posed almost insurmountable problems of linear perspective. Her body's vastitude broadcast brooding venality; nude she was unfashionable, clothed she was out of proportion. He had to create an image that would provide some semblance to the real Madame, while complimenting her, and making a tableau that worked in terms of composition and design.

It was an illustrative conundrum, but Bon Boullibonne faced it, unafraid and full of confidence.

He employed the clever and advantageous ruse of painting Madame as she wished to see herself. He had long known about that secret place shared by all women, and he knew that even the most exquisite wished that they were taller or shorter or fatter or thinner. They all longed for (and indeed prayed to the Good Lord for) their breasts to be firmer, or their thighs leaner or their mouths wider or their hair curlier.

Boullibonne knew this about women, and he could assess the whims of their vulnerabilities in the time it took for the artist's eye to assimilate the full detail of their basic construction. Vanity was his currency and he knew how to exchange it in order to avail himself of a price that benefited all.

La Grande Madame was well pleased with his interpretation of her magnificence. Given majestic grandeur as the goddess Diana, she was blissfully removed of her double chins, of her fat little fingers, of the jowls that had begun to dissolve her cheeks. She was given slender hands, and beautiful round breasts, and her eyes were restored to the brilliance of her youth.

The picture was admired by all and served to convince the viewer that La Grande Madame was a true beauty; there it was for all to see. Her husband, who had paid for it, was also well pleased, for when he became depressed by the deprivations that were presented by ageing, he could look at Boullibonne's dignified image and enjoy the suspended disbelief of created memories.

Boullibonne's lies were lies but they did no real harm. He believed in his right to sensualise depiction. Art was a licence to please.

Arriving in Paris with a reputation founded on his famous picture of La Grande Madame, work quickly came his way, and he completed a series of pictures of popular actresses whose mentors were willing to pay high prices to buy records of the beautiful women on whom they spent so much money and expended so much personal emotion.

Boullibonne's fresh brushstrokes complimented every tendril of hair, every swing of the hip, every gloss of the lips. He gave his patrons pictures that enhanced the lady's beauty and advertised her lover's power. Confirming these things for both parties, his works reassured them, and asserted a hold over the dreadful depredations of time and age.

Beautifying without qualm, he supplied odalisques immersed in dreamy languor, glowing with flesh tints, their bodies vibrant with incipient sensuality. The paintings were personal panegyrics to shapely sexuality and a calm exposure of aesthetic liberalism that aroused men and women alike.

He was particularly adept at the erotic allegory because he had learned that to place a nymph in Arcadia was to allow her to be ravaged by a centaur or a satyr. His subjects easily became Syrinx or Pitys, voluptuous and semi-clad, resisting the rapacious advantages of Pan, the shepherd god and phallic divinity.

The artist tended to use the young Comte Marcel Marello to play Pan both because he was a friend who needed the money and because Bon Boullibonne would have desired him himself if he had been more curious in that direction. All the ladies lusted after the young count; to present Marcel Marello in the guise of devilish deity was to present the promise of orgy to Boullibonne's studio, and Boullibonne always encouraged this. In his view his studio should be a place of recreation as much as work. He, as a voyeur, observed lewd proceedings with the pleasure of one who knew how to inspire himself.

The promise of Pan's phallus quickly spread around the court and every actress worthy of her name worked on her patron to produce Boullibonne's fee. It soon became known that this fee not only bought a portrait of great grandeur and beauty, but the sittings presented the young Marcel in the guise of allegory and, as the ladies soon discovered, this was a man whose groin was ready to deliver goatish pleasure to anyone who prevailed upon it.

Mademoiselle Bagneres-de-Bigorre was painted as a naiad rising from a cool pool of green water, naked except for the shower of the waterfall that fell about her in translucent streams. Marello, as satyr, took advantage of a lunch break to fall upon her, spread her white thighs, and fuck her on the floor amongst the dust and paint and discarded brushes.

Ninette was laughing and dreamy as Aphrodite, but she demanded more than one wood genii; she ordered a festival of hairy bodies and goats tails and elementary spirits of the forest, all muscled, all naked, all hard with their own sensual zeal, kissing her pretty toes, picking her excited nipple with sharp fingernails and one, one young god, kneeling in front of her, his mouth looking ready to kiss her mons, close enough even to lick it if he wanted. It was a daring posture whose devilish exhibitionisn was barely covered by the fact that it was art. It gave people ideas. It angered the prudish. It was perfect.

Many people wondered whether Bon Boullibonne would be able to top the *succès de scandale* of 'Aphrodite', but top it he did by persuading the actress Berthe Arbois to appear in an obscure allegory which required her to appear nude amongst mythological reptiles of dreadful proportions.

Berthe, a lovely redhead with pale flesh, had green eyes and an atmosphere of provocation that was instinctive rather than self-conscious or considered. She lay as a naked siren amongst the monsters of the deep.

They were horrifying, with jagged blue teeth and yellow eyes and long purple tongues, yellow claws and scaly tails, some wrapped around each other, writhing in the obscene force of their own sinewy mating rituals, but some slithered in attendance on Berthe, the siren herself. Shells on her nipples and a mother-of-pearl shield on her pubis served not to camouflage her nudity but to draw attention to it.

The lascivious creatures – some half-dragon, half-alligator, some contorted with men's legs and the faces of wolves – eyed her with lascivious gleam, a pack ready to spring, spit drizzling from gums, swollen red testicles hanging from the dark hair of dog-like loins. One vermiform creature was seen wound around her leg, the tip of its tail underneath the shield on her lower pelvis, painted with clear detail and obvious in its intent, for even the most naive observer must know that the tip of the monster's tail was rubbing against Berthe's soft vaginal ridges and exciting her with bestial amorality.

And Berthe? Boullibonne painted her looking upward, but not in the prayerful piety seen in icons of the Virgin Mary. Berthe looked upward as if at the point of orgasm, eyeballs rolled back into her head as if the attentions of the half-breed were exciting her beyond reason. And her face? On her face the smile that is usually only seen in the bedroom when the man first starts to find the internal triggers, that smile of knowing and pure pleasure. It is an expression of sexual enigma; it is not a laugh at a joke nor is it the spontaneous joy of everyday life. It is amused, it is grateful, it is purely female.

Bon Boullibonne knew this look because he had loved many woman and he had fucked some of them purely in order to study them visually. Berthe had that smile because once, while she was sitting for him, he had persuaded her to insert her own finger into her gash and show him how she pleased herself.

The Duke of Macon saw the picture of Berthe and asked Boullibonne to paint a picture for a gallery at his chateau in Vendome. Boullibonne sensibly provided an Olympian scene and asked all the most beautiful women at court to be the goddesses. There was a perfunctory allusion to the death of Dido, but the picture was an undisguised excuse to portray a suggestive display of erotic posturing; girlish body wound into girlish body as a bemusing welter of arms and legs.

Then came the longed-for accolade – the warrant of royal approval and the plum of the career. Madame de Pompadour ordered Bon Boullibonne to her apartment. He portrayed her as a vestal virgin surrounded by frenzied worshippers. After this he could do no wrong. Soon he was receiving commissions from the king and it was Louis who had commissioned the picture of the young women at Le Parc aux Cerfs.

Boullibonne had depicted them in Hades, infernal region of the underworld. This was a land that allowed licence to any fantastic creation that his mind was capable of conceiving and his hand was capable of illustrating. It was an innovative work, and one of great ambition, for there were many subjects and many scenes.

The artist unleashed the darkness that murked in the abyss at the bottom of his soul. His morbid illumination illustrated sins so varied and so dissipated that he was credited not only with inventing new vices, but with inspiring the onlooker to try out atrocious novelties that it had not been their previous inclination to commit.

The hallmarks of traditional Hadeian concept were found in this landscape. The River Styx (Hatred) was dark and bubbling with frothing yellow spume; The River Acheron (Woe) was the thick red of human blood; the river Lethe (Forgetfulness) was a turbulent current fed by the tears of nubiles who were pictured weeping on its shores. Fallen women tormented by spasms of unchaste guilt, they were lovingly detailed in naked discontent, each youthful body a beauty of sylphine nudity, each aureole of each nipple picked out with a detail brush, each tendril of the pubis immaculate in its reality.

Some bodies were knitted together, one on top of each other, a mesh of limbs and arms and necks and groins. Here a lady squatting down on the face of another, smothering her with the lewd offering of her minge; there a woman on all fours being guzzled from the back by the pert mouth of a hungry sister, all intertwined in a picnic of clit and tongue.

On a green hillock overlooking this scene, there was a horse painted in gold leaf and bearing a lone rider – a tall dark woman with flowing black hair that snaked down her back to her waist. She was clad only in a black mask and she was carrying a thin black whip.

Court circles knew that this was an accurate portrait of La Jeunesse, mistress of the poet Alain de Gentilhomme, whose pleasure (it was well known) lay in the merciless torture of her lover, a man whose back was well lacerated by his beloved flagellant and who willingly submitted to the correction of his wayward character. He had written many odes to the joy of her cruel caresses and the love that was to be found in the intimacies of a chosen flagellant. Now she was symbolised as the Queen of the Erinyes, the terrible trio of avenging harpies who had been born from the drops of blood which bled from Uranus's severed penis. Implacable, resolute, cruel, the Erinyes' duty was to ensure that men did not have too much power. They were licensed with the task to punish crimes, hound victims and drive them mad.

Bon Boullibonne's picture also showed the Titans, chained in lower Tartrarus. The Danaides, who had murdered their husbands with hairpins, were seen attempting to drink through sieves; Alastor, the Demon, penetrated the dead Medusa with his purple dick; and the vampire daughters of Hecate were engaged in a Sapphic rite of neck-biting and cunnilingus. Some immersed long fingers into the inner regions of their own vulvae; some contented themselves with biting necks or thighs or posteriors.

They were watched by a pack of dogs wearing leather masks chained to the wrists of the Keres, winged death spirits whose maniacal pleasure lay solely in the sight of bodies, welted and whimpering and transported in the transcendence that arrives with the rigorous melding of pain and pleasure.

Cerebrus, the Hound of Hell, was pictured, huge and drooling and wolverine. His gaping maw was a landscape of infernal scenarios. Bleeding gums sprouted long yellow jagged teeth from which the naked bodies of men and women were suspended in chains. Some were upside down, some were not, but all were shown being tormented by Boullibonne's gangs of demented demons, a race of dreadful creatures with distorted genitalia, scaly faces and pointed ears.

They were engaged in titillations of the suspended souls, some looping long crimson tongues into exposed sexual orifices, lapping anal sphincters or ruby clits until the supplicants seemed to actually moan out loud.

This painting, entitled 'Les Femmes d'Acheron' (an allusion to the Stygian river of Affliction) provided the backdrop to one of the greatest, longest and most abandoned orgies that Versailles had ever seen. Its event was recorded in many diaries and letters, but only the most adept writer could articulate the full gamut of sexual options that were entertained during this extraordinary rite.

The preparatory drawings for, 'Les Femmes d'Acheron' were completed during the three days that the subjects were gathered at Le Parc to be studied and drawn for the final picture. Twenty or so men and women assembled for this enaction of hellish torment; their sense of reality ebbed away as the boundaries between life and drama dissolved and unleashed the darkest desires of the heart and head.

Boullibonne lost all control. Later he blamed the wine. He had supplied many flagons from the finest vineyards, thinking to relax the ladies and encourage the young men, some of whom had travelled from Milan and even further in order to dramatise themselves as the classical heroes of myth.

The mixture of hard men and horny ladies posing for scenarios in a bizarre necropolis ignited a frenzy whose animal sexuality was brilliantly realised in the final picture. Ladies lips lapped men and women alike; stiff dicks visited places that they had never been allowed to enter. The Monsieurs Pierre and Philippe,

101

wearing only ivy headdresses, sodomised each other in front of an audience of a dozen excited onlookers. Mademoiselle Antoinette's smooth derrière received a lashing from a hirsute mercer (dressed as a demon) which left a tapestry of purple marks on her fine white flesh for a week.

Bon Boullibonne had completed, 'Les Femmes d'Acheron' some two months before Amy arrived at Le Parc aux Cerfs. The work had been received well at court. The king (wrongly thinking that the picture's hellish torments represented instructional morality and would help to redeem his endangered soul) hung it in a chapel where the abandoned scene of orgiastic excess angered a visiting papal nunciate. He called upon the Chief of Police and Boullibonne had actually been threatened with arrest.

Determined to lead a quieter life, the artist had decided to escape dangerous attention and lower his profile until the excitement of 'Les Femmes' died down and he could restore himself to the sanctity of privacy.

He contented himself with teaching the rudiments of line drawing to the young ladies at Le Parc. These lessons allowed him to ply his theories about philosophy and aesthetics and were enjoyable sessions held in the *petit salon*, a sunny room on the ground floor at the back of the house.

Bon Boullibonne looked at Amy, young, pert, blonde, a gleam in her eye, and he knew that she must be his next model. The tension of her incipient sexuality could be well exploited in the aspects of sensuality which were his particular talent to illustrate. He would paint her alone in a simple rustic setting that would offset the bloom of her skin and illuminate the innocence that she was on the brink of losing.

'You will be my Flora,' he said to her. 'The lovely Goddess of Spring.'

So she spent the warm afternoons in a leafy bower in a woodland on the edge of the garden. The sun spattered through a thin canopy of leaves and kissed her flesh, warming her body which was loosely wrapped in a drape of translucent silver silk.

Boullibonne's admiring eyes aroused her and made her want him. Boullibonne could kiss a woman with his stare and dizzy her with compliments.

He circled her, smelling of paint, his long hair, brushed, fine, showering his shoulders. He was smiling and giddy with the pure delight of being alone with a girl, naked, beautiful, and his to control.

So he circled her, whispering compliments into her ear, whispering compliments and frightening her with fantasies about her effect on him: how he wanted to fall on the ground in front of her and kiss her feet; how he wanted to nestle his fingers between her thighs and tingle her cunny until she shrieked out loud; how he would love her and marry her and make her the subject of all his paintings, the most beautiful woman in France. His muse. She would be written up in the notes of history; everyone would know who she was. She would be an immortal Venus in the historical annals of images, destined to live on along with Caravaggio's bacchantes and El Greco's saints and all the angels of the Renaissance masters.

If Amy had not been born with cynicism her head may have been turned by this man; if her mother had not set her right on the basic principles of reality before she had even set forth to France, she may have actually believed what he was saying and become damaged by superfice.

Falsity is a bad friend; it leads a girl along dangerous paths, paths where winds fan her ego and lies are the food of immature loves.

Bon Boullibonne did not care about any of this; he

103

was strange and wild and attractive but he was amoral and he did not consider the real effects that his flow of promises may have.

He talked to Amy of men and love and all the pleasures that were so easy for women to obtain. They only had to understand the warmth of their own pussies, the nerves of their own inner places, the subtle prowess of breasts and lips and hair and eyes.

She always became wet when Boullibonne was painting her; she often wondered about the cock in his black breeches and, one day, curiosity subsumed her.

'Why should I always be nude before you?' she said one afternoon when they were alone. 'Why should you not be nude before me?'

Undaunted and unabashed, he carefully took his organ out of the opening in front of his breeches.

She had hardly had time to register its significance, even its shape, before he was in front of her.

Placing his hand on the top of her head, he pushed her down into a kneeling position in front of him, so that her mouth was in front of the red bud that had forced its way through submissive foreskin.

Her mouth had fallen open, anyway, agape with surprise, and he eased his excited penis into it, pressing the wet top through her lips so that now he filled her mouth and she could not speak. She could hardly think. She hardly knew what was happening, for her mouth was full of him and everything was new.

She had been buggered by the Duc de Lausanne, but she had not seen his dick. She had not seen it or felt it or touched it; she had only known the sensation of its anonymous journey through her back passage. Here, suddenly, was volatile intimacy and enormous novelty.

Bon Boullibonne withdrew his penis from her wet mouth and, holding it in front of her face, said, 'Lick it gently on the tip, my darling. Lick it and then take it carefully into your mouth and suck me. Learn to do this and you will be able to have anything you want in the world. All men will be yours; the lovers will come and you will have everything.'

She licked the hot top of the offered organ as one might lick sugar off the top of a pastry, slowly, delicately, and with relish – tasting every morsel and enjoying the sensations and tastes on the tongue.

He liked this.

'Good girl.'

Then he taught her how to suckle a man until the full forces of his juices surged from his groin into the swollen sacs and finally, finally, down the agonised shaft and out of the dark spot in a flow of exuberance that moistened her face and her mouth.

Afterwards he took a clean cloth, gently wiped her face and kissed her.

'You are lovely,' he said. 'And you will have it all.'

The picture of Amy as Flora was unveiled with great ceremony at a champagne reception attended by nobles, ambassadors and the highest of high society. The picture hung over the fireplace in the Premiere Salon and was admired by every visitor.

Word spread that a new flower had opened at Madame de Pompadour's *maison de tolerance* and that the establishment was worth visiting.

This was something of a relief to both Madames Pompadour and Fontanelle. The competition was becoming more intense. Other houses were advertising themselves with vulgar lights and signs. Some had even started to display the girls in windows, déshabillé, rouged, and beckoning the men towards them. Virgins were getting cheaper; the hookers were on display; trade was becoming more and more difficult.

Le Parc needed the rujevenation of a new 'star'. La Petite Minette had finally agreed to marry the Duc du

Rochelles and had left the house to become chatelaine of his chateau. The king had lost interest in the nuns and they had returned to their abbey. Even Suzanne had been granted an annuity by a sadist from Sartres and had left to enjoy a dungeon lifestyle in some castle in the Pyrenees. Her letters announced that her arse was being lashed almost nightly, that there were two other 'wives' but, in general, she had a lot of free time and was enjoying herself.

Amy was now the beauty of Le Parc. Her wit and singularity would re-establish it as the leading house of luxury as well as make her famous. It was generally accepted that royalty was to be her destiny and it was only a matter of time before she became a *mistress en titre*.

Prepared though she was by flattering forecasts of fame (delivered by both her male admirers and by Madame le Fontanelle) Amy was nevertheless surprised when, without any warning at all, she was ushered into a drawing room and introduced to Louis XV himself.

The king had turned up without warning, as was often his wont. He enjoyed surprises and jokes and he liked the informalities that occurred when a monarch appeared unnanounced. It made for glimpses of reality that were rarely his to observe.

Madame le Fontanelle introduced Amy who swept the floor in a deep curtsy and was glad that by some inexplicable luck she was wearing one of her most beautiful dresses – a French *robe à la anglaise* of printed ivory cotton embossed with chinoiserie patterns that Madame Pompadour had made fashionable. It was a lovely thing, with cinched waist, and a poloponaise that bustled as an overskirt in a balloon at the back.

She moved, fresh and exotic, with the grace of one who knows her dress is the best and is working to her every advantage. It was by pure luck of the fates. She could have been in an ordinary sack for there were no planned visits that day; she could have been simple and summery, but the dress had arrived and she had decided to try it on.

Madame Le Fontanelle, relieved to see Amy presentable, served a cordial and some cake and swept out of the *salon royale*. This was one of the most luxurious rooms in the house. Dedicated entirely to receiving royalty and nothing else, it was little used and the shutters had had to be opened at the last minute. There were fresh flowers, placed quickly in a Chinese vase only because an equerry had ridden ahead and given the house twenty minutes' warning of the monarch's imminent arrival.

The king was rotund and middle-aged and the head of a superpower with colonies that stretched from Pondichery to Martinique. True, he had just lost a war with England (though he did not hold this against Amy personally) but he could content himself with heading the largest army in Europe. He was dressed in a silk suit of dark blue tricked with lace; his sword hung by his side and he was wearing riding boots embossed with the gold insignia of his family crest.

'I have been admiring Boullibonne's picture of you,' he said, smiling, and dropping the royal 'we' in an effort to make her feel at ease.

'Thank you, sire,' said Amy, curtsying. 'He is a great artist but he has flattered me beyond recognition. I do not think my own mother would recognise the girl in the picture.'

The king bowed and of course said, 'Nonsense! If anything the reality is more exquisite! It would be beyond the talent of any artist to accurately replicate the full charm of your person.'

Amy flushed, not because she believed him, but

because suddenly she was overwhelmed by being in the presence of one of the most powerful men in Europe. She had met the margrave of Moravia, danced with the archduke of Austria, received pearls from an overlord of Slavic possessions that stretched from Galicia to Slovenia. She knew how to address men with duchies and principalities and what to say to a tsarina but, suddenly, she was inexplicably silenced by the unexpected intimacy.

It was as if eighteen months at Le Parc had never occurred. She was a trained soldier who, in the final battle, did not know how to march to the front.

'I've embarrassed you,' he said kindly.

'No, sire. I'm sorry. It's hot today and I have forgotten my fan.'

He personally poured her a second cold cordial from a gold tray on a table and motioned that she should come and sit beside him on the silk sofa.

'Have you been busy with affairs of state, Your Highness? she inquired politely.

Louis XV was not known for being busy at anything but affairs of the heart and indeed had recently been personally blamed for losing a series of important military battles. But he waved his hand airily and said, '*Ah, oui.* I have just bought Corsica.'

Then he admired her dress, paying particular attention to the décolleté neckline. It was a dress fit for a duchess, he said, implying that if she fulfilled his expectations this was a title that she could expect to receive.

They talked of frocks and actors, of shows and books, and she liked him.

He, on the other hand, was smitten.

'I think I am in love,' he said to himself. 'Again.'

'You please me,' he said and, rising to a standing

position he rang a bell, summoned a servant, and bade the man to remove the clothes from his royal body.

The servant, accustomed to such tasks, could separate a monarch from his waistcoat and breeches in the flickering of an eye and, having accomplished divestment, backed silently out of the room leaving the King of France standing naked in front of Amy.

He lay down on the sofa, body in a languid prostration of enjoyable freedom, his white dick fat and erect in the middle of the bush of his groin.

'Pleasure me,' he ordered, without actually specifying what he meant and therefore leaving the field wide open to interpretation. A lesser woman might have been confused by the myriad options available to her; she may not have known whether to offer lips or muff or arse to her liege.

Amy performed the oral act that Bon Boullibonne had taught her and, though the king had slept with many many women, he had never received any attention as expert as this.

He could not believe the subtlety of her licks, the cruelty of her tongue, the deep cavern of the throat that so effortlessy swallowed the entire shaft of his manhood.

And then the beautiful angel lifted up her skirts, climbed upon him, sat astride him and lowered her warm wet pussy down on his pained cock. She eased herself wetly and up and own, using her cunt with the subtlety that she had used her mouth. It was as if it was her mouth. And she worked her thighs and her internal muscles so that his nerves felt every tiny niche of her warm passage as it swallowed the full length of his skin.

He came. He spurted. He rejoiced. He leaped around the room like a gazelle, full of the joys of love and relief. He felt young again.

Amy never regretted surrendering herself to the King of France. He paid Madame le Fontanelle the equivalent of £7,000, a goodly sum, indeed a sum that was said to be a record for such a thing in the whole of France. She was given £1,000, a useful nest-egg and one that gave her a feeling of safety every time she tipped the coins out from the velvet purse that she kept hidden locked in the jewellery box with the other mementoes given to her by the satisfied nobility of France. It was in this way that Amy Pringle accrued wealth and made the sum that was to become her dowry, a dowry that would purchase her a useful future.

The rumour soon circulated that Louis XV wanted to make Amy his premier consort and that, in the privacy of his royal apartments, he was talking about marrying her.

Madame le Fontanelle told Amy that this was the peak of her career. She could go no further. She luxuriated in visions of Amy as Queen of France.

But a complication arose that endangered the smooth path of Amy's course.

Madame Pompadour could not sponsor this turn of events. Of course she could not. To encourage this young English upstart was to elevate her from position of ordinary lady of leisure, sent to please the king occasionally when madame was busy, to a prime position at court. This would threaten madame herself, and she had not focused her energies of professional accession for many years in order to have her privileges removed by the very woman that she had advertised and offered to the king. She was aware that she had created a monster and she had every intention of destroying it.

Spies, ambassadors, politicans, courtiers, lackeys – all went into overdrive as all (battling in a cross-fire of personal motivation and self-aggrandising aspirations) circulated venomous disinformation about the king's new love.

Drama and conspiracy swirled from the dauphin's private staircase to the *salon des nobles*; from the Venus room to the antechambers and bedchambers.

Madame de Pompadour had many friends in the secret service; she was long experienced in the contradictions of intelligence, but even she was confused by the extraordinary fables that surrounded Mademoiselle Amy. She heard more than enough about the woman's talent, beauty, skill and magical sexual expertise; sexual expertise, of course, that she had been personally responsible for honing.

The ironies of the disaster were not lost on Madame Pompadour but she did not laugh. The final straw came when she walked into the king's own private cabinet and found Boullibonne's portrait of Amy hanging above the marble fireplace.

Word reached Madame le Fontanelle that Amy's life was actually in danger. The stakes were high, after all, and poisonings were not rare.

A messenger came in the middle of the night, one of the king's spies, despatched by Louis himself. He did not dare to stand up to Madame Pompadour (who was more powerful than him) but neither did he wish to be responsible for the murder of his one and only love.

He sent her a leather envelope sewn with gold thread and sealed with his seal. Inside there was a ruby necklace, a poem, a sum of £15,000, and a note warning her to hasten away from his shores by the next tide.

And so Amy left the Le Parc aux Cerfs in the middle of the night. Moonlight lit the path to Calais and she was carried on a packet to Dover.

Her mother, well satisfied by her achievements,

111

greeted her warmly and studied the changes in her. She was relieved that her daughter had escaped safely and was alive in the sanctity of her own native land but there was now the problem of her future.

She was advantaged by the money that she had earned at Le Parc aux Cerfs, a dowry that would come to her aid on the marriage market, but most of the eligible men of her age were already taken.

Ernestina Pringle had hoped that her daughter would make a match amongst the gentry of France but circumstances had prohibited this and now there was a danger of drowning in the choppy waters of the shark-infested social sea.

Energised by fear-based ambition, Ernestina swept around the houses of London. She showered her visiting cards in a blizzard, here and there, from Mount Street to Pont Street, from Chelsea to Pimlico and thus ensured invitations to a number of important teas which were necessary to attend if one was to be informed of all pertinent information.

It was at one of these gatherings that she heard the welcome news about Lady Miranda Fitzroy's early death, a death that liberated one of the most presitigious northern seats and made one of the richest young men in the land available to anyone who got there first. A viscount was not to be sniffed at and Ralph Fitzroy's name entered the top of the list that Ernestina Pringle had carefully pencilled in the tiny notebook that she kept in her purse.

There was some disgruntlement in matriarchal circles. Lips were pursed and fans flicked about cheeks with angry snaps. The mothers told each other that it was most unfair. Most unfair. They had married their daughters off to the various lords on a first-come first-serve basis. Now Viscount Fitzroy had tricked them all by marrying a person who died. If they had known that this was to occur they might have held back lesser engagements, avoided immediate marriages, and waited in order to push their own offspring towards this more attractive prospect.

Ernestina Pringle was the only woman left in a position to take advantage of this opportunity and she was further aided by an old friendship with Lady Hacclesfield, to whom she wrote immediately, suggesting that her daughter could be of comfort to her bereaved son in these, 'his times of terrible grief.' Thus it was that the negotiations had been officialised and Miss Pringle had been dispatched to the northern counties.

Chapter Five

There was only one topic of conversation in the servants' hall and that was the subject of Miss Amy Pringle. There was no end to the excitement that she was causing; everyone felt it, from the lowest scullery maid to the haughtiest upstairs maid. Old enmities dissolved and new relationships formed as men and women joined in a chorus of accordant interest. There is nothing like a scandal to bring life to the human spirit, and Miss Amy Pringle had provided just that. Her beauty! Her (rumoured) poverty! Her (rumoured) wealth! Her shameless nudity before the highest gentlefolk in the county! She was an adventuress! It was only a matter of time before her name would actually be in the newspapers and the smirch of publicity would taint them all with the delicious filth of prurience.

There was not only the matter of her naked posturing to discuss, but the imminence of the whipping that she was to receive from the master. This information, too, circulated the ranks, thanks, by and large, to the butler Headley, who had been ordered to tell the head

114

groom to bring a selection of whips from the stable in order that the master may inspect various types for suitability to the task that he had planned.

Miss Amy Pringle surely would not sit down for a week. She surely must make ready with a witch-hazel poultice if her gentle flesh was to recover.

Maids and menservants could barely imagine such a thing: the folds of a gentlewoman's dress pulled shamelessly away from her posterior, the silken folds revealing her noble flesh, subjected and subordinated, enforced to pain as ignominiously as any low orderly employed to throw scraps to the chickens in the yard.

Soon the rumours became embellished, the embellishments became lies and the lies turned into outright myths. It was not long before the glamorous arriviste attained the status of a goddess, imbued, in the eyes of some of the simpler souls, with magical gifts – Lorrie in the scullery insisted that a mere touch of Miss Pringle's hand was enough to cure any form of skin disease.

And now this dazzling star was due to be brutalised and broken down by the cruelty of the master of the household.

They all shuddered, feeling the tingle on their backsides as if they were to receive the punishment themselves. Their affectionate hearts went out to the martyr and they offered the silent support of sisterly spirits.

Prophesies and opinions were whispered from the time that the first fireplace was cleared at 4 a.m. to the first sitting of breakfast at 6 a.m. By 6.30 a.m. the gossip had climbed up the ranks of the kitchen hierarchy to Mrs Prenderghast herself.

Mrs Prenderghast, concerned in the main to ensure that a suitable lunch was made that day and involved in the complexity of suet and fruit, took less interest than most of her underlings in the momentous arrival

115

of this famous chattel, but she was far from immune, and she did not tell Mabel to shut her mouth when Mabel took it upon herself to reveal the exact nature of Miss Amy Pringle's litany of vices.

'I do not believe that the future mistress of this house arrived with no underthings in her luggage,' said Mrs Prenderghast. 'At the very least she would have had a trousseau! Her family is not poor. They would have provided the most excellent cottons and laces for her. She has pantalettes and stays a plenty, I'll warrant!'

'She has none, Mrs Prenderghast!' said Mabel stoutly. 'Milly told me herself. She has chemises, each with dear little gussets and muslin frills, and she has beautiful cotton stockings, made in Derby, all tricked out with delicate embroidery, and she has some black silk stockings, but that is all! Milly says she is a new woman.'

'New woman indeed!' said Mrs Prenderghast, face now vermilion from the steam billowing off the suet. 'New woman indeed! What is a new woman when it's at home? That is not a phrase I have ever heard from the pulpit at St Mark's and it is a phrase I therefore choose to ignore as not being amongst God's designated order of things. I'm an old woman and I am fast losing what very little patience I have left. Go and get the flour, Mabel, before I send you to Mr Headley.'

Mabel, not wanting her own poor parts to meet any painful fate, ran to the pantry to do as she was told.

In the laundry, a steaming cavern manned by twenty or so women of all ages, the topic was the same. Soapers and scrubbers, starchers and ironers, women whose special job it was to maintain the master's linen and women dedicated to preserving the mistress's delicate cambrics, all the specialists of the household wash met over tubs of hot water to chatter unanimously about the marvel that was lingering in their midst.

'I hear she bares her cunny with no fear of hell!'

'She cheeked the master, they say. Downright rude she was! They say he plans to put her in the stocks in the village and leave her there until her father comes to collect her!'

'They say that Mr Trenton Dastard is in love with her, that his very tongue has licked that cunny and that it swelled to the size of a pink rose and that she can make a lad go mad by merely looking at him!'

Similar tales were circulating amongst the men who worked in the stables, gardens and amongst the livestock that made Lancaster Hall's sprawling domain.

Weeders and cutters, pruners and keepers, dog-men and handymen, gardeners and grooms – they too revolved on this wheel of excitement. Somerley the under-gardener told Roberts the head gardener the full story as they were working on the vegetable patch.

'Fanny tells me that she has the finest white skin you have ever seen on a woman,' he said. 'Her breasts are round and full and her nipples are rouged especially by Milly so that they show through her gown when she walks about. Everyone can see when her teats are excited. They shrivel into little red hawthorns!'

Roberts, severing cabbages with his knife, threw one into a barrow with some verve. The tales of this immodest woman circulated in the rough wool of his gardening trousers, causing his dick to rise and chafe against the coarse weft. He shifted, a mixture of discomfort and delight relishing his senses and inspiring him with luxurious ideas. Sensuality darted through him. He longed to push his pulsing prick into the comforting warmth of a mouth. Any mouth would do. He turned around and stared meaningfully at Somerley, whose mouth was engaged in pouring out nonsense and could well be put to better use.

'Come here, Somerley,' said Roberts.

Somerley recognised the expression on his boss's face and he knelt down on the grass to comply.

Somerley knew his place.

Roberts eased his rock-hard dick through the fly of his trousers and pushed it into Somerley's wonderful wide mouth where its hot head was greeted with the delicious tickling of the under-gardener's strong tongue, a tongue that was equipped with a musculature of athletic skill.

Somerley had stamina. He could do anything with that mouth. Roberts sometimes wondered if this was because he talked so much and the exercise somehow toned his lips and throat.

Roberts did not talk much; he did not have to. He was handsome and he had savings. These things were enough to attract the things that he wanted.

Somerley sucked.

Somerley sucked like the good boy that he was.

Milly arrived for her breakfast at 7.00 a.m. to find her status heightened by proximity to her mistress. It was known that she was privy to the privilege of truth and everyone wanted a part of it.

The maid revelled in the luxury of attention and bathed in the balm that was her position of importance. The new prestige imbued her with a charisma that caused not only rough Tollard to stare lustfully in her direction, but more important men – the head gamekeeper, for instance (who had his own cottage), and Roberts, a man whose honed muscles and glowering expression were enough to turn the head of any woman who looked on them.

Immersed in flattery and gratification, Milly chatted

118

gaily to her admirers as she ate her breakfast at the kitchen table.

Roberts, who had arrived with a wicker basket full of fresh garden produce, even sat down beside her and partook of the bread and milk offered by Mrs Prenderghast.

He fixed Milly with his dark eye and grinned at her. Roberts' smile was full of the promise of demonic foreplay – and who can resist that? Particularly when it is accompanied by suggestive charm and witty parlay.

Headley found her thus, engaged in flirtation, and spoke sternly to her, asking her why she was not about her tasks, why her kerchief was askew, her hair messy? Even her hands were dirty!

He told her that she was already getting well above herself and needed to be brought down a peg or two if she was not to become diseased with the very depravity that her mistress was bringing down on Lancaster Hall.

'I am one step away from giving you a good spanking,' he barked at Milly, who flushed, as these sharp words were uttered in front of Roberts.

Roberts smiled cheekily, safe in the knowledge that his position did not fall under the jurisdiction of Headley, but of Lord Hacclesfield himself.

'I cannot think why you are in the house, Roberts,' Headley said pompously. 'Your duties are in the garden, I believe.'

'I brought in some cabbages for Mrs Prenderghast,' said Roberts, holding his ground and pointing to the basket full of vegetables that lay on the kitchen table.

'Well, you've brought them, now you can go and leave Milly to her work.'

Roberts winked at Milly and left.

119

Milly realised that she could quite easily ride Roberts, marry him and have his children, in approximately that order.

'He was doing no harm, Mr Headley,' she said, sipping her tea as if she was the lady of the house.

But Headley was not having any of it. If the saucy maid got above herself it would reflect on him and he did not wish to incur the wrath of the master. The earl was quite volatile enough as it was, and was capable of sending a servant to unemployment without any warning.

There had been seven sackings in the last seven months and Headley did not want to join the score of persons cast out into the wilderness without reference, for this was to face the reality of starvation.

He told Milly in no uncertain terms that she and she alone was responsible for ensuring that Miss Pringle arrived at the master's study at 9.30 a.m., not a second before, not a second after. If punctuality was not accomplished Milly would find herself in serious trouble.

Headley suspected that the maid was already colluding with her mistress to create unseemly sedition and he intended to keep her in line.

Dismissed by her superior, Milly meekly left the kitchen and went about the duties for which she had been directed.

Tapping on the door of Amy's bedroom at 8 a.m. she arrived with all the materials for Miss Pringle's morning rituals – hot water for the toilette, brushes for the hair, fresh linens for the bed, and a silver tray on which there was bread and a cup of chocolate.

Milly, poor Milly, sensing the difficulties that were beginning to taint her destiny, drew back the curtains and laid the tray on the bed.

'Good morning, miss,' she said. 'I am instructed to

aid you with your toilette and take you to the master's study at 9.30 a.m.'

Amy yawned.

Milly wondered at her careless insouciance. Had she forgotten the fierce reprisal that was her fate?

Amy sipped her chocolate in a relaxed manner.

'If we are late, Miss Pringle, Headley will whip me and you will receive worse,' she said nervously.

'Oh, nonsense!' said Amy, unperturbed. 'These men. You shouldn't let them frighten you, Milly . . .'

But Milly was frightened and she could not help herself. It was all very well for the mistress – she had no experience of the hard hand on the soft posterior. She did not know the smart of flaming cheeks and the ignominy of nudity in front of an authoritarian. She wanted to avoid it if she could and she wished Miss Pringle would learn to do the same, but the wild girl seemed to want to court trouble, to relish it as a dangerous mountain climb. She seemed to like the danger, indeed, risk seemed to be the sole spur of her existence.

Milly shuddered to herself. Miss Amy Pringle was lovely, she was exotic, she was like nothing on earth, but she was beginning to wonder if she was going to be able to cope with the stress of being in her proximity.

'I am glad I did not fuck Trenton Dastard,' Amy said haughtily. 'He looks like a mean kind of man to me. I bet he has broken hearts. Is he married?'

'I don't think so, miss,' said Amy, drawing a lilac dress from Miss Pringle's commode and brushing it down with a tiny silver clothes brush. 'Though I believe he has been engaged on more than one occasion. The poor Miss Davenport was quite ill after a failed affiancement. I believe she had to go to a doctor.'

'As I suspected,' said Amy, setting the dreadful machinations of her lively mind on how best to afflict Trenton Dastard and thus avenge the gentle sisterhood.

At 9.25 a.m., Milly's heart was beating painfully underneath her stays. She applied the finishing touches to Amy's hair with shaking hands.

'Calm down, Milly. Take a glass of ale or something.'

But Milly knew it would take a good five minutes to get down to the study. It was down the stairs and through a maze of corridors. She was not even certain that she would be able to find it. The master's private libraries and offices were located at an unfamiliar end of the house, far away from the kitchen and bedrooms that were familiar to her. Her duties did not take her further abroad than this and, though Headley had given her some instructions, she was nervous that the navigation would be confusing and slow and the journey would be hindered.

'Oh please, Miss Pringle!' she said anxiously. 'You don't know what the master is like!'

Her mistress seemed to be moving in slow motion.

'Lead, then,' Amy finally ordered.

Milly flung herself down the winding staircase as Amy strolled at a stately pace behind her. Milly darted and skipped. Amy moved as if walking down a wedding aisle. Past tapestries, suits of armour and portraits. Past inlaid mahogany cabinets and breakfront bookcases. Past bureau plats with marble tops and around plinths on which the heads of Roman emperors had been placed. On and on down panelled corridors lined with carved oak chairs that had been in the Hacclesfield family since the reign of Henry VIII. Finally, at the end of one of these seamless tunnels, Milly stopped at a dark wooden door lined with brass studs and an ornate brass door knob. Its very presence seemed to say 'Do Not Enter'. It was the portal that led to the master's realm.

Milly, heart thudding painfully, legs as jelly, tapped softly on the door. Amy nudged her maid out of the way and swept into Lord Hacclesfield's study just as he was barking, 'Enter!'

Amy marched into the room as if she was leading a parade. Milly, now behind, paused respectfully in the doorway and curtsied as Lord Hacclesfield's attention focused on them.

'Stay by the door please, Milly. You may witness what this insolent hussy is about to experience and I hope you will learn from it.'

Milly curtsied again.

'Yessir.'

'I may remind you, Milly, that I am not in general pleased with your work and if I find that your stan dards lessen even further I will ask Headley to implement measures that ensure the dutiful commitment that I expect from my staff. Those measures will be enforced with strict measure and they will be of great pain to you. I hope you understand this, Milly.'

'Yessir.'

He was standing at the end of a book-lined room in front of his desk. Wearing a dark tailcoat, white shirt, breeches and riding boots, he could not have looked more austere. There was a riding crop in his right hand.

Lord Hacclesfield had spent half an hour or so deciding how to punish Amy Pringle. He had considered a straightforward spanking, hard and fast on her bare backside. This would achieve many things. It would be humiliating and painful and instructive for her to be forced to bare her orbs to a greater authority in order to submit to indoctrination.

But he had decided against this in favour of a

harsher measure. Spanking a girl was all well and good but she would quickly forget; when the burning on her bum ebbed away only a faint memory would be left and she would all too easily fall back into indecorous ways. No. He decided that a spanking was not enough for Miss Pringle; a spanking instructed the simpler servants, it kept them on their toes, but they wanted to please him, they were easier to discipline. He gave them their food and they volunteered abnegation.

Miss Pringle was another entity altogether. She was not simple, nor had she shown any propensity to please. Lord Hacclesfield had genuinely wondered whether she was actually possessed by a devil. He had seen such a thing once, as a young man, when a girl in the village fell prey to screaming and seizures and had had to be saved from swearing dreadful profanities and fingering herself publicly.

He had instructed the groom to bring in the crop he used when hunting. It had a centre of bamboo and was bound in leather. The handle was embossed with silver and equipped with a leather loop for a more efficient grip. If it could spur a stallion on, it would be of use on the hide of Miss Pringle's cheeky arse and, hopefully, spur her to obedience.

He intended to streak her with six stripes across her bare bottom and then place her in a corner in the main hall so that the entire household would witness her abject humiliation.

He glared at Amy Pringle with stern *froideur*, an unsmiling man, tall and imposing. The crop twitched in his hand.

Milly shuddered but Amy walked over to him and glared at him with an intense defiance that, for a moment, he could not help momentarily admiring. He respected courage, after all, and this woman had cour-

124

age. The feeling was quickly vanquished by fury as sheer anger was promoted by her impudence. How dare she!

He clasped his strong left hand over the back of her neck and pushed her face down over the desk before she could say anything.

Holding her there with a vice-like grip so that her cheek was pressed against the polished wood of the surface, he barked at Milly.

'Come here, girl, and lift up the skirts, well above the waist, now!

Milly ran forward to obey. Kneeling on the floor, she took the hem at the bottom of Amy's long lilac gown and rolled it slowly past her ankles, knees, and up her thighs, placing it as an array over her back, so that now all that could be seen was Amy Pringle's bare white buttocks and the backs of her thighs.

There were new white silk stockings on her legs, ending at just above the knee, and flat pumps made in a lilac to match the dress.

So there she was, bent over that desk, unblemished buttocks framed by the drapery as a picture of vulnerable flesh.

Although some of the servants told each other that Miss Pringle did not wear underwear because her family could not afford it, this was not true. Amy did not wear underwear through conscious choice. She had discarded undergarments many years hence due to the fact that they were constraining, uncomfortable, and, in her view, often ruined the line of the clothes. She liked to be able to unwrap herself easily and smoothly and she did not like to be overheated or suffocated. She was a free spirit and she liked her body to feel free as well.

'I see, madam, that you are not wearing underwear. This will change. In the event that you must be received into this room again you will be modestly dressed. As it is, without appropriate coverings, you are flaunting bare-faced cheek and you will learn the error of this.'

Amy tried to mumble something, but the man's left hand was still pressing down on her neck and words were difficult.

'Do not speak, madam, or your count will go to eight.'

Milly stood aside.

Lord Hacclesfield, still holding Amy Pringle down, raised his right arm and brought the crop down on the sensitive white flesh of her naked buttocks.

He had a strong arm and a skilled one. He knew how to whip a horse and he had long known how to punish a disobedient girl.

He allowed the sting to spread deeply into her nether parts, then he brought the crop down again, slashing her orbs with intense fury.

Amy's body twitched and the flesh succumbed to the stripe, but she made no sound, no sound at all.

The whip cracked again across her buttocks, a stripe of searing fire, but still she was silent, and she remained silent as each stroke slashed down on her smooth round posterior.

Milly stared in awe as the pearl skin glowed now with four livid red weals. The mistress had uttered no word of agony. She had not even brushed her hands against her backside, in an effort to rub the pain away. She was as tranquil as a pail of milk.

Her implacability served only to infuriate Lord Hacclesfield, who would have liked to take the cropping from six to eight strokes and would have done so had he not been a man of his word. He did not believe in increasing punishments at the last minute; six strokes had been promised so six strokes must be delivered.

He took his time between the fourth and fifth stroke. He knew that pain took time to seep into the flesh and that lashes were more powerful if administered with this in mind.

He wanted this rebellious minx to know pain and to be dominated by it. He wanted her to be tormented by the realisation that he and he alone was the master of her every move. She was going to submit. No matter how long it took, no matter how many times those skirts had to be pulled over her unmodest behind, she was going to submit.

Another stroke.

'That is five, Miss Pringle. I hope you are now beginning to realise who is the master of this house.'

Amy, still silent, had entered a world of her own imagination that inured her to some extent to the immediacy of agony. But the pain was coming through now, and she knew the reality of punishment.

She had never been thus administered before, but she was becoming aware of its mysterious pleasure. Warm delight was creeping between her legs and making her moist. For a brief weird moment she hoped that he would drop that crop to the floor and simply take her from the back as she bent over the desk.

It was not to be.

The sixth penalty cracked on to the lower half of her bottom, the thin skin that edged the top of the thighs.

It was the hardest to bear as this was a sensitive place, but still she did not cry out.

Her white skin was now a tapestry of red lines, parallel stripes on display from the top of her buttock to the top of her thighs.

'Milly, lead Miss Pringle to the corner of the entrance hall. Ensure that her face is to the wall and that her skirts are neatly pinned up. I want every member of this household to see the reddened cheeks of this miss and know that no-one and I mean no-one is exempt from the rules that I make. Do you understand?'

Milly curtsied.

'Yessir.'

Amy followed Milly to the hall – a huge foyer which was dominated by a double front door and provided the official entranceway into the house. It was the most public place in that it was the area most used by the highest number of people. Not only did it provide the formal reception area for family and friends whose carriages drew up outside the main porch, but its central location provided access to the dining room, the ballroom, the withdrawing room, the library, a tapestry room, a couple of small galleries and the chapel, all of which commanded their own visitors.

People flowed through every hour all day, criss-crossing the stone floor in order to fulfil their individual tasks or proceed to the duties demanded by the areas of the house in which they worked.

Even the lowest orderlies could be seen, emerging from the servants' hall at dawn to clear the ash from the massive open fireplace and prepare it to be maintained by the hall-men and log-boys whose duty it was to ensure that baskets were full of wood and that warm flames crackled all day.

A doorman, dressed in the dark green of the Hacclesfield livery, sat permanently on a velvet chair beside the front door in order to open it when visitors arrived. His task was to usher them to the areas most appropriate to the time of day and to the reason for which they were visiting. Thus the mantua-maker would be shown to Lady Hacclesfield's private sitting room while friends of Bubb or Ralph would be led to their private suites on the first floor.

The family used the hall the most, running down the

central staircase all day, going to the dining hall for meals, to the withdrawing room, to the library.

Butlers and valets bustled about; maids carried food on trays; maids struggled with dusters and buckets.

The only people who had no business in this area were the tradesmen, the kitchen staff, and the laundry staff, whose activities lay in other parts of the house accessed by the maze of passages and stairways that wove through the back.

Amy's disgrace was witnessed by the majority of Lord Hacclesfield's household. Those who did not actually see her mortified posterior were told of it by those who had, and they had spared no detail, embellishing the picture with lurid descriptions in order to ensure the maximum effect on the listener. Thus the punishment became a horror story whispered from mouth to mouth and becoming more and more frightening as it circulated. Soon it was a fable of dark terror guaranteed to shrink the entrails of anyone who heard it.

Milly, as instructed by her employer, pinned Miss Pringle's dress up with clothes pegs so that her calves, thighs and the entire area of her buttocks were bared and displayed to public scrutiny.

She spent the morning standing in the corner nearest to the fireplace. Her face was to the wall, the cold plasterwork cooling her burning forehead, her flushed cheeks hidden in the shadow. Her hands were clasped in front of her.

The ministrations that she had received meant that her bottom glowed as red as poppies. This caused enjoyable sensations to pump into her groin and stomach where they slid as wet enjoyment into the cleavage between her legs.

Everyone in the house inspected Miss Pringle's marks. Nobody scurried past. They all ambled and stared as patiently and as with as much care as a tourist in an art gallery. The master had placed her there for good reasons – to humiliate the disgraced lady and to instruct others. There was no reason to avoid inspection and they did not. Embarrassment was no bar to their morbid enjoyment. Maids, valets and boot boys stopped in front of her and studied the view, scrutinising the harsh measure that the lady had received.

Tollard went as far as to kneel down behind her and press his fingers deep into the crimson flesh in order to see the white stain that his nosy fingers left behind. His nose was so close to the beautiful cleft of her bruised flesh he could smell her sweet scent, and feel the heat burning from her. How Tollard wanted to go further than this. How he wanted to peruse her pelvis with his fingers and force them slowly into her vulva, shoving and pushing until he heard her scream out for him. How he wanted to force himself into her as she crouched on all fours in front of him. Tollard sensed that this noble miss was excited. He was primitive in his senses and he could perceive such things as easily as an animal in the forest.

Amy felt these attentions, but she could not observe them as she was forced to remain with her face to the wall.

She did not know who was indulging themselves at her expense, but the traffic was heavy all morning as even those who had no business in the great hall made excuses to travel there in order to see her blushed abjection.

The consequence of this was not all in keeping with Lord Hacclesfield's ideas.

He had thought to make Miss Pringle an example with the object of reminding his staff that the necessity for total obedience was one that affected all members of his household, whatever their station. No person was exempt from his regime and Amy's arse should provide a deterrent to anyone who thought to rebel.

In fact, the display served to raise Miss Pringle to the status of martyr, and not only a martyr, but a martyr whose beauty was enough to turn the head of anyone who looked on her.

The men and the women of the household were aroused by flagrant exposure of her erogenous zones, which, painted red, incited even the dullest eye to sexual desire. The men longed for her; the women respected her unassailable dignity in the face of unfair treatment.

The fine lady was showing an example of defiance and courage and they could do the same. Some of them even began to have rebellious thoughts which was not what at all the earl had envisaged.

The following morning he voiced his concerns to his eldest son.

'Miss Pringle is insolent and wayward,' he told Ralph. 'She is not suitable to enter this family, let alone be your wife. She is offensive, flagrant and immoral! I plan to take her in hand and squash her impudence, but I am not confident of success.

'She is the most wilful, stubborn creature I have ever met within the human race. There are dogs like that, there are horses like that, but never have I seen a woman such as this. She is unfit to be counted as a member of the gentle sex.' Ralph nodded. He always agreed with his father.

'She has been allowed to stray,' he agreed. 'And she has picked up some dreadful manners. If Miss Pringle must be punished, then she must be punished; if she must go then she must go. I know that you will do what is right, Papa, and it will be for the best.'

Chapter Six

*B*ubb was in love with Amy. It was an affliction and an inconvenience and there was nothing he could do about it. He had felt weak the minute that he had seen her walking across the drawing room in her translucent robe; he had known he was in trouble then because he had recognised the familiar signs – heartbeat, stomach pain, a slight itch in the back of the throat. He had suffered from these symptoms before and he knew them well.

He had tried to force them away in the call of duty: she could not be his, after all. It was impossible. To court this danger was to risk everything. She was his brother's intended wife, she was destined to be the premier pillar of the future of the Hacclesfield dynasty, the structure upon which the family's fortunes would lie. To tamper with his father's schemes would be to tamper with the infrastructure that held his life together.

The frets that supported Bubb were firm but they could easily be tugged. His fortunes were inextricably enmeshed with his family. To incur the wrath of his brother and father would be not only to sever the relationships of blood ties, but to destroy his existence. His increments were supplied by the estate; his recreations were played on it; his friends lived around it. The countryside was his love and his life. But here now temptation beset him, dizzied him and made him feel most uncomfortable, if not actually frightened.

He had managed to assuage himself by giving the dowager a seeing to and then taking an afternoon out with his hawks. He had held a couple of meetings with the houndsman (to discuss the dogs' food) and he had planned a day's racing for the following week. He had even tried to read a book in an attempt to dispel the vision that kept forcing her way into his mind's eye.

He had managed to temporarily distract himself and, with these efforts, he had actually managed to forget the presence of Miss Pringle for an hour or so. He had begun to hope that his passion for her might have just been a passing fancy, the attraction of a spring flower whose scent and colour are momentarily ravishing to behold but quickly fade into a pleasant memory. But then, by chance, by mistake, and with great regret, he had seen Amy's person standing in the corner of the great hall. And it was a person half-naked. He had seen her bare shoulders, the back of her neck bent forward in supplication and he had seen her flaming buttocks bared in mortified exposure. He had been forced to walk around with a painful erection for the rest of the day.

An erection, in Bubb's case, was more than a physical presence. The huge size of his proportion meant that he was dominated by the changes that occurred in his nether regions. Though this is true of many men; most are not waylaid either by amplitude of painful hardness – not as the years go on, anyway.

Bubb's erections did not falter. There was never any

wavering or whimpering or demise. The bloodless incontinence of the sad man was never his tragedy to experience.

His dick was the core of his being and it dominated his inner life because of its pure physical presence. He had to have his breeches specially made to cater for it. It was well known to the tailors that the Hon. Bubb Fitzroy's proportions were particular and if he was to avoid chafing special gussets must be sewn into his breeches with invisible stitching that would then open out in a subtle fan to allow him room for the enormous growth that was his to enjoy when a stimulus was experienced.

Love, then, was the burden of Bubb's heart. Love and dishonesty, for he could not admit any of this. He was not a dishonest person. Nervous, shambling, unemployable, yes. Dishonest, no.

Breakfast on the day following Amy's disgrace presented him with almost insurmountable challenges, challenges that a simple man could not combat, for it was difficult to engage in a frenzy of emotion as well as concentrate on the grouse or eggs or white rolls that were being presented by the servants. Tea was the order of the morning but he longed for a stiff glass of brandy.

The meal comprised Amy, Bubb, Ralph, and Lord Hacclesfield. Trenton Dastard, bored, had returned to London. Lady Hacclesfield, as has been mentioned, tended not to rise until much later in the day, delayed by the aftereffect of drink or laudanum and by the intense toilette that she felt forced to maintain.

Amy was wearing a delightful dress of dusty pink velvet that was cut low over the breasts and which did nothing to advertise the chastity that was supposed to have been the result of her punishment. Forced to sit down on her bruised buttocks, which still flared as if they had been smacked only an hour before, the heat of the retribution still warmed her pelvis and her groin and seeped deep between her legs, making her feel alert with wanton desire.

Thus aroused, she surveyed the table carefully. Appearing to sup with ladylike manners and modesty, she was in fact secretly studying each man for the potential of their forecast.

There was Bubb, of course, big, blond, with an open face and blue eyes and a mouth that advertised both his generosity and his silliness. He was nice enough, and kind to her in this cold place of mannered patriarchs.

There was Lord Hacclesfield, dull totalitarian and arrogant autocrat whose basic sensibility was rendered uninteresting by his reactionary attitudes and his sad lack of intelligence.

Amy did not object to the efforts of Lord Hacclesfield to train her to his ways; it was a new experience, a battle that he was going to lose, but a battle that was throwing up pleasurable sensations of novel sexual enjoyment which it had not been hers to previously encounter.

If there was one thing that Amy Pringle enjoyed, even revered, this was the promise of new experience. She was a traveller. She wanted to see all the unknown scapes of life. And she was unafraid.

And finally there was Ralph.

Ralph. Her destiny. The very man to whom this show was dedicated. He was the purpose of the pageant, and he was supposed to represent the final scene of her life. They were being pushed together not by unknown forces, as is the course of haphazard romantic love, but by the firm palms of their various parents. They were arranged as cutlery and plates on a table are arranged, knife against plate, glass against glass, neatly fitting into a scheme of things and offering no brook to the established order.

Amy knew this was extraordinary when one looked at it with detachment and, though it was the conventional way of things, convention was not her skin to wear.

Life had taught her too many colourful lessons. Convention was dangerously dull and offered little obvious fulfilments to a person as easily bored as she. Nevertheless, there was something strangely exciting about being forced to address a strange man in order not only to make love to him but to spend the rest of her life with him. It appealed to her perversity because it was so opposite to her belief system.

Amy studied Ralph as one studies an animal that one knows one has bought. The money has changed hands; all that is left is the transport home.

She asked herself these questions:

'Can I make love to this man?'

'Do I want to kiss him?'

'Do I want to lick the tip of his hard dick and swallow his come?'

'Do I want to nuzzle the soft skin of his groin?'

'Do I want to rest my ankles on his neck and receive him full and hard deep into my centre?'

'Do I want to see him in the morning?'

She stared at Ralph and this was easy because Ralph was making no attempt to study her. It was as if she was not there. His aloof disinterest could have been rudeness or shyness, she did not know. It was strange to take so little interest in the woman that he was to marry, but indifferent he was and it drew her towards him like a magnet.

There was something about the arrogance of his bearing, the determined jaw line, the brown eyes, that made her want to smash him to pieces with a hammer;

but it also made her want to feel the warmth of his affection and see the intimacy of his soul. His unknowableness made her want to know him as surely as the rambler at the edge of a cave cannot but help wonder what lies at its dark centre. His handsome *froideur* made her want to explore him and it aroused the curiosity of sensual attraction.

She tried to catch his attention by the simple method of staring into his eyes and smiling in a way that most men would interpret as seductive. But he stared into her as if she was not there.

So Amy was surrounded by three men – one martinet, one cold fiancé and one Bubb who eased the tricky repast by attending to her, engaging her in conversation, and, in general, warming an atmosphere that would otherwise have been as cold as the winter on Everest.

'Somebody should show Miss Pringle around the estate, Papa,' he said. 'What are you doing today, Ralph?'

Amy sat up, alert. This was her chance to relish Ralph. An afternoon on horseback would be just the thing to show him her attributes – not only her expertise as a rider, but her qualities as a companion. As a woman. And as his future wife. Her heart actually started to beat and she realised not without discomfort that she was beginning to care about Ralph's reactions. She wanted him to like her and this was an unfamiliar feeling. Her life had been full of men who liked her enough to pay for the smallest trifle, who promoted her without question, who had fallen into her hands as easily as a blossom floats down from a branch in spring.

Something unexpected had happened. She was beginning to fall for Viscount Fitzroy, but Viscount Fitzroy was showing no sign of reciprocation; quite the opposite in fact. Lord Fitzroy was showing symptoms of actual distaste.

'Ralph?' said Bubb. 'Will you take Miss Pringle out this afternoon or not?'

Ralph's attention returned to the table from some distant land of his inner workings.

He shrugged coldly.

'I can't,' he said dismissively. 'I have a meeting about the hunt and I have to prepare for a trip to London. Papa and I are away for some days, as you know. I cannot possible find the time for this, er . . .' He waved his hand as if batting away a wasp. The words to describe either Amy or the outing seemed to fail his vocabulary.

She could not assess what it was he wanted to say – whether he wanted to insult her or find some pretty excuse to avoid her. She had rarely come across anyone so rude, and she had come across some very rude people in her time.

She tightened her facial muscles into a mask of indifference and calmly awaited the final decision that this absurd committee would doubtless make.

'Bubb,' said Lord Hacclesfield. 'You may show Miss Pringle the premises tomorrow afternoon. If you are to ride, please take Sally, not Formenta. Formenta would be too much for Miss Pringle, and please make sure that the groom knows where you are going. But first I wish to have a word with Miss Pringle in private.'

The two brothers rose from the table and left the room, leaving Lord Hacclesfield and Amy alone in the room.

The earl stood up and stood with his back to the fire, staring down at Amy as she remained sitting at the table.

She felt the heat of his dark eyes burning into her face and she felt the burning on her bottom. She knew he could punish her again if he wanted but he did not understand how little she cared about his absurd ways. He did not know that she was way beyond him in the mind game. She was learning to play him like a fiddle.

'Today is as good a day as any to initiate the regime to which I expect you to apply yourself,' he said pompously. 'I expect you to apply yourself efficiently and with good grace to the lessons that I have scheduled for you. These will be varied in their intent, but they are the lessons that I consider necessary to teach a good wife the essential requirements of her lifestyle. They will include embroidery, piano lessons, Bible study, singing, and some husbandry, though you will not of course be expected to take on any kitchen duties.'

Amy groaned inside.

Lord Hacclesfield was determined to avoid the mistakes that he had made with his own wife. He believed that to train Amy as a sensible wife for his eldest son would be to aid Ralph in the running of the estate and thus avoid the innumerable tasks with which he had been burdened and which, by rights, should have been undertaken by Lady Hacclesfield. He was determined that his son Ralph would have the pleasures of life that are supplied by an efficient partner and understanding companion. The woman who came to steer the domestic events of Lancaster Hall should be assiduous and sensible; she should not be the faded hedonist that he had allowed Aurelia to become. There was some logic, then, in the earl's instructions, but it subsisted of a rationale that Amy could not understand. A timetable of imbecilic tasks stretched out before her with as much attraction as the rote and reading of boring schoolroom Latin lessons.

'They will begin, madam, with the basic matter of your clothing. You will be modest at all times and you will start to wear underwear, and by underwear I mean stays, corsets, drawers and petticoats. I mean, Miss Pringle, the full modest understructure that befits any young woman of a certain social standing and who wishes to avoid the vices of a voluptuary.

'I have ordered a Monsieur Gerard to come from town with his assistants and I expect you to supply yourself to their demands with absolute obedience. They will make you the garments that you require and you will wear them. Is that understood?'

'Yes, my lord,' said Amy with her eyes lowered and her face bent towards the plate in front of her.

The earl was momentarily unnerved by her disarming servitude and checked her face to ascertain that she wasn't enjoying the dumb insolence of a private joke (he had come across such behaviour in one or two cheeky chambermaids but had quickly spanked it out of them). But she seemed genuine enough. Perhaps she was beginning to regret her transgressions and see the error of her ways. Perhaps she genuinely wanted to marry Ralph and understood the necessities required of his wife and wanted to acquire them.

The truth was that Amy had realised that she had to play Lord Hacclesfield carefully if she was to be allowed any personal liberty; that is, to pretend to obey him was an advantageous strategy whose final purpose was to avail herself of the things that she would need and want in order to survive the dreadful dull rigours of Lancaster Hall.

She did not want to earn Lord Hacclesfield's indefatigable hatred for to earn his implacable alienation would be to alienate herself from Ralph, and Ralph, in her view, had potential. She wanted to study him further in order to ascertain exactly what that potential was. Her own agenda was crystal clear to her; her purposes definite. And they would be easily implemented in front of a man as blind as Lord Hacclesfield.

'I will do as you say, sir,' she said.

'Good girl.'

The following morning various womenswear specialists arrived at the house in order to provide the accoutrements that Lord Hacclesfield had decided Amy must wear.

A guest suite was made over to these ministrations and Milly was in attendance to help with assorted tying and binding.

As each garment was fitted to the satisfaction of the merchant, Amy was then directed to go downstairs to Lord Hacclesfield's study in order to allow herself to be inspected, both so that he could check that the lingerie fitted correctly and that it was of adequate quality. He was not careless with his money and he insisted on the best.

His secretary Adrian noted down each item in a ledger book, described its appearance and recorded the price in a margin, thus providing his employer with an account of the expenditure and a comprehensive list of the under-wardrobe that Miss Pringle was now behoven to wear.

Adrian was not displeased by his work. Indeed, he spent some time immersed in arousing recollections of the days of his youth when women wore hoops which swung about the hips with provocative undulation and which inspired the sport of pushing them on swings. In those days drawers were not in fashion. A cloud of petticoats could, when tipped up, reveal a delightful garter, a stocking, or even, if the swing went very high, the tiny shrub that hid the lady's cleft, a place that it was no man's privilege to see unless by happy accident.

Adrian had never forgotten the day that Coraline's swing went so high that he, standing underneath, had seen the bare pink of her buttocks, the fur of her muff, and the actual crimson ridges between her thighs. Carried away by these glimpses of forbidden protuberances and flashes of female sex he had spent a night full of stiff insomnia, tossing and turning with undisciplined thoughts about ravaging her with lunging penetrative thrusts until she called out for mercy.

He had asked her to marry him the next day.

Amy spent the morning on a strange course where modesty was immodesty and underwear became an excuse for promoting nudity.

Madame le Fontanelle had often told her that a woman does not need to bare all to gain the attention of a man and that to reveal too much was the mistake of the desperate and the vulgar.

Madame le Fontanelle knew that marriage was a trap that must be carefully set and she often declared that, 'Men need the pleasure of imagination if they are to become husbands – to veil is to reveal, to display is to conceal.'

Amy forced herself to submit to the whims of the system, knowing that it would be to her advantage in the end. As the hours passed, with strange hands patting her posterior and stroking her flesh and easing her thighs into silk fabrics, she began to appreciate that there was pleasure to be gained from allowing one's body to experience the adventure of intimate apparel.

The stay-maker arrived first. A young man named Gerard (pronounced with a soft G, in the French manner), his inscrutable mien had given rise to the rumour that he had once been a spy.

Gerard looked as if he retained many secrets. Discretion was a component of his profession, and he relayed the inscrutability of a man who would not surrender his knowledge under the worst of tortures.

These characteristics were indispensable to his craft. He was allowed to see sights that no lady would wish to be circulated, such was their personal nature and secret shame. He had seen deformities of bones and rickety limbs; he had seen blemishes and scars, flat feet and knock knees. He had seen drooping breasts, and unwieldy bellies and all the crinkled, puckered, speckled imperfections that were usually only viewed by the lady in her own mirror.

It was his duty to conceal, maintain, curve and shape so that his customer conformed to the modern requisite of beauty, a requisite of perfection that he colluded with her to sustain in warranted delusion.

He could have told some horrifying sagas if he had so wished. He could have brought a duchess down with a slip of his tongue. But he was not stupid. He knew that his confidences were as important to his profession as those revealed to a priest in a confession box. He maintained a moral code of silence.

No gossip had ever been prised from his lips, and this might have been the reason why those lips were pursed in a constant expression of tight restraint. It was as if his face was forcing the muscles of his mouth to remain closed, locked securely, because he was afraid that his jaws would suddenly swing open like hinges and his mouth would spew forth all the evils of the world as they had flown out of Pandora's Box.

Gerard, tall, thin, blond, anally fastidious, wore an immaculate suit of light blue frockcoat and breeches. He exuded a complacent self-satisfaction that Amy disliked on sight and they surveyed each other with mutual distaste.

She saw a retentive prig; he saw an inconstant whore, ill disciplined, disordered and disrespectful.

She represented that prime anathema – the uncontrolled mischief-maker whose defiance of the convention meted out by his trade deserved nothing less than unswerving subjugation.

His assistants set up a complicated apparatus made of wood. On the floor was a platform with two niches and two silver hinges with chains. At the front of this, in vertical positions, stood two erect poles, on which there were leather wrist-cuffs and chains.

'Please remove Miss Pringle's clothes,' Gerard said to Milly in a tone that implied that this action was normal and the order was a directive that allowed no room for question.

Milly did as she was told.

Amy's primrose paduasoy robe dropped to the floor as the maid undid the ties at the back of the dress. She stood in the middle of the room naked except for some pearls in her hair and the ring that her father had given her on her finger.

'And the ring!' barked the corsetière.

'Sir!' said Amy. 'The ring provides no prohibition to your task. There is no need for it to be removed. No need on this earth!'

Gerard's wet lips curled with distaste. If there was one thing that made the bile rise in his chest it was the impudent contradiction of a silly young woman. He did not address her argument, judging it to be of no consequence, but merely caught Milly in the gleam of his cold blue eye and repeated his directive.

'And the ring.'

Amy was naked in front of this man, but she was strong and she was beautiful and she knew it. Gerard Brenton was a petty prig whose only correct destiny would be face down in a pool of mud with her foot on his neck pressing his face on to the filth until he breathed the dirt up through his nostrils, down his

144

throat and deep into his chest where, if right was right, it would drown his lungs and cause a slow painful death.

'The ring stays!' she said.

Gerard Brenton had not felt any emotion except greed and displeasure for many years, thus it was not irritation that propelled his body forward to two inches in front of Amy Pringle, but more a motivation that she should now hear exactly what he had to say, because he, Gerard Brenton, was the only valid authority and he could not understand why this obvious fact had bypassed this extraordinary young woman's attention.

'Miss Pringle,' he said with icy calm, 'Lord Hacclesfield has invested me with authority in this transaction. You will do as I say when I say. If I say the ring is to be removed, then it will be removed. It will be removed, Miss Pringle, if I have to cut your finger off.'

'Cut your own prick off, mister. The ring stays!'

The room went silent. The various assistants who had been banging nails into the wooden apparatus, or whispering instruction at each other, fell into mute terror. Milly's eyes widened and her breath came in painful gasps. Somebody's silver needle-box fell to the floor with a clatter.

Gerard Brenton could not believe that a naked wench could be quite so belligerent. Perhaps she was actually mad.

'Miss Pringle, it is my pleasure to inform you that I have been given licence to punish you in the event of any obstruction to my duties. If you wish me to lash you to this frame and whip your behind until I hear only the screams of a whimpering and scolded lass whose behaviour is no better than a naughty child, and who thus attracts the same treatment, then so be it.

'I can assure you that this measure will hurt you a

very great deal more than it will hurt me. Indeed, it will be my very great solace to provide the thrashing that you so richly deserve. But it will be a waste of my time and indeed yours.

'It is an inevitable fact that you are destined to do as you are told, with or without a whipping, and I suggest you do it with the least pain to yourself and the least draining of my own fluids.'

Amy pouted, and spent seven seconds wondering if the punishment was worth the stance. She decided it was not. It would have provided too much pleasure to this insufferable man.

She took the ring off and gave it to Milly.

Brenton, though largely immune to the subtle flow of emotions, experienced a tiny pang of disappointment. He had relished the thought of swinging a cane down on that cheeky behind.

'That is better. Now lean over these two poles so that I may tie you into a position best suited to the fitting of your stays.'

He tied her wrists to the two vertical poles and pushed her feet into the two niches that had been carved into the wooden platform. He then shackled them into place with two iron bars fixed with bolts so that her body was arrested by the shackles at her wrists and the locks at her feet. This forced her body to be immobile and allowed Gerard to stand behind her and pull the laces at the back of the stays with the force required to achieve the required effect of curvilinear precision.

The stay-maker, who smelled of lemons and an undercurrent of something most unpleasant that Amy could not identify, placed his clammy hands over her thighs and waist and breasts and pinched them in order to ascertain her size as a buyer assesses the size of a vegetable on a market stall.

His fingers lingered unnecessarily on her mons and he stroked the ridges of her pudenda with a smug leer.

He could do as he pleased and, though she disliked him intensely, this strangely excited her.

Gerard, seeing how the round orbs of her derrière were pushed out by his frame, and enjoying the sight of a freedom so easily curtailed, entertained a brief but enjoyable fantasy in which Amy was thrown into prison and forced to linger, pent up, powerless and behind bars.

The thought of her white skin stained with dirt, the flashing blue eyes glittering with hopeless hatred, the hair matted, the chemise torn with age and wear; these thoughts of Miss Pringle cooped up and controlled made him feel almost human.

He had to physically and mentally stop himself from either smacking her or fucking her or both.

If he had had the freedom, he would have forced those perky buttocks apart with his hands and pumped himself into her without a by-your-leave, but this was not his privilege. He had to maintain an aura of professionalism, and Lord Hacclesfield was an important customer. To submit to his own whims would have been to court a displeasure that would ruin him.

So Gerard Brenton satisfied himself by pinioning Miss Pringle into a position that allowed him to practise his craft.

'The number twelve, please,' he said to an assistant.

The youth opened an upright wooden trunk and sifted through its contents until he found the correctional garment that the Brenton family had spent two generations designing, perfecting and selling. The Brenton Stay was top of the range – each one was hand-made from several layers of stout canvas stiffened with paste. Several sections were stitched together with cat gut. Lengths of whale bone were

147

inserted into hollow casings to project the breast and minimise the waist. Armholes and edges were fitted with softer binding – made from kid leather – to avoid chafing.

Models came for all sizes, the larger being laced at the sides as well as the front and the back.

The number twelve was the standard model for young women. It was tied through a row of eyelets and leather laces that wove from the back.

The assistant fitted the coarse canvas panels around Amy's body where the stiff material irritated her skin.

Gerard stood behind her and started to walk away from her with the ends of the two laces in his hands.

The further away he stepped, the tighter the stays became as the thread was forced through the eyelets and the canvas panels tightened around her body.

'This will give you a fine shape,' he said.

'I already have a fine shape,' she managed to mutter, though the breath was fast being squeezed out of her body.

'Quiet, madam.'

He continued to pull the strings, on and on, until her waist clenched in, her bosoms heaved upward, and her back was forced into an erect stance that pushed her chin up and forward.

He pulled again, and now she was being pulled away from the vertical poles, her wrists straining against the leather cuffs, her buttocks forcibly moving towards him, as the waist became smaller and smaller.

Finally, as the tears began to well in her eyes, and the breath was now so short as to be almost non-existent, Gerard Brenton stopped and tied the laces with an immaculate knot.

The assistants released her wrists and unlocked the bars at her feet.

'Now, miss. Please go to Lord Hacclesfield and confirm that this is the shape that is required.'

Amy was bare except for the cruel canvas corset. Her bottom half was not covered and she had no shift to conceal her modesty. Her hair lay flat on a perspiring forehead; her body was boxed up in cramped confinement. She walked out of the room but she could not walk as she usually did, with a toss of the head – the walk of a woman who goes where she pleases.

Her steps were now small, her movement slow. She eased herself slowly down the stairs to the study and knocked on the door.

'Come.'

'You wish, you bastard,' she muttered to herself.

Lord Hacclesfield, discussing the ledger with Adrian, looked up as Amy entered.

Adrian's eyeballs bulged out of their sockets. A lovely woman, a future lady of this very house, was bare-limbed; unconcealed, all the flesh was his to peruse with private privilege. She was wearing no shoes, no feathers, no frills, no ruffles. Nothing. And her shape was accentuated to an hourglass with tight lace and canvas. His experiences had allowed him few sights of ladies' bodies, particularly ladies of the upper classes, whose presences were rare enough, and when he did see them they were covered in all the traditional habits of everyday guise. Adrian had never seen anything like it.

'Ah,' said Lord Hacclesfield. 'The stays.'

He got up and approached Amy across the rich Turkish carpet.

'I see that they fit well.'

He went round the back and tested the laces for tightness. He pushed his finger down the front of her breasts to see how they felt. He turned her around and inspected her pubis and her bare bottom as if he was examining livestock to see if he was going to buy it for the farm.

'That is fine,' he said. 'You may go. Tell Monsieur Gerard to bring his account to me.'

Mrs d'Angelo, the maker of chemises and under-petticoats, was more humane in her approach. A soft woman of 53 or so, she had been widowed early on in her marriage ('Thank goodness,' she told Amy, 'or I would have been the first to go – bored to death!') and had used her inheritance to start up a little shop in Bridgnorton, the market town three miles away from Lancaster Hall.

She carefully measured Amy with a gentle touch and warm hands whose fingers were efficient rather than cruel or probing.

'Lord Hacclesfield has said that you must have drawers, Miss Pringle,' said Mrs d'Angelo. 'They are the newest thing, don't you know? They were only introduced to London some four weeks ago and I must say they have gone very well, very well indeed. The queen herself has ordered 43 pairs from the royal pantaloonière, all in silk made from the palace's own silk worms and all embroidered with her coat of arms.

'I have heard it on very good authority that Her Majesty, in a moment of subtle discretion and in the privacy of her own bedchamber, told a lady-in-waiting that her royal bottom had never been so comfortable! She thinks drawers should be the law. Apparently she has even talked to the king about it, tried to get him to bring up the matter in parliament. Now of course everyone wants them. The ladies around here have seen them in the journals and I can tell you, I've got the work cut out for me this month. I've had to hire Nilly Tucket from the milliners to do extra hours, and poor Titty Woodlock is half blind from the sewing . . .'

She opened a leather box and produced a pile of

sheer silk knickers, cut low on the leg and trimmed with a Dutch lace that caressed the middle of the thigh. They were comfortable on the waist but fitted snugly, emphasising Amy's rotund firmness and pressing on to the skin tight enough to define the spheres of her buttocks and the curve of her thighs.

Amy, still wearing the stays, but now more modestly clad in Mrs d'Angelo's cream-coloured bloomers, went to the study again.

'Bend over, please,' said Lord Hacclesfield. 'And put your hands in front of you on the desk.'

Amy did as she was told.

Lord Hacclesfield pulled the bloomers down to her ankles.

'They fit well over the behind, but they are loose enough to pull down in the event that punishment is required,' he said. 'They will do. Please tell Mrs d'Angelo to make three more pairs in exactly the same style and to bring them to the house by next Monday.'

Amy left the study and stormed up the stairs to her own bedroom where Milly was waiting for her with a glass of lemonade and some sweet cakes that had been supplied by the kitchen.

'Get these bloody stays off me,' said Amy. 'I can't breathe.'

Milly was horrified.

'Oh, Miss Pringle, please! The master will see. He will check up on you! Please keep them on! You'll get used to them, I promise. All the ladies do. My Lady Hacclesfield, Mrs Prenderghast – they all have them. I wear them. You get used to them!'

'Untie me!'

Milly unfastened the offending laces, releasing Amy from her canvas prison. She looked on with nervous fear as Amy kicked the dreadful garment around the room and eventually threw it violently into a corner.

151

'Now,' she bade. 'Get my riding habit. I am to meet Bubb in the stables and we are to ride around the park. I will be back before the light goes.'

'But Miss Pringle – how will you ride with those cruel bruises on your bum? Will they not hurt you?'

'Ha! I've forgotten that already. It was nothing! I can't even feel it. He will have to do better than that, Lord Stupid and his switch; much better, if he thinks I am to pay any heed to him.'

Milly watched miserably as her proud mistress, wearing a deep purple riding habit of warm broadcloth, a lace jabot, a manly cambric shirt with ruffled sleeves, a dimity waistcoat, and a purple hat, swept down the stairs, the skirt flouncing behind her, the feather waving jauntily on her head. She knew, as surely as she knew that the good Lord had made heaven and earth, that their troubles had only just begun.

Bubb was waiting in the stables. There was a smell of horse and leather and straw; the groom was fitting a head collar on to Sally while the under-groom was polishing a saddle. Several geldings and mares stamped in their compartments, hard hooves clumping impatiently against the stone floor, tails swishing from side to side.

There was a sound of heavy breath snorting through flared nostrils. Bubb was grateful for these animal sounds because he was also panting, hard and fast, his chest heaving, and he did not want the stablehands to observe the rigours of the passion that, uncontrolled, pumped his body with weakening waves.

The pulse between his legs rose and fell with alarming force. The blood of lust surged down his body and, dizzy, he had to grip a wooden beam for support.

Subsumed by desire, he had been longing for this moment all day. He had thought of nothing but the hour when he would be alone with the object of his fascination.

He had not planned anything; there was no scheme for seduction. He did not plot. It would not have crossed his mind to do so; he was too simple for such manoeuvres. Bubb could only deal with the complicated moments of present reality as they rose up and challenged him. They were enough for him; sometimes they were too much.

Amy was late. She had been late all her life, so it was unlikely that a freak of nature would occur and that she would be punctual today. Two minutes, three hours, two days; she was unable to keep an appointment.

Questioned about this, she would usually say that it was not her fault. She did try to be on time, but the suspicious person might conclude that Miss Pringle, consciously or unconsciously, was keen to impose excitement. It did not matter where or when or how, as long as some kind of drama was initiated as a result of her appearance. This was the point of her tardiness. She wanted to be the lead actress of the opening scene. Amy would deny this hotly if she was accused of it. Nevertheless, it was true that her history told of many effective entrances made to grateful and appreciative audiences.

She was twenty minutes late and though Bubb did not feel any of the irascible affront that caused his father so much fury (he would not have dreamed of raising a hand to her lovely person, or raised a voice to impel her to his ways), he was driven nearly mad with piquant impatience and nearly tore down the foreflap of his riding breeches and manhandled his own meat into furious release of the painful juices, so intense was the torment of lust and love and the slow torpor of time.

And then, suddenly, silently, without warning, there she was, a neat figure at the doorway. An angel of beauty.

'So,' she said. 'I am riding Formenta.'

This phrase was issued as a statement of a fact, not a question.

'It is best not,' said Bubb. 'Papa is right about Formenta. She is very wild and unpredictable. It is best to go on Sally. She is a good ride and easy to control.'

'Rubbish,' said Amy, the feather waving on her hat, the whip snapping impatiently against her leg. 'Formenta will be fine with me. Saddle her up, please, Bubb. I don't want to go on dull Sally – look at her, she can hardly move, the lazy thing.'

They turned to look at the fat grey mare that had been saddled by the groom and Bubb had to agree. Sally had not been exercised enough and looked as if she was not about to rise above a sedate trot.

'But Papa –' The words did not come. He did not want to admit his fear of his father but neither did he wish to incur Lord Hacclesfield's wrath.

'I will take all the blame . . .' she said. 'If we are found out. Just give the groom half a guinea, Bubb, that will keep him quiet. Come on. Let's go! The sun will go down before we've got out of this stable.'

Bubb, very reluctantly, submitted to this demand but he knew it was not for the best.

'And I don't want the side-saddle!' Amy told the groom. 'Give me one of Lord Fitzroy's spare saddles, please.'

'But Lady Hacclesfield always rides side-saddle, miss,' said the groom. 'It is safe and comfortable . . .'

He wanted to add 'and ladylike', but he did not.

'I don't care what Lady Hacclesfield does or does not do. Please do as I say.'

The groom raised his eyebrows but sent them down again when he saw the look on Amy's face. Obediently he went to the tack-room and placed an ordinary leather saddle on Formenta's glossy chestnut back. The young mare snorted and stamped and would have tossed her head about if the under-groom had not been holding it firmly by her head collar.

The two servants led Formenta into the stable-yard and Amy followed. Assessing the horse's size and demeanour, she saw that the animal was not dangerous (as some horses could be, mad or stupid and out of control) but merely bored and ready to be given her head.

'Lovely girl,' she whispered into the lean nose. 'We'll be friends.'

The groom gave her a leg up and there she was, astride Formenta's back, her long black riding boots firmly in the stirrups, her gloved hands resting neatly on the reins, back erect, knees in, holding as good a seat as Bubb had seen any man take.

He leaped expertly on to his own chestnut and they trotted out of the stable and into one of the overgrown paths that led through the woodland and around the boundaries of the park.

Amy was right. She was an expert rider. Formenta gave her no trouble. Bubb had seen the horse cause more concern to grooms much taller and stronger than Miss Pringle. She seemed to understand the animal and to know when to push her so that they both enjoyed the ride.

Bubb could not imagine where she could have learned to perfect these talents. She seemed to have been born in the saddle and he thought, with a pang of regret, that Ralph would have appreciated this. The notion of Ralph caused a sharp remonstrance of conscience; though this expedition was not a betrayal to his brother, betrayal lay in the thoughts that fermented in Bubb's exhausted mind.

'I have no morals,' he told himself angrily. 'I will burn in hell and it will serve me right. But I do not care. I love her! I LOVE HER!'

This proclamation was internal, but it seemed so loud as to be external. He had to check himself to ensure that this strident confession was not actually vocal. They cantered up and down the hills of the green pastures that bordered Lancaster Hall. They directed the horses through fields and wound around hedgerows. The countryside spread out in an endless masterwork of greens, yellows and browns. The sky lowered, blue and grey. Lancaster Hall was a Palladian doll's house in the distance.

Bubb felt exhilarated. She enthused him with some unknown life-force that made him go further to the edge than he could ever have done under his own volition.

They stopped by a wide brown river where the family fished and the villagers poached. It moved along, slowly and easily, while kingfishers dipped down on it and long-legged fauna skated on top of it.

Bubb looped the horses to the branches of a tree and they sat down on a rug on the grass beside the water.

He brought out some ale and some bread and cheese from the leather pannier on his saddle and they supped, quietly, both drained by the exertion of the ride, both musing their own thoughts.

Amy's thoughts were about Ralph.

Bubb's thoughts were about Amy.

He did not think he had ever seen anything so lovely. He was a country man, but he had met many women. He was eligible, after all, despite being the second son. The sum of his annual increment was well known. He would inherit the mansion known as The Gate House and his brother would be an earl. These were enough to attract ambitious mothers and lissome daughters and the odd hoyden who had muscled into the competition when they had heard of the freak prodigy that snaked between his legs.

Some had been tall, some short, some pretty, some witty. Many had offered premarital favours for committed promises as to their connubial future. Bubb had liked them well enough, and he had enjoyed himself, but none of them had been like the woman who sat before him. She had fallen from some other place. It was as if she had been produced by supernature – more inexplicable than the headless wraith that was supposed to wander around the west wing of Lancaster Hall but certainly possessed of the same quality of unreality.

He stared at her with the unguarded honesty of his desire and she felt his stare. She was familiar with this kind of observation. She knew when men were feasting with their eyes and secretly arousing themselves with the sight of women. She often wondered how they managed to exist, so easily excited were they, the relentless gorge in their groins straining against the knowledge that consummation of their lust was by no means assured.

They must have to sit around in a state of agitation all the time. She could not imagine anything worse. If Amy felt aroused she never allowed her body to be pricked by the self-tease of denial; she knew how to satisfy herself, and if there were no friendly fingers or toys or dicks available, she would satisfy herself whenever and wherever she wished to do so. Often, so inclined, she would lie down wherever, fling up her petticoats and penetrate herself with her own hard piercing fingers until the heat had been quelled and the moment had passed.

Bubb was overcome. The bulge in his breeches was now so intense that he felt it like a third limb. The foreskin peeled back from the swollen head and the probe pushed up into the tight cotton, causing insufferable discomfort.

He swept her up in his arms and kissed her very hard on the lips.

The pastry dropped from her hand on to the grass where a militia of ants immediately started to stream towards it.

She was genuinely taken by surprise, not because she did not think that Bubb wanted her – but because he had not seemed to be a man driven by impulse.

Her breath was taken away and her rationale began to leave her. She felt the adamantine erection push hard against her legs and she remembered that Bubb's dick was notorious.

Curiosity and reciprocal lust overwhelmed her, but she said, 'My dear Bubb. Is this appropriate? I am supposed to become affianced to your brother, am I not?'

How little he cared.

He kissed her again, a hard keen tongue probing deep into her throat. Lip on lip. Having her. She laughed and submitted. Why not? She had not felt a good hard dick since she had been fucked by the King of France.

The purple skirt rode up, revealing new silk drawers, but they were not to stay in place for long. Bubb, heated beyond measure, yanked them down her legs and threw them on to the grass. Now there were thighs and pudenda and her white buttocks streaked by his father's lash. He stroked them tenderly.

'The punishment did not preclude the pleasure of your ride, I hope,' he whispered.

'Oh no,' she said. 'I have always been resistant to physical pain. My mother said I should have been a man, so strong am I!'

'I am glad you were not born a man,' he said, and flung her ankles above her shoulders so that the full flesh of her labia flowered in front of him and their lips, now flourished and dilated, allowed him access to the welcoming straits of her internal passage.

And now he pulled it out, the magnificent manhood of which she had heard so much. It was not a disappointment.

Bubb knew from experience that his tool must be handled with care, for ladies had been known to scream out in agony if this probe was propelled with clumsy force. Some of them could not take it. It was too much. He knew from experience that the insufferable size must slowly gain admission, oozing through the lady's excited lubricants if it was to cause enjoyment.

The broad head tipped itself into the opening and then through the inside of her, wedging itself into her passage, so that she felt it slowly move inside her, inch by inch by inch, until they were locked in the full gorgeous completion that only a big man can provide.

It was delicious to feel so filled, to feel almost endangered by sheer volume, and Amy allowed him to ride her as he wished, deep into the core of her being, his pelvis banging hard against her, his dick deep down inside her. She closed her eyes and gorged herself on gratification, enjoying the animal plunging that seemed to be crude revenge, but was, in fact, the only true inebriation.

He shuddered his finale and pulled out, knowing that the flow of his juices must not contaminate her future, and they lay briefly in the mutual transcendence of post-coital satisfaction, he stroking her hair, she enjoying the soft skin of his face and the knowledge that he was a real man.

'I want to marry you, Miss Pringle,' he said.

'You cannot, my dear Bubb. It would be dishonest of me to pretend that you can. Our destiny is barred by circumstance. You know that in your heart of hearts.'

She implied that she was committed to her duty and hoped that he would believe this, though the truth was that the challenge of Ralph was yet to be met and she knew that, large though Bubb's dick was, and sweet his noble personality, she would be too much for him. He would bore her and she would end up tormenting him.

Ralph Fitzroy, however, would not bore her. This she knew. Ralph Fitzroy would please her and challenge her and entertain her. He engaged her instincts, and though her rationale tried to quarrel with the intangible ideas thrown up by nonsensical passions, her rationale was losing.

'In the end,' she opined to herself, 'I am a fairly unpleasant person, and I should only be inflicted on someone who can recognise this, like it, match it and handle it. This person is not Bubb. He needs a sweet woman who will appreciate his gentle ways and never take advantage of his simplicity.'

They galloped down a long valley. He in front, she behind, her hair flowing, the hat having been lost hours before, but when he turned his horse around a corner into a field full of wheat, she was gone. It was as if she had fallen off the edge of the earth. There was no sign of her, no hoof marks, nothing.

He rode up and down for an hour calling her name, desperately, afraid of the dreadful conclusions that his mind threw up: that she had fallen and was wounded, that she had absconded and he would take the blame, that everything was to be found out – the illicit horse, the love-fuck. Everything.

He walked his tired horse home, alone.

Dinner that night was a gloomy affair. Ralph was sullen and Lord Hacclesfield was apoplectic. Purple in hue and slamming his hands on the table so that the china jumped up and down and the soup swirled into whirlpools in the dishes, he raged against Bubb and Miss Pringle and the crimes that they had dared go commit against his express orders. It was not enough that they had taken Formenta when he had specifically told them to take Sally, but now the woman was lost in the woods on a dangerous horse, causing Lord knows what mayhem, scandalising the neighbours, and possibly incurring personal injury that he would then have to pay a medic to cure.

He kept the vent of his spleen for the absent Amy, knowing that she had led his youngest son astray. Bubb did not have the gumption to plan such an excursion himself.

'That woman is going to have to go!' he shouted. 'She is not fit to be in this house, let alone a suitable wife for Ralph!'

'Oh, Father,' Bubb protested. 'Miss Pringle is spirited, but she means no harm!'

He looked over at his brother for support. Ralph stared silently into his soup.

'Why do you not defend Miss Amy, Ralph?' he asked. 'It seems fitting that a gentleman should defend his wife-to-be, does it not?'

'She is not going to be his wife if I have anything to do with it!' their father expostulated. 'I am going to order Jarvis to send a lawyer's letter terminating the contractual obligation . . .'

161

'Ralph!' Bubb snapped, trying to rouse his brother from whatever daymare immersed his senses.

Ralph lifted his eyes from the soup and stared coldly at Bubb.

'Frankly, my dear brother, I do not care whether Miss Pringle comes or goes. She cannot hold a candle to Miranda. No woman can. And that, sir, is the simple truth.'

Lord Hacclesfield's silver soup spoon clattered into the empty dish and he gesticulated at Headley to clear the bowls away.

The second course was eaten in silence.

Bubb sighed.

'Well,' he said, when a glass of port had fired up some courage, 'as far as I am concerned, Miss Pringle is lost out in the woods alone. It is dark and cold and she has nothing to eat. There is a possibility that she might die. I am going to take some of the men and search for her at first light.'

Lord Hacclesfield shrugged. He did not want the death of the dreadful woman on his hands.

'Do as you please,' he said.

Chapter Seven

*A*my was lost. She was tired and she was thirsty.
She wished she had not left Bubb behind in the
field. She had not meant to, but he was slow, and she
had lost him by mistake. Then Formenta had cantered
into the forest and Amy had allowed her to lead the
way, through the coppices and groves, down winding
paths, the golden sunlight showering through the shaking leaves. She had lost all sense of direction and now
the sun was setting.

She was not frightened particularly, but she felt a
little tense, and she was both hungry and thirsty. All
she wanted was a cup of water and sensible directions
as to how to escape from this woodland whose appearance was becoming more sinister with impending
evening.

And so, when she saw the cottage and the oil lamp
in the window, she knocked and waited. She could
hear whispering inside but at first no-one came to
answer the door. Irritated, she banged quite loudly
with her fist and considered kicking the door with her
foot.

The Magog sisters were excited.

'It is the Queen of Swords.'

'She has come.'

'The cards said she would.'

'We are ready.'

'Let her in.'

'Let her in.'

'Let her in.'

They floated as one across the floor of the cottage to the door and opened it, their three heads appearing in the jamb.

They were all clad in long scarlet robes, embroidered with gold. There were gold chains and pendants hanging around their necks. Their long black hair was braided and entwined with gold ribbon. Three identical white faces flashed with six slanted green eyes. They were like a waking dream.

Amy was not scared. She was fascinated, for they were beautiful. Three beautiful sisters.

'I'm ... er ... lost. I've been riding for ages. You couldn't tell me how to get back to Lancaster Hall, could you?'

'Come in,' said Octavia.

Amy followed them into the cottage where one room served as eating place, sitting area and temple.

The heat stroked her cold cheeks and ignited a flush. There were hundreds of candles and the smell of burning frankincense. A fire blazed in the grate and, in front of it, a lurcher lay chewing a bone on the floor.

An altar in one corner bore an effigy of the goddess Diana, some flowers and water and candles. An immaculate white pentagram had been painted on to the floor.

The three sisters ushered Amy into their epicentre, surrounding her with themselves, so that she was enclosed by their breasts and arms and warmth. She

164

allowed herself to be calmed by their maternal murmurings.

'You're cold, my dear.'

Olivia rubbed her as one would rub a child who was shivering.

'You must have come a long way.'

She allowed herself to be served some meat and a cup of honey-flavoured mead, traditional drink of potency, and she began to relax.

The Magog sisters, possessed of uncanny perceptions, seemed to know more about Amy than she knew herself. They told her that she was a unique woman in her experiences, that she had spent much time abroad and known important personages. She had met men who wore crowns and ruled the world.

'They rule the world,' said Sylvia. 'But they are weak.'

Amy agreed.

They told her that her father had died when she was young. They had seen these things in the cards.

They said that she was destined for greatness and would get what her heart desired.

Amy, fascinated and mesmerised, could not help but feel close to these three strange women, who seemed to feel so familiar and to know everything and who were operating to rules that were beyond the normal ken.

She forgot her plans to return home and allowed herself to be led by them into the magic of their intent. It was as if she was hypnotised. Her mind knew what she was doing, but her body submitted to their directives.

The three sisters slowly removed Amy's riding habit and laid it to one side, their 30 fingers working as one sensual organ, stroking her skin and gently exciting the gentle zones of her buttocks and neck and thighs.

Then Olivia took the waistband of the silken drawers and slowly pulled them down her legs. Now Amy was naked.

She was naked and she did not mind at all. She walked towards this mystical initiation as calmly as a gazelle walks towards a lake to drink.

The three sisters sniffed Amy's warm skin and smelled her odours as if they were the exotic scent of expensive oils.

'Ah, my lady has just received the act of love,' said one sister.

'She has enjoyed the large portion of Bubb Fitzroy.'

They cackled happily.

And she laughed with them, for it was true: her labia were still swollen and her inner passages were still humming with the delight of their recent reception. Bubb Fitzroy. Another place, another time, another world. She could feel the imprint of his dick, but she could hardly remember his face.

The sisters laid her down on the floor on top of the pentagram, spread-eagled her limbs on to the four points of a star and tied her wrists and ankles to four iron circles that were stapled to the ground.

So she was splayed across the pentagram, helplessly pinned down, her legs wide apart so that the roseate recesses of her lower lips curled out, vulnerable and swollen with the complex pulses of new desire.

'The juices of your matrix symbolise the nuptial ascendant,' said Octavia. 'The unguent of venery will be taken and used for great purpose.'

'They are love pure and divine, the magic of passion, and they will help to find the way to the starry spaces,' said Sylvia.

Then each of the three Magog sisters took up athames, daggers of the witches, whose faultless steel glinted dangerously in the candlelight and Amy, staring up at them from her bed of immutable supplication on the floor, suddenly felt the novel flicker of apprehension; a heartbeat, not much more, but she was, after all, surrounded by the three wild women, unknown and odd, playing with the waves of the occult.

'Oh, round circle of pure magic,' said Octavia, 'with this powerful athame I cut away all the cords that bond us to the mundane world.'

They placed the knives ceremoniously on the point of the north and took up three wands, charged by many evenings of mystical rite, and the same ones that they had used since they were initiated.

'Oh, round circle of pure magic,' said Olivia. 'With this pure wand I wave away all the evil spirits of the other world so that we may be protected in safety in the temple of our dreams.'

The Magog sisters swayed as one, circling Amy with small footsteps, then dancing faster and faster as Sylvia played a flute and emitted a strange tune made of unfamiliar notes.

They swayed faster and faster, muttering incantations to the goddess Diana and invoking her powers.

'Beautiful huntress of the night . . .'

'Bring your power into our place.'

'By the light of moon and sun.'

'Grant our wishes every one.'

Olivia passed a silver chalice full of wine and all three sisters sipped from it.

'So mote it be.'

'So mote it be.'

The triplets knelt down on the floor by Amy's side and, bending over her, they rocked their heads so that their soft black hair flicked over her skin and tickled her with soft tendrils.

Each woman took it in turns to insert their fingers

into her ever-widening orifice, pushing into her with easy force and manipulating her until the pulses of climax rose from her labia to her pelvis and then, as spasms, up her back to her throat and mouth. She had never felt anything like it. Vibrant with endless ripples of bliss, she laughed, and the laughter came as a witchy cackle of weird triumph. The victorious joy of orgasm. That ultimate joke. Then she moaned and pleaded, she begged into the night for things that she did not even know existed. She did not know where she was. She did not know who she was.

They had not finished.

'Shout out your desire,' said one sister (she did not know which). 'Shout out your innermost secret, the need of your soul. Ask the Invisible Ones for the need of your essence and your wish will be granted.'

'So mote it be.'

'So mote it be.'

'So mote it be.'

Confused beyond any capability of rationale, Amy did not know what she wanted. She could not work it out logically in the throes of ecstasy. They had reduced her to an unthinking mass by the force of deft exploitation. She was dreaming in the space of true knowledge that only appears to the lucky few, and often creeps up without warning when one neither expects it or wants it. Oddly, though, she knew that the dissolution of the Amy that she knew to the uninhibited ranting female essence was not a distortion of herself. It was herself.

Now, in the semi-dark, the fingers provoking her every nerve, her erogenous recesses vitalised and her mind enlightened, she was transported by magical excess. The face of Ralph Fitzroy rose as a vision. His face, the dark eyes, the stern mouth, stared at her and it was not as if he was in her mind's eye. He, it, was a concrete presence floating in front of her as clearly as one sees a chair or a table or a rock. He was three-dimensional. If she had been able to lift her fingers from the hooks on the floor she would have been able to touch his face and feel the warmth of his skin.

Love surged as a passionate force through her entire body and she jolted.

Her mouth opened wide and the words that came out as a scream did not feel as if they were being spoken by her.

'I want Ralph Fitzroy!' she shrieked. 'I want Ralph!'

'You shall have him,' they said as one voice. 'He is yours.'

They were still kneeling beside her bound body. Now they moved to the cunt conjunction of her legs, and, crouching in front of it, they took turns to lick her clitoris. They licked it until she thought her mind would leave her and that this was their intention; to repel her very life, expel it into an invisible world, and take her body for some cause of their own.

Now the juices gushed from between her legs and flowed on to the floor, creating a pool.

The Magog sisters mopped up this viscous fluid from the floor with silk swatches of fabric and held the stained squares to the candlelight.

'The lubrication of sex magick.'

'Prime sigil of perfect mastery.'

Each dark woman leaned down and kissed Amy gently on the mouth. Then they took handfuls of salt from a silver urn on the altar and threw it over themselves, its grains glittering as sparkles as it showered the air.

Slowly they undid each other's robes and the red dresses fell to the ground. Naked, they rubbed each other's bodies, a triumvirate of self-stimulation and sisterly knowing, one and three, three and one, the fingers of Olivia in Octavia, Octavia rubbing Sylvia, round and round, murmuring, kissing, arousing each other with perfect knowledge of one woman knowing her three cunts, her six nipples, all organs blending into one organism, all nerve endings unifying but also triplicate.

'Oh, goddess, great and true, join us in this protected circle.'

'Bring us the man that we desire.'

'Bring us a son of the earth.'

'Borne from the blood of Uranus's wound.'

'Bring us a man mighty enough to fight Zeus.'

'Bring us, oh wise one, the Titan of our dreams that we may traverse the circle of wyrd from girlhood to womanhood.'

'Bring us the King of Gigantomachy!'

Amy, transported by magic and sex and in some inner world of her own, now hardly knew where she was or how she had got there. Neither did she care.

She lay on the floor, physically restrained, emotionally drained, her mind travelling between waking and dreaming. Her body had been ripped apart with muscular contortion, her spine revitalised with multiple spasms, her very being charged with life.

There was no sense of abnormality but neither was there any sense; she did not know if she had been drugged by some witches' infusion, a narcotic, perhaps, placed with subtle fingers into the mead, or whether she was simply the guest of three sylphs of the sexual night.

The room went cold. Two candles flickered and went out. And somewhere, far away at first, the night filled with the clumping of footsteps. Nearer and nearer they came, louder and louder as they did so.

The Magog sisters quiet, naked and still, paused to listen.

The feet came closer and closer.

The hairy head of the dog jolted up and he whined, fear in his eyes.

The door of the cottage swung open.

He was not a real giant, in the mythical sense, towering over churches and head above the rain clouds, but he was very tall none the less, freakishly tall, too tall to ride a normal horse, for instance, or to walk through a normal doorway without bending over to avoid knocking his head on the top of the frame.

He was about seven foot and aged, if one was forced to guess, between 28 and 30.

Well built, with firm stomach and a wide chest, arms that looked as if they could have pulled an apple tree out of the ground, thighs the size of some women's waists, his eyes were dark blue and his hair sat as a thick black mop on the top of his head.

He wore leather breeches made of tanned deer-skin that were held together by rough hand-sewn stitches and a belt from which various implements hung. These included a screwdriver, for instance, a whip, some keys, a small saw, and a leather pouch full of water.

He was big and he was handsome. The Magog sisters stared. There was enough of him to go around; no-one would have to fight to gain his attention. Their lives would be full of ithyphallic satisfaction as three separate orifices could gorge themselves on the lucky manifestation that was their one giant-husband.

Love beat violently in three hearts.

'I am Jotunheim,' he said. 'I am the son of the woodman Willard and I am delivering the logs that you ordered from the mill. They are outside on the horse's cart.'

The three women did not care about logs. Silently they sidled forward. Their foreheads reached to his chest. They rubbed themselves up against him, allowing him to feel the force of their soft breasts and thighs and lips. Six hands caressed his groin. Octavia, leader as always, reached into the flap at the front of his breeches and brought out the instrument that they had so often seen in their dreams. They had often whispered about the penis of the giant when the three of them sat by the fire in the evenings, thinking of their man and how he must be. How rather than who, that was the important thing. They did not care who. They just wanted the stamina of masculine energy and a totem that they could respect.

Octavia brought out the megalith and it raged with force. She had to hold it in two hands. Lovingly she caressed the soft skin and felt its satisfying hardness.

'This is the One,' she whispered. 'Oh, this is the One.'

A deep growl rumbled from somewhere above her head – the emission of pleasure from a vast, deep throat.

One woman would not have been enough for a giant, but Jotunheim had three, and this was about right for him. His sexual desires were three times the size of any normal man, as was his genitalia. This was an icon of grandeur, the like of which no human could imagine, the like of which could spawn the fertility frenzy of any pagan fertility rite.

The sisters (particularly Octavia) thought that this man was to be the slave of their desires, but they were wrong. He was not destined to bow to their witchy ways.

The currents turned like a tide.

'Kneel on the floor before your master!' said the behemoth Jotunheim in his deep baritone.

The Magog sisters had never been spoken to thus, but they did as they were told. Forced down by the power of his authority, their senses were in their groins, causing heat and need, the very element of fire that they had invoked.

The three women dropped to the floor and on to their knees. Their foreheads touched the floor in front of his feet.

The giant gazed down at them with calm majesty.

The Magog sisters kissed his boots.

Six buttocks trembled, three cunts slathered with expectation. They were his.

The giant reached down and lifted them up as one body. Throwing them over his Herculean shoulders he carried them to a fur-covered day-bed that ran along the wall of the cottage in front of the fire.

Now they were on their backs, these triplicate women, and all of them spread their legs with humble obedience, displaying their witches' lips and opening themselves to the object of desire, all three pelvises gyrating helplessly.

Jotunheim detached a china bottle from his belt and spilled anointing oil on to the wide spread of his hands, rubbing the unguent into each huge finger. Now lubricated with the sweet-smelling fluid, he carefully massaged the three bodies as if they were one, equally playing with all breasts, gently manipulating all nipples, using his fingers to find all their places.

Elevated, excited, the Magog sisters removed the giant's clothes with perfect coordination because they had worked as one all their lives. Jerkin, shirt, breeches, all were taken until he too was naked, a vast expanse of smooth muscle and soft skin, his gorgeous cock still as straight and hard as any stone in any ancient circle.

The Magog sisters surrounded him and embraced him. Sylvia tickled the nerves around his anus, Octavia stroked the balls that hung like oranges between his legs, Olivia sucked as much of his head as she could in her mouth. This would take practice, for there was much of it and her muscles were unaccustomed to this kind of work.

Jotunheim pushed them gently away from him so that they were on their backs on the sofa.

'Please take us, sir,' moaned Octavia.

And her sisters whispered their agreement as a murmur of sibilant need.

Which one first? Which one last? Which one in between? What order of sisters should Jotunheim fuck? This apparently complex decision did not hinder him for a second; he took them with an instinctive sense of irony. Olivia, the quietest, the least aggressive, she got that magnificent dick first.

He eased himself into her and she shouted out loud. Her lucky sisters, so closely joined by their triplet nerve systems, felt her pleasure resound in their heads and groins.

Tears sprang to Olivia's eyes.

She was full.

As all her passages contorted to pleasurable frenzy, the giant man took Sylvia in the same way, sliding his tense muscle into her, and fucking her with strong, slow, easy lunges, driving her into the place that she had longed to go for many, many months.

Finally Octavia. He forced himself into her harder than the other two, sensing that that was what she wanted. He plunged, hard and rhythmic, and she did not want him to ever, ever stop. On and on, until, at last, she surrendered to him; the constrictions of ego left her and she abandoned herself to his control.

She screamed out her climax and her love. She felt the deep loss as he withdrew.

Jotunheim's juices flowed as a river from the recesses of his muscular pelvis.

All four of them were soft now, the sisters full of grateful affection, the giant appreciating the treasure that he had found. They all embraced. He would stay with them for ever. It was destined to be a happy household. How could it not be?

It was dark. Amy was untied. Gentle hands helped her into her clothes, gentle lips brushed her face, her hair was brushed and she was given more mead and something to eat. She came to her senses – or to some semblance of chill reality, anyway. She hardly knew where she had been, but she knew what she had seen. Jotunheim helped her on to Formenta. Then, riding his own horse in front of her, a flaming torch in his hand, he led the way to the path out of the woods.

Formenta plodded easily towards the lights of Lancaster Hall and Amy, relaxed by a deep feeling of centred calm, reflected on the scene that she had witnessed and some of the extraordinary sensations that she had experienced.

'Lord,' she said to herself. 'And I thought I had seen everything.'

It was 11.30 p.m. when Amy finally walked through the front door of Lancaster Hall. The house was dark. Only one figure loomed in the great hall. It was the figure of Lord Hacclesfield, who had been sitting by the dying fire in a coiled constriction that combined fury and worry.

He had already heard tales about Amy's wild riding. A poacher had told a forester, a forester had told a clergyman. Soon it would be all over the county – how the future wife of Lord Fitzroy rode about dressed as a man, bare-backed and savage, on top of the very horse that he had forbidden her to ride.

He heard the door click open and saw Amy enter.

He was not a superstitious man, but her arrival caused his skin to tingle and his body to feel sensations that were most uncomfortable to a man who wished to

175

recognise reality at all times and who needed the security of familiarity. The man was controlled by fear-based inflexibility. This was his safeguard and, when removed, it meant that he was as cold and dangerous as any soldier trained to protect defences.

'So, madam!' he thundered. 'Now you arrive!'

His being a pyre of fury, he did not allow her to speak. Driven by anger, he merely grabbed her and physically dragged her up the stairs to her room. Pushing her into it, he slammed the door shut and locked it.

She heard his expletives as he stamped down the corridor away from her room.

Amy lay on her bed in her riding habit. The smells of the cottage lingered in her hair and clothes; the sweet oil, the mead, the fire. Her cunt still tingled, her head was still there. It was as if Lancaster Hall was the dreamworld, and the sphere of magic sex was the real one. Sense and non-sense mingled in an unfathomable quantum zone. Her consciousness had been raised, her strengths strengthened, and all her options opened out in a wide spectrum of pleasing possibilities.

Falling to sleep, still clothed, she thought, finally, of Ralph. It was confusing. She hardly knew him. He was a numinous knave. He should be wandering on the outside of her thoughts, not central to them. But there he was, manifest as a man of her dreams.

The next day Milly informed Amy that she was to remain locked in her bedroom until Lord Hacclesfield and Ralph returned from London, which would be a journey of about seven days.

'A week!' Amy shrieked. 'A week? I can't stay in this room for a week. I will go stark staring raving mad. It is June, for crying out loud! The sun is out.'

'That is what the master has ordered,' said Milly.

'You are to do needlework and embroidery and read the Bible. You are to have your meals brought up to you three times a day. You have to wear your stays and underwear at all times. And you are to write a long letter of apology to Lord Hacclesfield explaining that you have done wrong and that you know it. If you do not do these things you are to be thrown out of the house and you will not be allowed to marry Lord Fitzroy.

'His Lordship is going to send you up an official letter of directions with Headley later this morning. I only know all this because they were talking about it in the servants' dining hall. The official instructions are to arrive with Headley, and he has been ordered to supervise you. Please be careful of Headley, miss. When the master is away he becomes full of his own importance. He is like Genghis Khan, miss. All blown up with his own position.

'He thinks he is a lord himself because he has so much responsibility, you see. He thinks he owns the place. I wouldn't put it past him to punish you if he wanted. He gave Fanny a good hiding this morning and the master had only been gone two hours. She hadn't done anything! Spilled a bit of milk, that's all. Mrs Prenderghast was against her having her bum tanned just for that, but Headley did not listen. Pushed her over the kitchen table in front of everyone, tossed up her skirts, pulled up her petticoats, and beat her cheeks red with a hard wooden spoon. She was kicking and crying and begging him to stop, but he went on for about half an hour. She was still weeping when I left ten minutes ago. Don't give Headley an excuse, Miss Amy. He'll have you over his knee, I know he will . . .'

'He had better not,' said Amy, jaw tightening into a

177

hard mask of resilience. 'If that man lays a hand on me he will not even be able to imagine the consequences.'

Headley, swollen with the authority of his own importance, arrived at 12 p.m. and unlocked the chamber where Milly was attempting to persuade her mistress to make a start on the sewing swatches that had been sent from Lady Hacclesfield's linen baskets. There were sheets that needed darning and pillowcases that needed to be relaced – dull jobs that were usually delegated to the upstairs maids who served Lady Hacclesfield in her private suites. Lord Hacclesfield had, however, ordered them to be rerouted and he expected to see this job, and others just as boring, completed by the time he returned to Lancaster Hall.

Headley entered with ostentatious pomposity. Slowly, and with stupid drama, he unfurled a long yellow document on which Lord Hacclesfield's directions had been inscribed by his own feather quill – Adrian being ill that day.

Deploying the tone of a town crier, Headley read with the sombre monotone of a small-minded man who has just enough imagination to relish his tiny seconds in the sun.

It was a list full of the excruciating monotonies that Milly had prophesied. The maid had been right. Amy was expected to spend the term of her imprisonment engaged in darning and needlework and religious study with particular emphasis on edifying tales of morality that had been hand-picked by the earl.

These tales, for the most part, described the lives of young women who had voluntarily suffered sins of the flesh in order to enter the kingdom of Heaven. They were dutiful and innocent and pure and would have made you want to run a mile if you met them in real life.

Lord Hacclesfield's suggestions would have sent anyone mad unless they had actually taken vows to marry God and had entered themselves into a Carmelite convent.

'Lord Hacclesfield will expect you to be able to recite twenty separate psalms by heart by the time he returns,' said Headley. 'You are allowed to choose which ones to learn, but I am to hear them to ensure that progress is being made, and in the event that it is not, I am instructed to take you to the stables and switch your bare bottom eight times with one of the canes from the old schoolroom. If you cry during this punishment I have permission to gag your mouth until the whipping is over. If there is further disobedience, Lord Hacclesfield has allowed me to increase the punishment to twelve hard lashes. In the event of bruising, Milly will apply the herbal poultice that is currently being formulated by Mrs Prenderghast in the kitchen.'

Amy stared coldly at Headley. There was enjoyment to be had in the sensual pleasure of an arse-paddling, that much the earl had taught her, but as far as she was concerned this should be connected with foreplay rather than with an unattractive servant who she could not fuck if he was the last man on earth.

If she was to be punished she would take pleasure in her punishment and she would manipulate it to the enjoyment of her own whims. She certainly would not allow this menial to have his own pleasure at the expense of hers.

Headley would have to be managed, tormented if possible, and this would entail intelligent duplicity designed to achieve her own ends. Amy had plans. But her plans did not include giving Headley any fun.

Headley stared at her with a dreadful smile whose only communication was that of smug triumph. Yes, he wanted to see those bare cheeks bobbing up at him, ready to be streaked red with pain. Yes, he wanted to humiliate that lady and have her under his control. Yes, he wanted to hear her cry and beg. He hoped that she would disobey. How he hoped she would disobey.

He carefully refolded his employer's letter, left the room and locked it again.

Milly stared gloomily out of the window. There was Roberts bent over a flowerbed, weeding the earth. The sun was shining on his broad back and he was wearing a straw hat that, on some, would have looked absurd, but on Roberts cast a dandy stylishness that was inherent to his mien. Roberts had taste and he had confidence. It meant that he could wear anything and look like a man who had allowed himself to expect the best. Milly's heart beat with instinctive lust and passion, but her spirit was depressed.

She saw a boring week stretch out before them, a boring week that would inevitably throw up some transaction and end in both their backsides feeling the brusque reality of the schoolmaster's cane.

Amy, being Amy, was not to be beaten down by these atrocities. Locked up she might be, but she still had her imagination, and she had her allies. There was fun to be had in these confines. It just took a little nerve and a little persuasion of those who were less brave than she.

'Oh, Milly,' she said. 'Cheer up. Come here.'

She lay on the bed and lifted up her skirts.

'Take these silly drawers off.'

Milly, excited as always by her mistress's demanding sexuality, walked over to the door and listened in order to assure herself that Headley was not engaged in his customary practice of listening through the keyhole.

Then she did as she was told and pulled the soft silk pants down her mistress's beautiful thighs. She folded them neatly and placed them on an elegant chair whose upholstery was velvet and whose legs were carved in the modish cabriole style of the French court.

Amy splayed her ankles so that the tongue of her clit poked out for Milly to see.

'I am wet,' she said, matter-of-factly. 'Perhaps confinement and punishment excite me in ways whose mysteries I do not know. Feel me, Milly, I am ready for a fucking but there is no hard man to give it to me. Shame! Where are they when you need them? Never available, that I know. Never available with their hearts and never available with their cocks.'

She was thinking of Ralph when she said this, for it had not, in truth, been her experience to suffer many unavailable men. Men had always wanted to ravage Amy Pringle. They had clustered towards her all her life, but as a consummate minx it was her prerogative to turn her head the other way and pretend that she did not see them clamouring with need, passion and devotion.

'. . . Oh, Milly, come here, my dear, come here. I am frustrated, Milly. Finger me! Make me come. You're so good at it.'

Milly did as she was told. She knew her mistress's little secrets now – the wet recess of her sex and all the nerve endings that conspired to spread bliss.

She pushed three fingers deep inside and manipulated until she felt the translucent juices pour on to her hands.

Milly liked to feel her mistress's humid excitement, and she liked to see her expression immersed in the love that must be shown to the one who provides welcome climax. But it was an unusual power exchange and one that Milly was not yet used to; she the maid, Amy the mistress. Amy was supposed to have the power, but, in these circumstances, Milly was given as much control as it was possible for a woman to have. She could withdraw her finger and leave her mistress desperate, though she suspected that she would not have the nerve, and that if she did exercise these facilities of torture, her mistress would become cruel, maybe even take on the role of punisher.

So Milly fingered Amy and with artful hands brought her slowly to the unbearable tension that precedes orgasm, those tantalising seconds when promises have been made, money has been extorted, and the secrets of war exposed.

'Ah yes, my love,' said Amy, wondering if she should surrender the idea of making it with men and simply move Milly to a little house in Margate where they could live in peace, untroubled by the tartars that currently controlled their lives.

'You make me feel so good, Milly.'

She shuddered, cried, and relaxed.

Visions of Margate and sapphic heaven dissolved. She was back. In the room that was her prison, in the life that she was not sure she wanted.

'Your drawers, miss,' said Milly, bringing them over to the bed and making ready to help Amy put the mandatory underwear back on.

'I think not,' said Amy.

'But Headley! He will check. Your drawers are on My Lord's list. He was very specific. Underwear must be worn all day and every day!'

'Let him check,' said Amy.

'Oh, miss!'

'Enough of that, Milly. You're such a scaredy-cat. I have decided we are going to make ourselves some entertainment and that this entertainment is going to help your love life.'

Milly blushed. Her love life? There was only one man for her, and she could not rid him from her mind.

Amy, uncannily perceptive (and more so since her

experience with the witchy Magog sisters) said, 'You are in love with the gardener Roberts, are you not, Milly?'

'Yes, miss.'

'How is the romance proceeding? Well, or with difficulty?'

Amy knew a difficult man when she saw one and the gardener Roberts looked like a difficult man. Attractive, yes. But difficult.

'Oh, miss,' said the maid, 'he keeps his knob buttoned in his breeches as if it is locked in there and he has lost the key.'

'Perhaps he thinks it is a dangerous animal and he is afraid to let it out,' Amy sniffed, unimpressed. 'And there's nothing wrong with that. Men shouldn't put it about as carelessly as they do. They have no control, Milly, no feeling for consequences. They go about without a by-your-leave.'

'But he has my by-your-leave,' said Milly. 'I want him to kiss me and fuck me and do everything to me. I want to marry that man!'

'Well,' said Amy, 'I think you should. But not until you have ensured that he is a good and proper lover with the proportions that you deserve. One does not want to end up with a small man, Milly. It is a recipe for disaster. Small men have small dicks and small minds.

'Their personalities have had to adapt to their sad shortcomings and as a result they are cursed with the knowledge that they can never satisfy a woman as she needs to be satisfied. They become bullies and sadists or dreadful boring show-offs. Sometimes their emptiness drives them to become very rich, sometimes they take it upon themselves to go out and conquer continents, but whatever they do, Milly, whatever they do, they will not escape the simple tragic fact that they have been poisoned with a small penis.'

'Yes, miss,' said Milly, who had never heard such an outrageous philosophy and could barely understand it. Most of her information arrived from the pulpit at St Mark's and through the tittle-tattle in the servants' hall. The latter tended to stress the importance of money and housing over the matters of a man's physique. Roberts had obtained prestige because he laboured at the top of his profession, because he was known to have savings, and because he had a house with more than one room that he did not use.

'Go to the greenhouses and instruct Roberts to bring some fresh fruit to me,' said Amy. 'Anything that is in season, I don't mind, but tell him to deliver it tomorrow afternoon. By then, Milly, we will be ready for him.'

'Yes, miss.'

The next day Roberts arrived with the fruit as requested. He also brought a bunch of cultivated roses because he was a gentleman and he knew what ladies liked; they were fresh and pink and they smelt as all roses should.

The head gardener knew the circumstances of Amy's punishment – the servants spoke of little else – and he knew that Milly had been detailed to direct her immediate domestic needs. He could have no idea, though, as to the exact machinations that these young women were capable of; very few people would have been able to. Amy Pringle was a singular woman. A sexual adventuress and an unashamed minx. She moved outside her times and bucked all trends. Roberts was not a stupid person, but his life had been confined to the garden, which he loved; his cottage, for which he was grateful, and the occasional trip to the tavern. He was aware that something was missing and grudgingly agreed with his mother when she informed him that he needed a wife. He was 28. It wasn't healthy for a big good-looking man such as himself to move about the world like a solitary ghost. Roberts liked women, young and old, but he was not always aware of the exact meaning of their actions. He was a man's man; he spoke man's language and understood male ways. Women were fascinating creatures but he (he often admitted after a glass or three of ale) knew very little about them. Very little indeed.

He was vaguely aware that they liked respect and they liked flowers and he brought both these things to Amy Pringle's chamber.

He wondered why he had been personally called to visit the imprisoned lady's chamber. An under-gardener or house-boy could have as easily delivered produce from the gardens. Mrs Prenderghast had advised him against the mission, saying that Headley would not like it if he found out.

This information was enough to engage Roberts' complicity. Anything that annoyed Headley was worth doing. The expedition wafted a peccant promise which Roberts found very difficult to resist.

Milly opened the door.

She was not wearing her uniform; indeed she was wearing one of her mistress's light shifts and her strawberry-blonde hair was loose. Her locks fell down her shoulders, her arms and breasts were barely covered, and she wore delicate gold bracelets.

She was not the Milly that Roberts had seen before, bobbing curtsies in the livery of Lancaster Hall, eyes lowered, blushing and shy.

There was a tiny gloss on her lips, natural or cosmetic, Roberts did not know, but it accentuated them and made him want to push her against the wall and kiss her.

This was a new woman. A siren. Roberts knew immediately that something unusual was about to happen but he still could not imagine the nature of its specifics.

Amy Pringle also looked delightful in a simple blue chemise of the type that ladies only wore in the most informal circumstances; when at their toilette, for instance, and in the privacy of their own boudoirs. It was not a nightdress, exactly; one did not sleep in it, but it provided none of the constrictions of more formal wear. It, again, was loose and flowing, and cut low at the back and bosom, allowing prominence to Amy's full beauty.

She wore simple small pearls on her neck and on her ears.

'Ah, Roberts,' she said. 'You have brought the fruit. Thank you. Please come in.'

Roberts entered, gave the basket to Milly, and stood to attention in the middle of the room like a soldier awaiting his orders.

'I am bored, Roberts. A lady needs entertainment and your master is a cruel man.'

Robert did not quite know what to say to this, nor could he envisage the scene that this gorgeous woman had in mind.

'A lady needs her pleasure and I think you are the man to supply it.'

Roberts gawped and could not imagine what she meant. A game of piquet, perhaps.

'Take your clothes off, Roberts.'

'Miss?'

'You heard. Take them off.'

Robert was not unadventurous, but he was a little nervous. He was the man, after all. He liked to have control, and it had been usually his experience to have this privilege.

Still, an order from a superior was an order.

Roberts did as he was told.

He removed a linen shirt, his leather breeches, his gardening boots and his hat to reveal a proud body of perfect tone that was all a man should be – hard from years of physical labour, taut at the back and on the thighs, a chest that leaned towards smooth rather than Neanderthal. His skin glowed with health and he was brown from the sun. He flicked the black hair from his face with his hand and grinned at the two women. He was beginning to enjoy himself.

'Lie on the bed, please, Roberts,' Amy instructed.

Roberts lay down on his back, relaxed. Milly stood on an ottoman at the end of the bed. Amy stood next to the bed.

'I have decided that you should attend more to Milly,' said Amy. 'You have been downright rude in your dismissal of her attractions and I think it is time that you began to learn of their full extent. Milly is going to fuck you, Roberts, and she is going to judge for herself what kind of a lover you are. But first I am going to assess your cock to ensure that it is good enough for my maid.'

She crouched over the prostrate body of the gardener and kissed him on the mouth. Her blonde hair tickled his face and her smooth skin rubbed against his chest. His dick sprang up immediately – it needed no attention. It was there, stiff and ready on parade. He groaned and sank into the beginning of the journey to release.

'Watch, Milly,' said Amy. 'I learned this from the artist Bon Boullibonne and it has often been of great use to me.'

Gently she touched the twitching dick to ascertain

187

its girth and its hardness. It was a good dick – not the biggest she had ever seen, not as big as Bubb's, but wide and long and, at first inspection, well able to satisfy.

She peeled back the skin at the top and licked the tip with a teasing tongue. Roberts groaned again and the dick swelled to twice the size.

'My,' said Amy. 'How you swell.'

She sucked now, moving her mouth up and down on the end of him and he, forgetting himself, pushed her head up and down on himself as if controlling her.

She pulled away.

'Control yourself, Roberts. You will come when I say so and only when I say so, do you understand?'

'Yes, madam.'

She teased him some more with her mouth and he had to exert every control he had not to splurt himself right in her beautiful face.

'Good boy,' said Amy, seeing his desperation. 'Now it is Milly's turn.'

The women swapped places. Milly sat astride the primed prick of the gardener while Amy went and sat on the ottoman. Ensuring that the correct points were in Roberts' eye-view, she removed her chemise, spread her legs, and began to rub herself with agitation.

So now Roberts, lucky Roberts, had a woman watching him with her crude hands up her sluttish fanny, while the maid, the pretty maid with green eyes and lush white skin, was riding him.

Roberts filled Milly up to her stomach. Amy fiddled and fingered until she thought she might die without orgasm. The girls were ready to go, so now, and only now, could the man be given permission.

'You may come, Roberts, now, please, right now,' said Amy.

He released the full force of his load deep into the

maid as the maid threw back her head and cried out the primal shriek of release. Then seconds later Amy too vibrated into climax. There was a second or two of silence. Their heads were elsewhere.

And Roberts was in love.

'Oh, miss,' said Milly when he had left. 'Thank you. I think I am in with a chance now. Did you see how he stared?'

They were both lying on Milly's bed, semi-naked and sucking on the peaches that Roberts had brought from the garden. Milly's thigh intermingled with Amy's leg and they stroked each other's hair.

'Yes,' Amy said kindly. 'I think you are the one for Roberts.'

The words had hardly left her lips when the door snapped open on its hinges and Headley entered with the demeanour of a jailor who has received interesting details from an informant, details that would guarantee him a promotion.

Amy lazily looked up, but Milly jolted upright and covered herself up.

'What is going on here?' the butler shouted.

'I can explain, sir,' said Milly, shivering like an animal caught in the snow.

How Milly planned to explain that a maid and her mistress were lying in déshabillé and in each other's arms at 3.30 in the afternoon was anyone's guess, but, anyway, her words were stopped by the tempest that was her boss.

Headley could hardly conceal the delight that bubbled under the guise of shock and fury. But he knew that, as disciplinarian, he was now within his rights and he planned to enjoy this moment to the full extent.

He marched over to the bed and shouted, 'Get up at once, you sluts.'

Both girls rose from the disarranged white lace of

the mattress, Amy with dumb turpitude, Milly twitching with nerves and fear.

Headley did not say anything else. He simply marched the two down the stairs, through the front hall, over the lawn and into the stables, where, still silent, he pushed them both over a wooden frame used to store saddles. This meant that their bodies were almost doubled over, their feet were on the ground, their faces were pushed low, almost to their knees, and their bottoms were pushed high.

He roughly grabbed the flimsy garments that they were both wearing and shoved them over their backs.

Four perfect round orbs stared at him, as white as snow, and beautiful in their rotund perfection.

They were cheeky arses and they were going to get flayed. Headley felt dizzy with excitement. He saw the weals before he had even inflicted them. He knew that the wenches deserved what they were about to get.

Bent over the frame, side by side, the two girls could hear each other breathing. Milly was panting and whimpering, Amy was silent and calm.

'You will have six each, on your bare backsides, and afterwards you will both write letters to Lord Hacclesfield describing the crimes that you have committed. You have broken at least three directives, I believe. You, Miss Pringle, are not wearing the underwear ordered by His Lordship; you have not learned the psalm that he wishes you to recite. You, Milly, were out of uniform and in a bed. I need not say more. You will be very lucky if you do not end your days in the workhouse.

'There will be three strokes for Milly followed by three strokes for Miss Pringle. This will be followed by another three on each bottom.'

Headley took the cane that Fanny Mutterton had been ordered to bring from the old schoolroom and switched it in the air, enjoying the noise of the whistle through the air. He slashed it against a wooden post to test its flexibility and then positioned himself behind the four clean white orbs that were presented to him.

Milly first.

The first swipe cracked against her poor sensitive skin and she cried out loud. The second underneath it, the third, the hardest, underneath that.

Milly burst into tears and her body was racked with sobs.

Now Amy.

Three hard cruel strokes, slash, slash, slash, beat against her buttocks with quick succession. Then a pause. The weals flared up, the pain seeped in. She felt it with the detachment of a scientist studying a phenomenon. She did not cry.

Milly again. Headley could see the tail of her muff dripping delicately below her stomach, the delicious backs of her smooth thighs, the arse now striped with three crimson lines.

Again, three. Crack, crack, crack. Milly continued to sob and now she rubbed her flaming cheeks with her hands in an attempt to rub away the searing pain.

Again three for Amy. Crack, crack, crack. She shuddered to herself. It was painful. My, how she hated Headley. My, how she hated the bloody earl. Was Ralph going to be worth this? Was it worth waiting for him in the midst of punishment and discipline and smacking?

Amy was marched up to her bedroom and locked in. Milly was dismissed to her bedroom in the attic with instructions to put on a clean uniform and to stay there until she was told to come out.

Headley spent an enjoyable evening writing to Lord Hacclesfield and detailing the punishment that had

had to be meted to Miss Amy Pringle and her maid Milly.

Amy spent the next day locked in her bedroom with her meals delivered by a maid she did not know. She stared out of the window, tried to read, even tried to sew, but the confinement was beginning to make her feel mad. It was with some relief, though also with shock, that she looked up to see Bubb climbing through the open window. This was on the second floor of the house and entrance was no mean achievement. Bubb, it turned out, had manufactured a rope out of twine and ivy and had clambered up like a hero of a fairy tale.

'Oh, Bubb,' said Amy, hugging him. 'I'm so glad to see you.'

Bubb hugged her back.

'I've missed you,' he said. 'How I've missed you. Can we not run away, Amy, and be together?'

'Oh, Bubb. I am so sorry. It is not you that I love. It is your brother. It is Ralph.'

Despondency struck as shards of glass into Bubb's entrails but he knew, despite the wracking disappointment, that she was right and the circumstance was right. Destiny formed Ralph and Amy; it had been designated. He had to stand back and let her go.

'Bubb,' she said, 'you have to help me escape from this place. I cannot bear it any longer. I am spurned by your brother, smacked by your father . . . I am alone and I am bored, bored, bored.'

Bubb helped Amy Pringle climb down the ivy rope to the lawn and helped her saddle up Formenta. Then he rode with her to the Newcomers Tavern outside Bridgnorton and waited for her until the stagecoach arrived that would take her to London. She was wearing her travelling suit and carrying a small leather bag. She did not have much, but she did have hope.

192

Chapter Eight

Ralph met Trenton Dastard at Trite's club. The poet was, as always, engaged in a tankard of ale, a game of cards, and several severe quarrels with the various libertines of rank and fashion who had turned Trite's into the nucleus of London society.

The club was owned by Benjamin Trite, a willowy figure of indeterminate age and unfathomable character who understood the needs of his milieu and had long been pleased to provide for them with a glad hand and an open palm.

Benjamin Trite believed in vice as some people believe in God; that is, he believed in the inalienable right of man to follow his inclinations to whatever end they wished and that much truth lay in extremist pursuits for they were the honest answer to the questions posed by the dark mysteries of the mind.

Trite was not judgmental, nor did he look down on the uncontrolled ardours that controlled the behaviour of his clients as surely as if their limbs were being twitched by unseen puppet masters. Profanity and impurity and untrammelled attraction to the perils of life had made him his fortune and provided him with the entertainment that is necessary to achieve some release from the harsh rigours of everyday reality and the boundaries of selfhood.

Trite was a consummate voyeur. He liked to look and he remained detached. Thus he was secure.

His philosophy had gestated when, during his Grand Tour, he had met the Marquis de Sade and this occasion had changed his life. The young Trite and the old debauchee had enjoyed stimulating repartee and a session or two at the castle known as La Coste. The Marquis liked to be whipped and Trite had been willing to comply, flailing the seigneur's naked buttocks with a flexible broom made of birch twigs that was possessed of both spring and sting.

Never had Trite seen a man who had not been to Eton enjoy so much punishment with so little outward expression of distress. On one occasion de Sade abducted a secular canoness from outside the very gates of her abbey. Pushing her into his black stage-coach, he had pinned her roughly down on the seat.

There and then, watched by Trite, the canoness had been flipped over on to her stomach, her grey habit had been trussed up above her waist, her white buttocks displayed, and, to the rough rocking of the fleeing carriage, she had been sodomised to the full extent of all possible satisfaction. Hard, fast, violation *in extremis*; the innocent maid's vocal shrieks of unbelieving joy had been drowned out by the drumming of the horses' hooves.

Trite had watched her expressions of surprised happiness and had been surprised himself. Abduction and anal rape as symptoms of foreplay were not something he had formerly entertained as being within the possibilities of the sensual spectrum.

These experiences had left an impression whose

messages had resonated within him, stayed with him and continued to form the foundation of many of the decisions in which he was further enabled and ably supported by his beautiful French wife Francette, who he had bought from the Marquis de Sade for 200 livres.

Francette was a very unusual woman. Her father (needing to escape a prison sentence) had given her to the Chief of Police when she was sixteen. The Chief of Police had introduced her to the delights of cages and handcuffs but the compatible arrangement had ended when he suddenly died at the age of 32.

This unexpected finale had released Francette. Furnished with perverted desires and cognisant of the nature of mens passions, she was well equipped to fight in the battlefield that was dominated by her opposite sex.

Moving forward with determined drive and subtle ease, Francette quickly availed herself of the opportunities that she saw in the man's world. Strong in her self-assurance, she was aided by a belief in her own beauty which her detractors (a group made of spurned lovers and jealous women) put down to pure delusion. It was true that Francette was not quite as exquisite as she thought she was but she walked about with such dignified *froideur*, such deep faith in the lustre of her person, that a mirage was created and her audience fell in with the truth of the messages that she conveyed.

She was lovely enough, but the reality of her physical appearance was not of the supernormal proportions outined in the many complimentary paragraphs that described her divinity in the nation's newspapers.

Francette knew that she was being idolised beyond the mundane truth of her personal gifts. She knew this because she was neither stupid or dangerously vain. She understood the essential joke of life. Nothing was serious. This, of course, drove her lovers nearly insane, because they too were jokes, never to be taken on as substantial propositions because, in the eyes of Francette, they were amusing and that was all. Some were more amusing than others, but that was basically what they were there for.

Financial support, recreation, entertainment – these formed the purposes of men. She could not take them more seriously than that. They could be kings or counts, admirals or doctors, to her they were all the bastard children of some mistaken matriach, disabled by ego and undermined by simplicity.

She did not let them know that she thought they were ludicrous. As we have said, she was not stupid; indeed she performed the drama of flattery with great conviction, but her heart remained unimpressed and unconcerned.

The young and sensate read this and railed against it. They picked up the subtle messages of amused disdain and it drove their egos crazy.

The older men did not bother to observe the subtle inuendoes of female awareness; they saw a young sensual woman gifted in the arts of love-making, beautiful of hair, breast and buttock, and interesting in conversation without breaking the slim threads that held their manhood together. They were further protected against insecurity by their power of purchase – that is, they could easily obtain control with their money.

Francette, then, was the perfect cocotte. She had been courted by the most illustrious men in Europe, most of them noble (by birth rather than in spirit – the two are not genetically connected), many of them powerful, and she had managed to commit herself to their happiness without denying herself the satisfaction of younger lovers, the so-called *guerluchons* whose privilege it was to make love to the grander courtesans in the knowledge that the *objet* of their ardours was being adequately maintained by another man's purse, thus liberating them from paying the bills for this costly benefit.

Francette's daily rates were very high and this enabled her to allow herself the occasional luxury provided by the poor man's prick. It was the industry of love and she understood it.

The Marquis de Sade had met her when her accounts were being paid by the Chevalier la Pienne de la Boulet and by the Comte Beauvosin, neither of whom knew about each other. Bedecked with diamonds, availed of three monogrammed carriages, enticing her men undressed in a déshabillé made of the whitest and most delicate laces, Francette lived in the grand style of the successful demi-mondaine and ruled over twenty or so servants in a vast town house on the rue Courteauvillain.

Her unassuming mien disguised fiery passion and extraordinary sexual imagination. This composite was quickly read by the Marquis and it quickly bewitched him. The mixture of sluttish humility and perverted prowess was, in his view, perfect. She was a woman to whom he could and should devote himself. He negotiated a take-over bid, ousted the other men, made over an annuity to the lady, and consequently purchased sole rights and complete monopoly.

Francette had willingly engaged herself in the mad deviations so enjoyed by her patron. She was being paid to submit and submit she did, willingly, abjectly and with a beautiful grace that made him pride her above every other doxy he had encountered. Inextricably linked by the bond of sexual tension, that connection between two people who whenever they see each other know they must fuck, the Marquis and Francette spent many hours in lustful arrangement of exotic interlude.

She, painted black by his servants, hair a shower of gaudy feathers, naked except for a long bull whip, would lash the prostrate and bound lover until he bled.

He engorged his every whim. He told her what to do. She did it. The very order would make her wet. The very idea that there was no recourse to argument made the cream bubble between her legs and her very entrails yearn to submit to the violent plunging of his ever-stiff cock. He was a cruel tyrant but a great fuck.

Surprise and attack were the mainspring of their love.

He would appear in her boudoir unnanounced with his servant, a good-looking, well-born youth of 24, following behind.

'Strip, madam,' he would say.

If she hesitated the servant would take her and violently rip off her clothes without caring if they were torn or ruined.

And he, the master, would always be hard, the stiff dick ready to go, poking with fierce white threat from the gap of his breeches.

Sometimes he would push her down over a writing desk and merely lunge into her from the back; sometimes through her rectum, sometimes driving into her wet cunt, with unbounded stamina that could go on and on for hours, until she felt her vital forces melt into exhaustion and she would fall to her knees, exhausted and satiated.

Sometimes he would lash her behind with the leather thongs of a cat-o'-nine-tails so that the heat rose and the pain melted into the pleasure and the tears would run down her face, releasing her from all the inner woes and old worries and bringing her to the transcendent calm of catharsis.

Sometimes he would watch as his servant took his pleasure on her. The wanton Francette, having put up the fight of the modest maiden (a pretence that they all enjoyed) was then pleased to have her buttocks slapped and to be pushed into some ignominious but convenient prostration – perhaps tied so that her ankles were behind her neck and all orifices were revealed, perhaps chained to the wall.

The Marquis, then, would manhandle the servant's organ until the servant could think only of release and the master, always in control, always the one to dictate, would, with sneering asides, instruct the servant on how best to pleasure the fine Francette.

'Put it in her mouth.'

'Pump her throat.'

'Thrash her!'

'Spank her.'

'Bang her until she screams.'

'Take her up the arse.'

'Switch the bitch.'

'Fuck her hard.'

Sometimes, at the end of this, both men would gently kiss her, caress her affectionately, and carry her exhausted to her bed, where she would lie down and sleep for hours on end, deflated by the vigours of endless copulation.

Francette was the best that the Marquis de Sade had ever had but she was expensive and her upkeep was beginning to drain resources already exhausted by the compulsive profligacy that had condemned him to insoluble debt.

Benjamin Trite put in a fair offer and de Sade submitted with some relief. He made over his mistress for the reasonable (though not bargain) price that sometimes arises when the the seller is facing a state of embarassment thanks to having little business sense, a characteristic that often arrives with inherited money, an artistic disposition and psychotic hedonism – the three chracteristics that composed his character. He had allowed Francette to thrash him one last time; he had taken her backside with loving violence, and then, with regret, and even a tear, he had bid *adieu*, assuring her that their parting was more to do with impecuniosity than disaffection.

Francette married Benjamin Trite and acclimatised easily to London life. The couple had spent five years or so building up a business whose sole aim was to supply the demands of the richest and most dissolute men in England.

Francette was an invaluable partner. She knew exactly when to exact her wiles to divert the attentions of the gambers so that her husband could maximise his advantage. She combined the mixture of girlish innocence and worldly knowing that intoxicated the senses of any man who looked at her.

They did not know whether to deflower her or send her to Newgate. Politicians fell like ninepins at her feet and even the most retarded country peers found that lust pumped through their bodies as if it was pure love itself.

Francette and her husband were willing to go down many routes to please the disparate tastes of the clientele from whom they made their fortunes, but they were devoted to each other. Enjoying a bond of love that was not only unusual in these circumstances, but unique within the stormy social currents in which they swam, there remained a true link of respect and friendship.

Trite's relationship with his clientele was a creative collaboration. Each fed off each other with symbiotic sensuality that entailed a cross-pollination of venal ideologies. That is, while the clients sometimes provided Trite with innovative ideas about breaking taboos and pushing forward the boundaries of licentiousness, so he too led them to new ways of sin with some inventions of his own.

This fertile collusion enabled everyone to combat the boredom that was the disease of this class and the ruin of many who had set themselves up to cater for the business of its desires.

Trite ensured that his establishment retained an edge of intemperate carnality that tainted its reputation and consequently caused it to continue to be an attraction.

Some people were actually frightened of Trite's. In the early hours of the morning, when those who lived in the London night walked home by dawn, and those who rose at the same time commuted in the opposite direction, a traffic of types would criss-cross by the light of the morning sky.

Pastry-cooks and seal-cutters, ballad-sellers and fruiterers hurried past the infamous black door with their heads bowed and their eyes lowered as if to merely glance at the devilish place would be to be involuntarily pressed into its sinful service as if the dark windows were evil eyes against which no person could defend him or herself unless thoroughly doused in the water of some holy chalice sanctified by the Church.

The door had once been daubed with the white cross of salvation by protesting members of the Society for the Reformation of Manners. This had attracted some attention. The society, as a result, recruited 30 new members. Trite's, meanwhile, attracted 200.

The lights were always on at Trite's (or Number 33 as it was sometimes known); the glow of the gas lamps at the windows would often light the faces of the *beau monde* who paused to look out – fabulous bejewelled *poules-de-luxe*, and haughty autocrats. Often noises could be heard: a drunken brawl, the clatter of steel on steel, women's voices, thumping and singing. Every night the late hours rent with shrieks of sexual ecstasy or the sounds of some action more animal and more violent than this.

It was whispered that murders and necrophilia were committed there and the bodies were secreted away by an invisible army of the night. It was said that hordes of naked women were kept in dungeons and that an apothecary supplied the most powerful aphrodisiac known to any doctor of medicine. This medication was so effective that it had been known to grant the oldest men uninhibited action in the longest orgies.

Penton Mewsey, a man of 65 years old, had successfully fucked 43 women over a course of three days, an achievement (it was said) that had earned him the respect of George III and paved the way to his job as Chancellor of the Exchequer.

Meanwhile, a strange individual named Blewbury St Isle had, under the same influence, penetrated a group of girls from Southwark and was said to have banged them so hard and for so long that their lives had changed. Having been relatively innocent girls from the provinces, they turned into turbulent hussies whose quest it was to fulfil their fannies and allow their arses to be screwed by all and sundry in a daily life spent with their skirts over their shoulders and their white thighs flashing up their tufts of black moss, making tongue faces with their mons, begging for rough violation to remind them of the fair night that they had been so efficiently split by the thick fat penis of Blewbury St Isle.

'He was a strange man,' the watchmen and coachmen would say to each other as they passed the door of Number 33 and talked of the things that were supposed to happen behind it.

'His carriage was green.'

'His wig was green.'

'He only ate spinach.'

'He came from Salisbury, did he not?'

'No, from Brighton, I believe.'

'They say he now has four wives and thanks to the powders of the apothecary he can fuck them all day and night, night and day, and they all live in sexual bliss.'

'It's not the way of the Lord, I know that.'

'Tis not.'

'Still. You can't help envying the man.'

'You cannot.'

These last tales were tall but they were true. Sexual vigour had sold itself as a right to the men who frequented Trite's thanks to the supplies of Armand, who rented a small room at the end of the alley that ran down the back of the club.

Armand's tiny shop was a dark room lined with shelves full of dusty bottles and lit by candles.

It was always dark, largely because of its location in a narrow stone corridor and also because Armand only opened up at night when there was most activity and the gentlemen who circulated in this profane vicinity were most likely to purchase his requisites.

He slept on a wooden platform during the day which was the reason, perhaps, why his general appearance was yellowish in hue and his eyes were large and round like those of a nocturnal animal. He was old, but, in general, he was well tempered, and he genuinely believed in the efficacy of his products.

He did not take them himself as there were no occasions in which they would be of use. His days were spent on his palliasse alone; his evenings at work. There was church on Sundays and that was it. The life of Armand was simple, but sex did not feature as an occupational pastime.

The sensual pleasures available to him came in the form of the tales of success told with enthusiasm by the lords who frequented his shop and purchased his products. No lord, young or old, could resist revealing details of their sexual escapades when they had been fired by Armand's potions.

Women had been truly and wonderfully fulfilled by the simple onslaught of their artificially hardened organs and the apothecary was the confession box that heard it all.

Few can pass through life without witnessing how many are the tolls that are exerted on men's organs and how soft they can make them.

A flicker, a shadow, a whim, some invisible portent – all can reduce an erection and fell it with more ease than a blade on a trunk.

Armand's exotic products, imported from far-flung places, provided disinhibition and guranteed the stimulation necessary to sustain the precious but neurotic flame that is man's virility. His potions and fluids were in demand and he plied his trade well, availing each customer with a fortifying description of the medicine's history and the tradition of its efficacy.

He prided himself on his variety, on the comprehensiveness of his stock and on the freshness of produce such as the nectar from the wild orchids that were grown under glass by a specialist in Chiswick.

Armand supplied cantharides made from the dried remains of the blister beetles and he sold the root of the yohimbe tree, known to make a man as hard as steel and to increase the volume of ejaculation threefold and ten.

He sold pulverised agate and pastilles made of ambergris. He sold testicular cervi (deer testicles) and coca (as used by the Incas). He stocked tiny bottles that were said to be full of the sexual scent of the elephant and he even had some red leaves that he insisted were from the legendary plant known as the satyrion.

There were bowls full of pine-nuts and olives and dusty bottles full of coloured liquids. There were books containing sex spells and a wooden chest full of muira puma. In one corner a wicker basket held coils of live snakes. Their energising blood was sucked straight out of their tails following an incision with a small silver knife that Armand kept for that particular purpose.

The Duke of Bavaria was particularly keen on this route to ecstasies; the snake blood gave him bouts of priapism that lasted as long as three days and rejuvenated his love life, restoring him to the adoration that he had enjoyed as a youth.

Armand's most effective and popular powder, though, arrived in tiny stone ampoules and was exported from the shores of India. This mixture was comprised of three ingredients (tagara, kustha and talisha patra) which were crushed together in a human skull and then mixed with saffron and utpala leaves. A peacock's eye (taken from a dead bird) was added to this and the potion was charged during a time when Venus glowed with full force of its ascendant energy. This was boiled with ghee, enticed with honey, and distilled to the syrupy mixture that was exported first by elephant, then by galleon, to the portals of the apothecary's shop.

It was exclusive stock. And expensive. But no price was too large for a product that brought the life-force back to the groin.

Francette had benefited from this last miracle cure which was known as the Spirit of the Lotus. Having fed it on a silver teaspoon to Lieutenant St Blaise, she was pleased to see the gorge swell and his fattened girth chafe against his breeches.

'Ah, sir,' she said, kneeling in front of him. 'You want to feel my mouth on your tip, my hand on your hard shaft, admiring it, stroking it, revering its threat? You want to hear me begging you for it? You want to see the need drip down my legs, the pulse redden my clit, the lie of disdain in my eye?'

'Yes,' he said throwing himself on her and kissing her violently on the mouth. Prostrate on the soft Turkish carpet, flailing helplessly under the weight of his body and the force of his strength, she allowed herself to be taken.

He pushed her silk skirts above her waist and she was pleased to feel the full hard quotient of pleasure-mongering lunge into her cunt, into her hot roots, to the very womb itself. He banged her relentlessly for half an hour until her entire body melted on to the unrelenting dick. After that she always looked on the lieutenant with warm affection.

'The apothecary's cures work,' she told her husband. 'Armand sells true aphrodisiacs.'

They were alone in their bedroom and she lifted her white lace nightdress above her thighs, spread them, and showed him her vermilion vulva which was still swollen from the good screwing it had received.

Her husband licked the tip of his finger and stroked her crimson display with curiousity, gently touching the smug swollen vulva with moist tip.

'Ah, Francette,' he said, inserting a digit deep into her. 'You are still wet. Is this for the good lieutenant or is it for me?'

She looked deep into his eyes with the pure devotion of an old love.

'It is for you. It is always for you.'

'Spread them, madam. Now.'

He pushed her legs so wide apart that the muscles in her groin were almost strained. Her opening widened in front of him, and he thrust his tongue into it, French kissing it with vehement passion.

She groaned.

She was so lucky.

But the tongue? The tongue is never enough.

'On all fours, you little slut.'

Francette did as she was told. She loved the pretence of jealous retribution; the hard husband avenging himself on her and punishing her wicked ways. How great it was to be allowed to roam and then to be punished for roaming – a delicious double bind from which there was no escape. How great to know that he cared so much – it was a true and wise love that allowed so full a play of all the drama of human emotion enacted in the safe sanctum of trust.

She waggled her cheeks at her husband like a cheeky hussy who did not care. He pushed her nightdress up her back so that it fell around her shoulders and neck. Then he slapped her rump with his hard palm.

Taking her as a furious husband claiming conjugal possession, he repossessed her. And she came back to him. Easily. As she always did.

The club had started humbly in Pall Mall where Benjamin Trite once rented a bachelor apartment. The same Grand Tour that had introduced him to the Marquis de Sade had also taken him to Spain where he had discovered the intriguing game of hombre. He had introduced it to his friends and they would play every night on a card table in his rooms. It was a regular and enjoyable party whose evenings were enlivened not only by the vagaries of the game but by Francette, who was quite often given as a prize to the winner.

Hombre entertained its players with a complexity of

rules and a reliance on luck that entranced those members of the elite whose minds were bored and their pockets big. Estates were quickly won and lost during games that went on through the night and during which Trite served the finest clarets to ensure that the gentlemen's exuberance quickly overcame the little judgement with which they had been born.

Undermined by these ruses, Prince Wurtenburg, a fat German from Munich, had had to sign over his gracious home overlooking Hyde Park to Trite after a long and painful session in which he had been ruined by six 'matadors'.

Crowds began to meet in Trite's private rooms and the gatherings that had begun as a card game played by friends augmented until Trite had to bring in more tables and introduce several new games. The numbers became uncontainable and he decided to put the enterprise on to a commercial footing.

He purchased two neighbouring houses in St James, both large, and both located a phaeton's ride from Mayfair, which housed the majority of his clientele – a shifting collective that liked to confine itself to the borders of Bond Street and Park Lane.

He devoted several rooms to gaming, installed a dining room furnished with the finest period furniture, as well as a smoking room, with elegant giltwood and satin suites, and lined with shelves of leather-bound books, many of which had been written by the members themselves.

The top floor held several bedrooms, a necessity in the light of the fact that games often went on all night and, by the end of them, the participants' capacities (such as they were) were exterminated either by the shock of loss or (more commonly) by advanced inebriation which meant that they did not know who they were or where they lived.

Several comfortable four-poster beds were offered to those who needed to collapse on them, and collapse on them they did, sometimes fully clothed, sometimes writhing in naked lust.

Young gentlemen would fall on top of each other. Dizzy with drink, blind with uninhibited passion, they discovered things about themselves that they had only formerly suspected but were now released with abandon and joy in the safety of a place where all proclivities were celebrated.

Francette had particularly the enjoyed the evening that she had come across the Lords Hollybush and St Maizey in the green room. Both beautiful, both in their mid-twenties, both possessed of smooth glowing skin and toned muscles, long limbs entwined with long limbs as lip enjoyed lip and two heads of glossy brown curls intermingled. The men had spoken of love for each other then Lord Hollybush had inserted his fine hard white prick into the offered buttocks of his lover, on all fours in front of him. He had slowly eased himself in, grinding with care and then pistoning in and out until both groaned out the joy of true release.

The heady waft of sodomy permeated the air of Trite's and did much to enhance the excitement of its calling.

Some youths actually began to live in the club. There seemed no need to go to their homes, which were full of wives and children and demands for payment. Trite's was safe. The company was amenable and all their needs were supplied.

A natural entrepreneur, Trite had seen the wisdom of employing young French women to deal the cards and cause amusing diversions with beauty and cleavage. The women did not speak. They did not have to. Their appearances said much about them and their appearances served to keep all but the strongest players' attention away from the cards in their hands and on the fine white breasts of the women whose chests tended to be placed so close to their faces that they could smell the very sweetness of their scents.

Trite introduced all games of chance – from piquet and quinze to faro and hazard, a lethal dice game that had caused at least three dukes to shoot themselves.

Trite's may have just become another gentleman's club if it had not been for the regular appearance of several influential opinion-makers.

These included the thrusting politician Charles Fox. Brilliant, articulate, inebriated, powerful, Fox's apartment was so near to Trite's that he would often appear in the morning, unpurified by ablution and still wearing his nightclothes. He would place himself with royal dignity on a velveteen cushion, imbibe a morning concoction of sweet Hungarian wine (heated to blood temperature), read the newspapers and hold court until he passed out.

Charles Fox attracted an influential elite that began to grant the club some notoriety. Benjamin Trite knew that guards officers and viscounts were all very well, but he would not be made until he had received the royal seal of approval, and, in particular, the patronage of the Prince of Wales, who would gurantee commercial longevity and confirm the club's stature as an exclusive temple of the *beau monde*.

Excitement, then, arrived in the form of Beau Brummell, whose opinions tended to predict those of his friend, the prince.

Brummell had approved of the club largely because Benjamin Trite and his wife had initiated some research and ensured that some of his many tastes were catered for.

Brummell was vain, obsessed by clothes, and loved by many women, but, as Francette discovered, his

210

favourite activity was to disport naked in front of mirrors, thus guaranteeing himself an admiring audience – that is, multiple images of himself. The irony was that the fastidious style guru who had devoted his life to the introduction of fashionable detail and must-have modish appurtenance preferred uninhibited nudity.

Francette ordered a small third-floor chamber to be lined with the best French gilt mirrors. There were some valuable pieces and they were placed on the walls in a collage of gold and glass.

'This,' said Brummell when he entered it, 'is a splendid room! It will be my favourite salon in the whole of London – perhaps the whole of Europe! My dears! What mirrors! What fine glass! What chandeliers! They can only come from Venice! Venice, the new centre of the fashionable cogniscenti! I cannot wait to tell my little Prinny . . .'

The excited dandy threw off his sateen accroutements then danced and pranced around the room accompanied by a Vivaldi concerto played with energy and passion by a violinist.

Champagne was served in elegant flutes and the various bucks who accompanied the Lord of Fashion wherever he went sat around flattering him on the classical musculature of his physique and the wondrous sheen of his faultless skin. Brummell was lean and toned and proud of his body. He knew it was as good unclothed as clothed.

He spent the evening posing in front of the mirrors, studying himself with interested intent, and bathing in the gaze of the various young men who were content to sit on the chic French furniture and appreciate his beauty.

'I have had a lovely time!' he trilled to the Trites as he left, now dressed, purple cape flapping, the matching purple feather in his hat shuddering as his head bobbed and juddered.

The next evening he brought the Prince of Wales.

The Prince of Wales immediately lost £10,000 at faro and proceeded to embroil himself in an unseemly mêlée that ended in Horace Walpole falling down the stairs and cracking his forehead open on the wooden floor.

The royal bloodstain remained on the floor and was pointed out by all the members to new members as an interesting landmark. Many tales were told about how the shed had occurred. Some were true, some were not, but tales will always be told at places like Trite's where handsome men had little to do but fuck and gamble and drink – the last two of which were responsible for the huge fortune that Benjamin Trite had managed to accrue.

Trite was a rich man but he did not have many real friends. He did not drink, which was a repellant in itself, and his origins were unknown, a state of affairs that unnerved the milieu in which he moved. He had no title and no family that anyone knew. No-one knew who he was, so he was seen as a vulture amongst those whose carnage he picked with cool aplomb.

Trenton Dastard was not a proficient gambler. He succumbed to his need for flamboyance rather than the solid subtlety of intent that is, in general, needed to succeed in the more sophisticated card games. It is a realm where dogged obstinacy does not make up for lack of judgement.

No-one could remember when Dastard had last won anything at all. But still he went on, encouraged by the knowledge that debt was the currency of this market and calmed by the fact that most of the libertines surrounding him had lost a very great deal more money than he had. Lord Fontayne had recently lost his wife, as well, though there were many who thought that loss was not quite the right word for it.

Dastard liked to live dangerously. He liked to be on the edge. What fun was life if running with doxies did not risk death from syphilis, if travel did not risk highwaymen, and if love did not risk death by duel. He was a poet. It was his duty to stare into the abyss.

Ralph hated Trite's. He only went there because everyone else did and there was nowhere else to go if one wanted to remain associated to the deranged group that one laughingly described as one's friends.

He did not particularly like drinking or gambling; he did not care much for London gossip and he did not even like Trenton Dastard that much. He was compelled to the club by forceful social necessity rather than any natural inclination. If one visited London one went to Trite's. It was a rigmarole to which one had to submit, like it or not. He resented this. He wished there were valid alternatives. But there were not.

And so it was with an aspect of some gloom that he clumped up the polished wooden stairs, past the portraits of various royalties, past the regent's famous bloodstain, and handed his sword to the valet. Swords were not allowed to be worn at the club; it was a rule that had been made in the interest of members' safety. Drink and gambling losses are a dangerous mixture and can ignite morid fury in even the coolest men.

Trite had learned his lesson the evening that Lord Boatman had killed his younger brother after an unfortunate game of piquet. The incident had not been honoured by the fact that the various members of Trite's then took a bet on whether the younger Lord Boatman was actually dead or not and, when the physician arrived to bleed the frantic youth, complained that this action was unfair on the bet.

The young Lord Boatman had not survived (Browne

Candover had made £600) and there had been some unflattering paragraphs in the newspapers about the slack morals of the younger generation, and in particular the younger generation that surrounded the prince regent. The king was said to be most displeased. Trite banned swords and all pointed objects from then on.

'Good evening, John,' said Ralph.

'Good evening, Lord Fitzroy,' said the valet, bowing low and placing Ralph's weapon amongst a selection in a carved walnut stand.

'Who is in tonight?'

'His Royal Highness the Prince Regent, the Beaus Brummell and Nash, and Mr Dastard, of course.'

'Jolly good,' said Ralph, attempting a semblance of cheerfulness that was impeded by the unerasable memory of his first wife that he carried in his head with as much clarity as if he had worn a picture of her in a locket around his neck.

'There's a good claret out, I believe, sir,' said the valet kindly, perhaps recognising the customer's ennui, which was a common enough condition amongst the young lords of his acquaintance.

God, thought Ralph. It'll take more than claret.

'Good evening, Ralph,' said Benjamin Trite, who never used anyone's title and was, in the opinion of his members, a man without manners or respect. They would complain about him amongst themselves, and this amused Trite because he was empowered by the fact that most of them owed him exorbitant sums of money. It was only due to his complicit gentility that they were not all languishing in the debtors' prison in Fleet Street.

This gentleman's club was a domain full of tense relationships inspired by the vices of metropolitan life and founded on self-gratification, compulsion and hedonism.

214

Ralph signalled to Dastard that he had arrived and repaired to the smoking room where Beau Brummell was sitting delicately in one corner wearing a violet wig, a matching mauve and white silk suit, a pair of silver stockings and purple shoes. Holding a frilled silk handkerchief delicately in one hand and sniffing its floral scent occasionally, he was emitting witty epithets to the detriment of the rest of the clients for the amusement of the Prince of Wales, who was sitting next to him. A silver tray of port sat between them and they had consumed most of it.

On the other side of the room two young lords from Norfolk were whispering about the scandal of the prince's horse Escape, whose jockey was currently embroiled on charges of running a rigged race.

A Whig and a Tory were describing the latest atrocities suffered by the aristocrats in Paris, their dialogue decorated with lascivious attention to detail.

'They say that the Marchioness Bonmarcher was boiled alive.'

'And that her husband's parts were scattered all around the street.'

'Then eaten by the hungry poor in a dreadful picnic in the palace gardens.'

'No!'

'Yes. Delicious apparently. Or *delicieux*, as I think they say over there.'

Trenton Dastard swept in having lost a sum of £100 which he said was nothing as compared to the Duke of York who had just lost the entire revenue of the Bishopric of Osnaburgh.

The conversation turned, inevitably, towards women, spawned by the sight of the Earl of Borg, who was lying on the floor, exhausted by a night in a bawdy house near Cheapside.

'He has familiarised himself with low women of all

shapes and sizes,' sniffed one dandy, flicking open a snuff box and delicately pushing it into his left nostril with his left hand, a technique that he had copied from Beau Brummell.

'The cock has shafted baggages all over London and now he comes here to show us the results of his vices.'

'He'll have the pox, to be sure.'

'Ah, but I hear that Jamaican Lil likes to be taken as a dog in the streets – and who could resist that?'

They fluttered their fans and ordered more champagne.

'You look as if you've been exhumed,' Trenton said to Ralph as a way of greeting. 'What ails thee, young man?'

Ralph swept his black fringe off his forehead and stared gloomily into the middle distance. He didn't know what ailed him.

'Perhaps he is having a dark night of the soul,' said Beau Brummell, giggling with high-pitched glee.

The Prince of Wales slapped his fat thigh so hard his wig toppled to one side of his head.

The noises were too loud and the colours were too bright. Ralph wondered if he was going mad.

'How is the lovely Miss Pringle?' said Trenton, who had been genuinely impressed by Amy. No woman had managed to reject him with such haughtiness – her pride aroused him and he had often thought about her, particularly in naked compromising postions, bound and gagged, or face down on a pillow, presented in all her perfect glory by obedience to him. But these were the stirrings only of his febrile imagination. Miss Pringle had turned him down but somehow he could not hold it against her. He even admired her for it. It was a novelty, anyway. Women never turned Dastard down. He liked novelties. God, he would like to thrust his tongue into her cheeky mouth.

'Who?'

'Your affianced, I believe.'

'Oh, her.'

Ralph was so immersed in his own gloom that he had to spend some seconds recalling Miss Pringle's face.

'I think she fares well. I don't know really.'

'You should go to bedlam, Ralph,' said Trenton. 'That girl is something special. Take it from me, my man. I know women . . .'

He smiled smugly. It was true. He did know women in that he had slept with hundreds of them, but he had only gleaned a minuscule amount of pertinent information. His critics sometimes observed that these failings were apparent in the ignorant imagery of his poesy, but Trenton thought that they were jealous. His dick had dipped in many quims and he had availed himself of a wide expertise. His opinions on the gentle sex should not be dismissed, particularly by a person as naive as Ralph.

'I know what you need,' said Trenton. 'Come on. Get up. Let's get out of here. Let's go to La Grisette where the beautiful Francette, goddess of St James, will make us welcome. To her parlour where games can be played and the women of the world can be yours for £50 a night, and upwards!'

Ralph felt like going home but he didn't have the energy to resist. To follow Trenton was more fun than going home alone. He needed the distraction and a night of lewd entertainment would at least provide temporary distraction from the grey cloud that seemed to be floating around his head.

'The problem with you, my man,' said Trenton, 'is that you don't get out enough. You sit stuck in that country . . .'

Ralph followed him down the stairs, out of a back

door, down the dark alleyway, past the tiny apothecary.

'Evening, Armand.'

'Evening, Mr Dastard. Anything for you tonight?'

'Don't need it, Armand. I'm as stiff as a poker . . .'

They stepped around to the house next door which was entered via a small stone porch to a green door marked '34'. A small sign in black and white letters said 'La Grisette'.

Chapter Nine

*L*a Grisette was owned by Benjamin Trite and managed by Francette. It was one of the largest and
most luxurious bordellos in Europe. It was also unique
in that it did not offer only women to men, it also
offered men to women, an innovative sideline that had
proved so lucrative that the custom was being copied
in brothels all over London.

Retaining impeccable standards of cleanlinless, a
famous cellar, and some of the most beautiful men and
women on the market, La Grisette had become a legend, as famous as Le Parc aux Cerfs, but more popu-
larly known as its client base was wider spread and its
employees were broader in their skills and age groups.

Around 50 or so men and women worked at La
Grisette. Hand-picked by Francette, they were chosen
from all walks of life and from all countries in order to
ensure that all tastes were catered for and all proclivities acknowledged. La Grisette was sophisticated and
it was international; its rooms were filled with sensu-
alists borne of far-flung regions who brought their own
cultures into play and thus coloured the atmosphere

with exotic tones that put this resort far ahead of the ordinary bordello where a fuck was a fuck, one came and went, and the simplicity of sex could be cold and dull.

La Grisette was fun. There was entertainment. There was choice. It was expensive, but it was generally agreed that it provided value for money. Where else could one find belly dancers one evening and Greek hetarae the next? Where else could one buy a eunuch for £30 a night or watch oil-covered nubiles indulge in a Sapphic rite of nipple painting, hair brushing and foot worship? Where else could a woman pay to fuck the Tsar of Russia or spend the night enacting the fantasies that, hitherto, had been forced to lurk in the dark constraints of her mind?

The ladies who came to buy the men were well born, monied and bored. They would arrive in the night, protected by the shadows. Spilling out of their carriages, ushered through to the luxurious suites, they were cared for with gentle politeness and discreet service that befitted the manners to which they were accustomed.

Hailing from some of the oldest families in England, travelling from counties north and south, they expected to receive correct hospitality. Francette understood this. She knew that her ladies must feel at home, relax, feel able to demand exactly what they wanted and then feel the satisfaction of getting it.

Her attention to these details had resulted in the success of the business whose annual turnover continued to surprise and delight her devoted husband.

A club atmosphere aided efficiency and Francette had formed friendly relations with every member. She knew them all, men and women, by name, by family and by connections. She knew their inclinations and she knew what they wanted and, as importantly, what they did not want.

This was dangerous territory. The nature of this information gave Mrs Trite enormous power. She had access to details that could have brought some of the greatest families in England down to their knees with scandal. She was furnished with knowledge that could have actually affected the defence of the country and the laws made in it.

The more intelligent customers were well aware of this and each dealt with it in their own way. Most of them kept their distance, thinking that polite noblesse oblige would protect them; others attempted to form the bonds of intimate relations that are the foundation of loyalty and respect.

Francette navigated these tricky waters with skill and panache, but she was, in the end, the consummate businesswoman and never indulged personal feelings at the expense of her profit margins. She loved her husband and her son and nobody else. She retained affection for some of the idle liasions that she enjoyed, but watched them with a cool eye, knowing that all who came to both the club and brothel were vulnerable. Herself included. The wrong enemies could force her out of business overnight while the right friends could grant her a place at the centre of the web of connections that formed the infrastructure of power.

The ladies who came to La Grisette regularly tended to require the same service; their habits were known to the attendants and the house would be informed of requirements through handwritten notes delivered by messenger a day or so beforehand.

Many were simple. They came to La Grisette to be pampered, attended to, worshipped, and then to receive the kind of hard grinding fuck that had only existed at the beginning of their long, dull marriages,

221

and, in many cases, not even then. They wanted to luxuriate in surroundings that were soft and sweet-smelling, where the constraints of social protocols did not exist, where they could achieve the climax of the erotic reveries that had held them for so long.

The young needed to feel safe; the old needed to feel young. All of them needed to feel that they were unusual and beautiful; all of them needed the basic empowerment of a man's powerful insertion, that combative exchange of fluid energies that fuels women and exhausts men. This contraflow drains the life out of marriages and affection was often replaced by cards, boredom and imagined (or real) physical decrepitude.

Regular customers who were familiar with the voluptuous mores of La Grisette would fall in with a mode of regular play. Confident in their choices they tended to buy the same men each week and ask for the same things. There were few true adventuresses who indulged in any lust for experimentation – though there were *some*, of course.

The newer arrivals required tender encouragement for they were often very nervous. Whatever their age, young or old, if new to these games they blushed and stammered, their hearts beat and their eyes flickered. They shivered with anxiety. Some did not know what they wanted; some knew but could not admit to it.

Many women who visited Francette's bordello simply wanted a massage and a slow fuck – sensual, easy, affectionate. They paid for the tender attention of a young man who would rub sweet-smelling oils into aching muscles, stroke the thighs and breasts with knowing fingers, until slowly, easily, she was ready to receive him.

Others wanted to be taken by force. There were several who wanted three in a bed, and, in particular, the dual possibilities provided by two men. This was an unfashionable idea that was difficult to achieve in the real world. When it comes to threesomes, men prefer to lie with two women. Male duos are hard to come by; the accomplices are waylaid by penile insecurity or by lack of experience and the confines of machismo. They compare erections rather than concentrate on the pleasure of the woman. It is a difficult dynamic to obtain to the satisfaction of all. La Grisette prided itself on overcoming these petty inhibitions and training men to the skills required of these particular *ménages*.

Some ladies needed to be taught and some wanted to teach. There were many who wanted to be virgins again and a few who were virgins and were willing to pay for rampant defloration. And there were many who wanted revenge – to punish a symbol of oppression for the wrongs that had been committed. There were furious scenes of cathartic passion where the energy of the room would crackle to a hellish electricity whose danger was only contained by the sang-froid of the professional man.

The male supplicants were more expensive, for these evenings often meant that their smooth white flesh received the black laces of a whip, or that their arses were paddled into two deep purple blemishes. These bruised moons could stay with them for a week and prohibit similar activity during this time. Few women felt inclined to spank the behind of another woman's punishment toy; a bruise was the sign of territorial right. It had to fade to make the fantasy work. A fresh bum was a good bum; made to order.

These vixen bitches of the night were offered boys whose predilections lay in subjugation. Those who enjoyed punishment were punished and the truth of revenge was obfuscated by complexity because nobody was really hurt.

David liked to be tied up and left in a room, naked, until his mistress chose to offer him a sip of wine, or to fondle his ever-excited balls, or to slap him hard in the face with hands dressed in silk evening gloves.

John, once a prizefighter on the street, was a compact man, and very rough. Scarred as he was by his profession and broken by former blows, he was willing, for a price, to receive the punches of the many women who had wanted to hit out for years. He could take kicks to the chest and stomach while his black eyes, whose expression said nothing of the rigours of his history, stared with innate passivity. Uninjured, he could survive these womanly bouts without a qualm.

Did the brawls arouse John? The answer to this came when the combatant slipped her palm through the flap in front of his breeches and circled her fingers around a thick brown swollen cock. John was not oblivious to the arousal of slap and bite and blow.

The furious women would ease themselves down on top of his swollen shaft and take their pleasure with piston movements astride his groin, coming as they wished and without caring about his climax. He was paid, after all: the ride was theirs to enjoy. He did not matter.

Several of his clients liked to witness his excitement. They would leave him without screwing him then relish the thought of his exquisite need as they clattered home in their carriages, the jolting rhythm of the ride vibrating their inflamed pudenda and soaking the seat beneath them. This nether weeping would turn to overflow as they thought of the ride that John would not be allowed to have.

Not all good sex is consummated sex.

Francette ensured that a wide variety of men were available because all ages were requested to provide different services.

Some were young, muscled and beautiful with classic chiselled features; handsome is as handsome does. Some were African, some were Indian, some were German. There were men who were tall and well built who looked as if they could throw you over their shoulder because they could. There were men who looked like women and women who looked like men. There were short men and medium men, men with thick hair and men with thin hair, men who smiled and men who sulked. There were men you wanted to hug and men you wanted to kill. And there was one midget, a manikin named Manolo.

Manolo, documented as one of the smallest men in the world, enjoyed a vista that was unavailable to most of his sex, as his eyes tended to be parallel to a woman's pubis. This lucky birthright granted him observation, knowledge and technique that ensured an expertise in oral sex that was unparalleled.

Manolo's employment was esoteric. He could hide underneath skirts and tables without causing inconvenience, and he could devote himself, with tongue and tiny hands, to stimulating the thighs or puss or other zones while his mistress played cards or carried on other pastimes.

Some evenings were spent underneath a piquet table. As two ladies played their hands, Manolo would go from one to another. Crawling underneath their skirts, pushing his face between their thighs, he would lick their clits with his tiny tongue, enjoying the ripples of flesh that ebbed around his ears as pleasure asserted itself. He would relish the moans that emitted from the table above him.

The trick was to carry on playing one's hand, a trick that many ladies could not learn, so good was Manolo at tickling their sensitive button and igniting climax. Cards would be thrown on to the table in a swirling blizzard as the lady threw her neck back and groaned out her joy. Then Manolo would remove himself from the confines of her silk skirts, crawl underneath the tent that was her partner's petticoats and perform the same act until she too was made incapable of play.

Manolo's life was spent in a strange terrain, surrounded as he was by the fabrics of linings and by the pulpy folds of thighs. Existing in dark places, full of flesh and the scent of human arousal, his tiny mouth could kiss a vulva in many different ways just as a mouth can be kissed in many different ways, his lips grappling with her moist mons in a range of imaginative options.

Having inspected the nature of its petals first, for he knew that all were different, he would gently pull back the labia to inspect the crimson recess. He knew what he was doing. A marriage of instinct, experience and observation made his skills miraculous.

He could take her swollen labia into his mouth and suck, or he could lunge his tongue into her salty passage in a knowing intimacy unknown to most men, for Manolo's proportions allowed unusual access.

He would tickle and torture, persevere and probe, until the lady, her face far above him, a face that he rarely saw, was an expression of surprise then smiling gratification.

'Sometimes I wish I could see eyes as well as thighs,' he would say.

His room was a skirt and his view was the ripe fruit of excited genitalia. His own tiny prick would be tough all day, stiff in the permanent excitement of his job. It was a good life, made even better by regular remuneration.

Anthony, an actor, was often employed to satisfy the lady's tastes for abject flattery. Anthony played the part of the lover who, having rejected the woman, had found he had made a mistake and, tormented by unrequited passion, begged and pleaded to be allowed back into her life.

He performed these scenarios with genuine tears in his eyes, on his bended knees, groaning with beautifully enacted pain.

What better arousal than an ex-lover brought down by misery? For who wishes happiness on those who have departed? Who blesses the mercenary merchants of dull emotions who row their boats away and never look back? They are dead but they leave bitter memories and turn love into hate and the lady has no recourse.

It is a common enough thing, the retreat of men, for they lose interest, of course, once the juices have spewed out of their bodies. Their ardour wanes, the excitement dulls, their soul detaches just as the vulva is becoming interested and she is getting going. It is a realm of biological impossibility and crass imbalance. Suffice it to say the experience was universal and Anthony's services were in demand every single night of the week.

The young Mrs Appleby, in particular, enjoyed kicking Anthony over on the carpet so that he lay there in a prostrate pile of misery.

He would beg for forgiveness and shriek that he had made a mistake. He would go down on his knees, hug her skirts, and weep. He would sit next to her on the silk sofa and describe the qualities of her character – her beauty, her wit, her unique gifts – and how he could not live without them.

Eventually, depending on how she felt, she would allow him to kiss her on the back of the neck. If his humility was very woebegone and her cunt flowed with the arousal of his convincing agony, she might allow him to insert his fingers, three or four, and push her to an orgasm. But she would never ever allow him to fuck her.

He would threaten suicide, claim that he was going to drink poison, hold a knife to his throat. His death threats soaked her with the flow of fantasy as warmth spread from her stomach and aroused her with the narcotic essence of triumph.

A part of her knew that this was an enactment, of course, but somehow her imagination allowed her to enjoy the sight of his sorrow, believe in the wretched suffering and relish it as compensation.

Mrs Appleby had been in love once, not with her husband, it has to be admitted, but in love with another, as in love as it is possible to be. She had had passion, hope and a future, until the evening that it ended for no reason at all. He walked out of her life and she never saw him again. It was as if he had been killed and nobody had invited her to the funeral.

Anthony's brother Atlas, also an actor, was an expert in the scenes for those who wanted to be taken as if they were innocent again. These tended to be the older women who had seen it all and knew that the cynicism of age had somehow ousted the innocent optimism of youth. Sexual predators with macho self-confidence, they could drive into any erotic scenario and stalk a man until he fell. They could and would pursue, but the harsh realities of the chase sometimes cracked their patina of determination and they would want to be innocent again, to remember what it was like to know nothing, to be seduced by unfamiliar lips and gentle persuasion.

Beaux and Bonne worked together. Blond, bisexual, with smooth brown skin and toned muscles, they were identical types and their dicks were of equal size which meant that they did not have to fight the stress of competition when engaged in three-play.

And threesomes were the game in which they excelled.

Beaux and Bonne got much pleasure from each other because they were in love with each other, but both were blessed with a lucky desire to please ladies and to satisfy them.

They were soul brothers and easy sisters and no lady could say that she had experienced revelry if she had not purchased Beaux and Bonne for one evening.

They worked in a salon on the first floor. One of the most luxurious, its walls were lined with pink and gold silk wallpaper and the ceiling featured a baroque painting of Neptune and various sea monsters, all composed in light blues, whites and greens. A fire flickered in a marble fireplace on which there was a bust of Julius Caesar; but the room was dominated by the bed, a magnificent divan shrouded in opulent musky pink curtains of thick velvet and matched with a pink coverlet embroidered with gold thread and hundreds of tiny beads. The light flickered from candles on a crystal chandelier and there was a smell of fresh lilies and strawberries which were arranged in glass receptacles on tiny gold tables.

Beaux and Bonne, with perfect coordination honed by experience and confidence, would serve the lady a glass of wine from a silver tray. Then both would fold her into their arms and envelop her, one kissing the back of her neck, one fondling her breasts, both occasionally pausing to kiss each other on the lips.

Beaux would untie the laces of her bodice and ease the dress slowly down her body while Bonne would stroke the back of her neck with his hands and tickle the length of spine until shivers travelled up and down her back to her stomach and to the cleft of her cunt where it transformed into the ooze of carnality.

Knowing this moment and seizing it, Beaux would

thrust his fingers deep inside her then massage her vulva, pumping it to the full swollen fruit that was insurmountable desire.

He could feel her mound, wet and warm and wanton in his hand, while his boyfriend investigated places the lady hardly knew she possessed.

Sometimes she would fall back into the arms of Bonne, who would catch her naked and helpless, pelvis gyrating with the unshamed request for the hard thrust of vigorous copulation. As delight fused her, she would open up to the two men, her lips ready for their tongues, her inner passage emblazoned with flaming red flora. She needed it, she wanted it, and both men could supply it, long and hard until she would beg them to stop.

Beaux and Bonne knew that there could be no failure in this last phase of disinhibition. Premature ejaculation was a sackable offence at La Grisette. It was an unwritten law that no man came before their client. Those who spluttered or sank were sent back on to the streets from whence most of them came.

They were paid to provide satisfaction. A dissatisfied customer meant an angry customer, an angry customer had to be given her money back. Furthermore an angry customer would gossip and word would get round that a true man could not be acquired in this bagnio.

It would only take one limp dick to sink the house of La Grisette. Jeering and laughing are not aphrodisiacs and nor do they enhance the charisma of a house whose mystique subsisted on supplying all the occult tones that are the kaleidoscope of human sexuality.

So Beaux and Bonne would take it in turns. While Bonne held her legs up by the feet, Beaux would lunge in, hard dick grinding into the overflow of her slippery canal, forcing himself hard up so that she felt him all the way and could only shriek out that this, yes, this was money very, very well spent.

As he felt the gush of his spasm reach the fore, he would quickly draw back with perfect timing, just as the bead of cream glistened on his end, but before the current came and, while he recovered himself, Bonne would go in, pumping with granite dick, soft on the outside, hard as stone on the inside. After this, Beaux again.

She would think that she had had enough. Her cunt was full, her entrails had been handed over to them; they were in her, up her, all over her. There was only these two men. She lost herself. It was enough.

She would shout at them to stop but they would carry on until they knew for certain that she had been transported by the rhythm of true climax and that the tremors of pleasure had vibrated up and down her insides.

There were older men who fulfilled the eternal paternal roles that mesmerised and sustained and were always a popular ride on the sexual carousel. Distinguished daddies with steel-grey hair and hard hands and authority could make between £25 and £75 a night.

Lady St Michael, 25, would arrive every Wednesday at 7 p.m. in order to dine with Hunter, a glowering man who would chastise her manners and threaten her with punishment until she burst into tears. Eventually, after she had showed him that she could behave herself, she was allowed to sit deep in his lap and be fed by him.

Hunter was much in demand because he was unknowable and he never let his role slip. He was the person that the lady created and she never knew who he was in real life. After the session he would slip away to some private room down a dark corridor while the lady settled into her carriage. A footman would wrap a rug around her legs and she would think only of Hunter and the evening when she would see him again.

Hunter would and could do anything. His sexuality lay in his basic strength. A lady was powerless in his arms; only her mind was superior and her mind was of no use in these circumstances, particularly if her mouth was full of his tongue, or covered over by his ham hands. To be fucked by Hunter was to go down in the full force of pure masculinity; to be pinned down and banged, to abnegate control, to allow it to happen. Many women were awakened by Hunter. Their bodies realised new sensations that they had not experienced, deadened as they had been by unknowing husbands or lack of interest or embarassment and ignorance. To fuck Hunter was to discover a new realm and to learn interesting lessons. To buy him regularly was to indulge ideas and to go further with the experiments of love.

His fingers and his hands would probe every orifice with arrogant knowledge, opening her up, making her as vulnerable as it was possible to be. Cunt, anus, mouth – they were his. She could not struggle. She could not leave. She had bought herself this strange cruelty for £100. He was one of the most expensive in the business. Sometimes there was fear; sometimes moments of disgust; but never embarrassment or mortification. Hunter believed that it was everyone's right to enjoy themselves by any method that pleased them.

So all the Francescas and Emilys, Janes and Amelias, found out that sex was sordid and sordid was good. They learned to worship the hard white dick of Hunter, to stroke its soft skin and know its ways. They learned to suck the tip and to swallow the hot juices that erupted from the end of it. They learned to embrace his rigid organ with the muscles of their inner pass-

232

ages, to feel his every lunge, and to embrace it with their thighs, groins, every nerve of their vulvae.

Hunter knew who to slap and who to kiss. He knew who to rape and who to slowly seduce with whispered affection and sincere flattery. He knew when to pounce and when to humiliate.

Lady Amelia went down on him the night that he threw a glass of red wine in her face. Lady Francesca, arrogant and spoiled, would polish his boots in order to earn the grace of his favour. But shy Emily, whose marriage had only been consummated once, was slowly undressed and caressed. Then, with care, she was laid out on the bed on her back, her thighs were pushed apart, and she was slowly penetrated, hot tip first, inch by inch the prick disappearing into her, so that she felt each tiny movement, every part of its length as it soothed itself into her entrails. Now Emily knew everything.

Suzanna, Lady Osterley, also knew much. She had arrived at La Grisette as an unhappily married mother of three. Her husband, the scion of the Osterleys of Somerset, had long since taken up a mistress, having done his duty and created his heirs.

Lady Osterley, energetic, in her thirties, possessed of a lustrous beauty that arrives with a combination of health and good humour, had been drained of her essences. The smile had begun to leave her face. She had forgotten how to laugh until a friend led her to La Grisette and, surveying the men there, she plucked the two that were to become her favourites. She never learned their names and she did not want to, though she never forgot to tip them at Christmas with a generous bonus that earned their genuine affection.

They were not her friends, they were her lovers, paid to be so, paid to conform to the emotional constrictions required of the transaction.

Sometimes the ineffable complexities of love did arise and Francette had to exert diplomacy as an elopement could bring scandal to La Grisette and scandal could mean closure.

Anthony, the actor, found it difficult to extricate himself from his roles and he often fancied that he was actually in love with the women who had paid him to pretend. There would be moaning and beating of the brow; he would go off his food and profess that death was an attractive alternative to the torture that he was suffering. Francette would have seriously considered firing him if he was not one of the highest earners in the house.

Several women fell in love with Hunter but, fortunately, most were sensible. They had married for money and with money they would stay, partaking of the delicacies that money offered with enjoyment rather than the surrender of common sense. The cycles of love tended to be short; people recovered. Life went on.

The facade of La Grisette was respectable enough; there were stone steps, railings, a grand door with stone carving. Nothing indicated the commerce of unrestrained ardour that was bartered inside.

There were three storeys. The ground floor was divided into a series of reception rooms some of which were 'themed' for fantasies. These, decorated with all the plush extravagance that money could buy, were designed to please the eye and comfort the body.

The Moorish room, always popular, was a sanctum created to represent the imagined seraglio of a past sultan of the Ottoman empire. A scented place of silk-covered divans and glossy pillows, low tables bore garlands of flowers and jars full of lemon peel. Several multicoloured birds sung in gold cages. In one corner, on a plinth, there was a solid gold statue of Vishnu, Lord of the World.

Painted panels showed scenes from the Perfumed Garden, the ancient work of Umar ibn Muhammed al Nefzawi, whose pages outline eleven sexual positions.

The artist had painted men and women in various configurations of erotic possibility – some standing on their heads, some entwined like trees, some taking it from the back – but all intent on achieving the godhead of sexual union as promised by the ancient philosophers of Arabic lore.

A sunken bath steamed behind a mother-of-pearl screen. Here the houris would bathe, massage their skins with scented oils, apply kohl to their eyes, and jewels to their belly buttons. Many of them wore a gold ring in the nose, others wore anklets, bracelets, toe-rings and a belt around the hips on which there were hundreds of tiny bells.

The dancers who worked the Moorish room, six in all, were costumed in the traditional outfit of belly dancers, though for the purposes of prostitution these were customised to enhance their appeal. The glittering bodices were cut low to reveal all aspects of cleavage and nipple. The harem pants were made of translucent silks to reveal the shadow of the dark pubis as it flowed around the thighs of the dancer.

The women were full and fleshy, chosen to appeal to men who preferred the female form as a soft composition of curves and contours. Plump, moon-faced, rotund but graceful, the dancers would shake their wide hips in front of the gentlemen, who gathered to enjoy the evening's entertainment.

Swaying to the sound of cymbals and drums, they would gyrate their pelvises and offer up the pulpy mass of their stomachs in a jiggling show of frantic display. Arms fluttered, hands like leaves; eyes, defined by their black lines, flirted. The lips, glossed, offered everything.

The clients were also porcine, as adipose as the sultans of old whose weight was a status symbol that reflected wealth and power. As the courtesans of the past had done, the dancers of La Grisette accommodated the swollen bodies with *daq al arz*, thirteenth position of the Perfumed Garden, which saw them mesmerise the client with gyrating breasts, provoke exquisite reaction with undulation then straddle the man with their thighs, allowing themselves access to the excited organ twitching underneath the folds of his distended belly.

The royal room was a domain of gold leaf and mirrors, painted in the china blue seen at Versailles, and attempting to imitate its luxuries with painted wall panels and chinoiserie.

There was also a small theatre. Many actresses worked at La Grisette and were more than willing to present exotic theatrical presentations. These took various directions, from straightforward naked posturing enhanced by silk scarves to more sophisticated stage shows written by professional playwrights and properly directed, lit and choreographed.

A successful 'run' could last for three months. Miss Kazzaz's erotic dance with a python attracted packed houses for more than twelve weeks.

No-one had ever seen anything like Miss Kazzaz. Her body wrapped in an eight-foot-long snake, she and the reptile seemed to be as one, wound around each other, woman and serpent, serpent and woman, her brown skin melding with the glossy scales of the tail and body, the animal's diamond emblems, yellow and gold, undulating against the brown and black of its glittering skin.

The finale, her *pièce de résistance*, was a dangerous

feat where she encouraged the snake to explore her body. Trained by some secret method, its head and cold eyes would slink down her belly to the black moss between her legs, nuzzle between her thighs and reappear up on the other side. Caressing her buttocks with cold coils, it would slither up her back and reappear at her shoulder where its terrifying mouth would gape open, revealing enormous jaws with crimson recess and pointed fangs. It looked as if it was seized with the death thrust of the jungle predator, but Miss Kazzaz would simply grab the snake by the back of the neck and gently kiss it before shimmying away from her spotlight and into the dark of the wings.

Most popular of all, though, was an abridged version of *Romeo and Juliet* performed naked. Adapted by John Fontaine, a popular playwright, he had penned an erotic masterpiece of contagious venality that charged the pulses and loins of anyone who saw it.

Fontaine had turned Shakespeare's love story into a tale of consummated bliss. The audience was treated to scenes of violent coition performed by Angelo as Romeo and the petite Phylida as Juliet. Both of them were uninhibited exhibitionists. He thrust his prick into her pubis and both threw themselves into a performance of the throes of lust as a rakehell on *joie-de-fille*.

First love, last love, any love – it mattered not. All that mattered to the audience was the sight of two young bodies engaged in passionate intercourse.

The scene allowed the paying public to hear every groan, moan and whisper, to smell the scent of arousal that rose hotly from both groins, to see the beads of sweat glow on her smooth arms, belly and stomach, to see her unfold for him and he to penetrate her – all enhanced by the chemistry between two lovers who wanted each other in real life.

Above the theatre, on the first floor, lay a set of

rooms known as the Temple of Pleasure. These, in general, were suites and bedrooms with the most luxury, reserved for the most expensive men and women – the stars of this sky whose skills now made them glitter with the charisma of sensual success.

La Grisette had released some of London's most notorious harlots into the city, harlots who had been bought houses in Grosvenor Square, who moved in royal circles, and, in some cases, ran them. Nina dela Mare dripped in jewels and was known, consequently, as 'The Chandelier'. Her sister Za-Za rode in a carriage painted gold and white which was lined with fur and decorated with the crest of the Duke of Hinton-Houghton.

They were the super-breed, a species promoted by the newspapers, by their own greed, by exquisite beauty and by a self-sustaining legend that had kept them at the top of their profession for nearly a decade at a time when the average *horizontale* was fortunate if she lasted as long as the strawberry season.

Luxuriating in an echelon far above the common tart, their financial power was encapsulated the day that Rena Powell announced that she did not get into bed for less than 200 guineas, a claim that was validated when she threw the Duke of York out of her house when he offered her 50.

All these great and greedy women had started off in the suites that made the Temple of Pleasure at La Grisette. They had managed to promote themselves up the hierachy and out of the house by enviable dint of athleticism, wile, imagination and insurmountable skill in the realm of oral sex.

The Temple of Pain was on the top floor of the house and had been designed for the desires of the deviant.

A series of panelled salons were painted black and gold and were lit by candles in ornate sconces. Several dark mahogany chaise-longues with emerald-green upholstery were placed around the rooms. Rich black curtains hung from the windows, always closed, for light was never allowed to enter this warm shadowy place.

A range of polished glass cabinets displayed the equipment that was available to the mistresses and their victims. There were polished dildos in black ebony and coils of iron chain. There were horse whips and birch rods and paddles. And there were crystal decanters full of different brown and orange liqueurs.

Secrets were played out in these cells of fantasy and all the demands of the flesh were attained.

Francette oversaw this realm, but the daily activities were organised by Madame Jasmine, a tall hermaphrodite with a head of lush red hair.

Once boyish, but now in her middle years, she looked like a beautiful man. An excellent androgyne, her shape was masculine – narrow hips, muscular arms, strong shoulders, sinewy neck. She had a strong jawline, wide sensual mouth and small breasts for a person of five foot eleven. Her spell lay in her sexual mystery. Age had brought something that it does not always give to youth – it brought dignity, grace and the attribute of self-knowledge.

Madame Jasmine had class. This distinction, set as an example, had trickled down to her establishement which also had class. The men and women who worked to her authority were properly looked after. Time off was allowed, personal problems were understood and heard. Madame Jasmine did not brook laziness or dishonesty. She devoted herself to cultivating the qualities that ensured standards – such as sexual imagination, attention to detail, manners, wit and panache.

Adam Neville, a writer of scatalogical pamphlets so

crude that a warrant had been put out for his arrest, was one of Madame Jasmine's regulars.

They would repair to the central chamber of the Temple of Pain. She, red hair piled on the top of her head in an arrangement of black ribbon, would appear in a leather corset that turned her into a mobile hourglass. This was teamed with shiny black wool stockings and black silk shoes with diamond buckles.

Slowly and with great care she would unlock one of the fine display cabinets and pluck a whip from within.

'On your knees, sir!' she would snap, and push him violently.

The writer would drop down, crawl about on the floor in front of her like the dog that he was, moaning and apprehensive in the knowledge of what was to come.

Madame Jasmine would ring a bell and two attendants would arrive. Regular aides to the Temple of Pain, they wore uniforms of black silk breeches, black waistcoats and black shirts. Burly, they would lift Neville up from the floor and push him face down on a chaise-longue, where he would be securely tied by the wrists and ankles.

At a flick of Madame Jasmine's fingers, Neville's breeches would be ripped down his bottom, down his thighs, and left halfway down his calves where they acted as a further constriction.

And so his arse would be in the air, ready for the whipping that was so dreadful but so satisfying when delivered by the strong male-female arm of the cruel redhead. At this point he would already start to beg for mercy. He was a coward, after all, not a man at all. He snivelled and complained, moaned and groaned, and the effect of this was to actually irritate Madame Jasmine and stimulate her to commit futher torment. Often she would brandish a bunch of twigs, bound like a broom, but made of willow that was softer and springier. The flail would snap down on his quivery flesh with a bite that, depending on the direction of the blow, left a rose blemish that stretched all over the buttocks, or harsher more defined lines of red lacing.

He would beg her to stop, but she knew that he was hard, that his dick was full of urgency and chafing against the velvet of the sofa as his pelvis convulsed and the target that was his arse jerked from side to side.

She knew that he loved it.

The punishment would last a half an hour or so and the lashing was so intense that Adam Neville would wonder if he could bear it.

Madame Jasmine would throw the twigs to one side and sweep from the room, leaving him to think of his sins and to remember all the reasons why he was the lowliest of the low.

Pain and pleasure would mingle with his essence and engulf him in irrational thoughts. He would often spend a further £100 to buy penetrative sex, or, at the very least hand relief.

Madame Jasmine did not perform these services, considering them to be rather beneath her (although she did not actually admit this) and, anyway, she had never enjoyed these intimate particulars. They were not to her taste. An underling would perform the extra duties and finish Neville off with hand or mouth or hole.

Trenton Dastard was a regular customer at La Grisette, where he was more popular with the ladies who worked there than with Francette who did not favour those whose financial balances were so unbalanced.

She was fond, however, of Ralph Fitzroy and greeted him with a smile when she swept into the smoking chamber where he and Dastard were lounging.

241

Ralph jolted dutifully to his feet and bowed.

Francette offered him her scented white fingers to kiss.

'Madame,' he said.

'My lord.'

Dastard ambled slowly to his feet and awarded her with a perfunctory bow which she acknowledged with cool disdain that was just short of actually being rude.

'Mrs Trite.'

'Mr Dastard.'

'We come to, er, cheer Lord Fitzroy up,' said Trenton. 'Who have you got for him?'

'Ah well,' said Francette with her secret smile. 'There is one beauty who I know that Lord Fitzroy will like.'

'Have I met her before?' said Ralph, who had been pleasured by many of the women at La Grisette.

'Non, je ne pense pas,' said Francette. 'She is a new girl. And one of our best – she is in demand every night of the week. I have had to turn people away – and she is fussy. She won't have everyone. Her price now, I am afraid, is £120, but this grants you exclusive rights for the whole night and to stay until the morning if you wish.'

'Expensive,' said Trenton, who always tried to keep his own fees down to an average rate of £25 and this was only ever achieved after hours of negotiation and because his regular girl, Lavinia, was in love with him.

'She is worth it,' said Francette.

'I am sure she is,' said Ralph gallantly. 'I am sure she is.'

He climbed the stairs to the second floor where several doors led to the range of suites known collectively as the Temple of Pleasure. One or two doors had tiny circular windows in them which allowed the casual passer-by to watch the scenes therein. This service was provided free of charge for the mutual pleasure of both voyeur and exhibitionist.

Striding purposefully towards Number 10, he stopped occasionally to observe the activities in the chambers along the way.

In Number 5, a small white room tricked with gold, a brown-skinned man with dark eyes and gypsy looks stood in front of Letty St Blaize, the eldest daughter of the Earl of Stress and the wife of Milton Mowbray, an equerry to George III. She, a young woman of 23 or so, was a dainty little thing with wild dark brown hair, dancing brown eyes and painted red lips. Her smile expressed amused flirtation and bold banter.

Wearing a loose cotton chemise that fell off the shoulders and slipped down her arms as she waved them, and with her hair in disarray, she was perched on a tall stool. The gypsy and Letty were playing the kissing game.

The winner was the first to snare the other's lips with their own.

Her lover, a £50 a night man named Guillame, dipped to kiss her, his fringe flopping over his forehead, a cool smile on his lips, but Letty turned her head away and his mouth banged her ear. She laughed and taunted him. Called him a slow old thing. He dipped again, she turned her head again. He blew the air. She giggled, waved her arms so that the cotton chemise fell from her shoulders and revealed the smooth white of her chest and the long graceful neck.

He, irritated now, grabbed her small face in his two large palms and forced her to be still. Then with one hand he wiped the lipstick from her mouth with a stroke, smearing the red paint over her chin and cheeks. She silent now, taken aback, was still. Covering her eyes with his left hand, the tall man pulled the girl's face towards his mouth with his right hand and clamped his mouth firmly down on hers. Forcing her lips open with his tongue, her jaw fell open with surprise and allowed him in. His tongue fought with hers, he held her so that all she could do was indulge him in the combat that he was destined to win; tongue wrestled with tongue. Finally her shoulders relaxed, she fell into him, she gave herself up to the intimacy of his mouth. He had won.

In Number 7, Princess Mahalia, a dignitary from the Congo, was amusing herself with Jeroboam, a tall Jamaican of liquorice grace and a lean black body willing to submit to any whim that the princess desired. She, lewd, lay on the floor with her feet in the air, holding her thighs with her hands. Then she dropped her legs and put the base of her feet together and shielded the opening of her labia with them.

He pushed her feet out of the way, enabling him to enter either her front or back passage. He plunged his sturdy organ into her damp snare which opened and closed to receive him, controlled by the expert ligaments of her thighs and buttocks, thus enabling her muscles to kiss the length of his cock as surely as her mouth would have been able to.

In Number 8, Hunter, fully clothed, was forcing his hard cock into Lady Francesca's mouth. She, kneeling in front of him, was unwillingly performing the deed. She had submitted to his order but she did not like it; her mouth was full of him, tears were in her eyes, she seemed about to gag, but she took him obediently.

Hunter thrust his pelvis aggressively into her face, and came, allowing the cream to pump into her mouth. She withdrew from her position, stood up straight and leaned forward towards his face as if to kiss him. He moved his face forward with a smug smile. She spat his own semen into his eye.

Ralph, excited now, turned the brass door knob of

room Number 10. Flickerings of excitement quickening his body, pulses that were the fine line between apprehension and impatience.

The room was small but luxurious. Dominated by a bed protected by rich red and gold curtains, these were drawn back against the wall. Candles flickered on a cabinet by the side of the bed, but they did not give much light and Ralph's eyes took some time to become accustomed to seeing the shapes in warm gloom.

She lay on the bed and she was unclothed except for a pair of opaque black stockings that ended halfway up her thighs and for a plain black mask that fitted her eyes. This was all. Her body, perfect, was white and smooth. He did not think he had seen anyone so well proportioned. The curves came where they should, the buttocks were round and provocative, the upper arms were sensual without being fleshy. This was a woman at the peak of her beauty.

He did not say anything because he did not have to. That was the arrangement. No trite platitudes intended to clear the way for consummation; no insincere small-talk designed to flatter virtues that patently did not exist. No lies. Ralph had paid for silence; it was with silence that he was most relaxed, where he felt that little could go wrong, and where he felt he could focus with more effect on the pleasure of both parties.

He stood at the end of the bed while she watched him undress himself. He did this with a casual grace. Sexual self-confidence lay at the bottom of Ralph's psyche; he was not sure of everything, but there was a part of him that knew he was attractive, that his body was fine, that there was nothing to be ashamed of. She, gazing at his strong shoulders, his tight buttocks, his lean strength, retained an expression of enigmatic *froideur* which hid the impatience that was beginning to take control.

At last, naked now, his dick thrust forward from his pelvis with grand intent and much promise. Easing himself towards her, he kissed her passionately on the neck, on her beautiful breasts, between her thighs. She gave herself up to him without question, easily, immediately and with fond supplication.

She knew that his dick would be good and it was. He wound himself slowly into her, sensing all her bodily nuances, for he could not see her face at all. The silk stockings rubbed against his thighs; he held on. He immersed himself in her. He held on. Her pelvis rose to dance with his, a perfect rhythm, two souls, two bodies, one unit. She let herself go, and, as the contractions of her inner self kissed his soft shaft, so too did he.

Silently he rose from her, dressed and left the room.

There had been no speech.

Only the veil of anonymity.

He walked back to the rooms he kept in Mount Street and tried unsuccessfully to sleep. Something had happened to him and he was not sure whether it was a good thing. The masked woman haunted his thoughts and he could not dispel them.

He tried to think of other things. He tried to remember when he was next due to hunt. He even tried to remember some ribald moment shared with Trenton Dastard. They all ebbed away to the force of the presence that she now exerted on his inner life.

He went back to La Grisette the following night. And the night after that. And the night after that. His days became about the nights; his life was about the masked woman. But still he had only made love to her; he knew everything about her body, about her soul, about the essence of her pleasures, but he knew nothing about her.

She did not break the rules. She remained silent and

masked as she had been instructed, quietly submitting with tact and imagination to the rules that he had provided. She enjoyed supplying what he wanted and he assumed that she was merely one of La Grisette's finer girls, who were always intelligent and sensate and knew how to please a man however complicated he was.

An *horizontale* did not reach the top by display alone; she had to have brains as well as beauty. She had to be better than the others and this meant developing the art of intercourse to a level where she provided an experience that was unique to her. Thus she earned her money. Thus she gained status. Thus men fell in love with her.

Ralph realised that he had deluded himself and that he was not immune to the spells cast by the girls to whom one gave money. He had paid girls at La Grisette over the years and had remained detached. They had been charming and entertaining and pretty but he had not fallen for them. He had not thought of them after the evenings were over except in the simplest sense of erotic flashback. He had not longed for their company, wondered about their lives, wanted to know who they were when he left Francette's house.

He felt disabled and irritated but he realised that he had lost control. He realised that if he wanted to buy more rights to her he would have to set her up somewhere and make her his offical mistress.

On the seventh night, impassioned with pre-coital love, he suddenly and without warning pulled the mask off her face.

'Miss Pringle!'

'Lord Fitzroy.'

'Miss Pringle! What are you doing here?'

'Well, I am afraid I just got bored at Lancaster Hall. I was locked in my room the whole time and that ghastly Headley caned my backside. There was no entertainment. So Bubb helped me to escape. I thought London was a better option. I've known Francette for years. We were in Paris together.'

Ralph did not know whether to be pleased or infuriated.

'My father was right – you're an amoral minx.'

'Oh, sweetheart, but you love me so . . .'

She was right. He did. And there was nothing he could do about it. She was like an incurable infection that could not be bled away.

He sighed. He knew he was beaten. The rest of his life stretched out before him as a clear landscape. He could see it like a vision. It could be lonely and sad or it could be entertaining and interesting.

'Miss Pringle,' he said. 'Will you be my wife?'

'Yes,' she replied.

Chapter Ten

The news of Viscount Fitzroy's engagement to Miss Amy Pringle was greeted with a mixture of derision and horror by those who lived in and around Lancaster Hall. Lord Hacclesfield, overcome by the scandal, suffered an immediate coronary and died. His fortune went, as always intended, to Ralph, the son he loved. The irony was that this rich legacy would also be enjoyed by the scarlet daughter-in-law who had cast the fatal shock to his heart.

Lady Hacclesfield, optimism raised by the death of her husband, told her friends that, in her view, the match was a suitable one. Miss Pringle had the courage and energy to be of genuine support to a man destined to run the vast business that was an hereditary estate. There would be responsibilities. Lady Hacclesfield knew this because she had spent many years conscientiously avoiding them.

Miss Pringle would take the lead and organise things and fill all the roles that filled Lady Hacclesfield with fear and fatigue. Lady Hacclesfield looked forward to spending her dower years fanning herself and enjoying the sedentary life thanks to the wise choice made by her son.

'Miss Pringle is bossy and intelligent,' she told Lady Marsh-Motcombe. 'Two things I will never be.'

'And nor would you want to be, dear,' her friend replied.

Bubb announced his decision to go into the Church. This bad news reverberated as a gale-force wind around three counties and the ladies of all the great houses launched an epistolary campaign to dissuade him for an act which would deprive the nation's womanhood from one of the finest cocks in the free world. It was a shameful waste. Journalists even began to allude to it in newspaper columns, criticising an unnamed lord for this ungentlemanly act.

The pressure was intense but Bubb was adamant. He had found God and the spiritual life was the one in which he found comfort and fulfilment. It was a tragedy, but everybody was forced to live with it.

The love that existed between the affianced couple was an interesting mixture of abject affection and tense counterattack. Ralph was his father's son, and, since his father's death, had also taken his name. The new Earl of Hacclesfield, was fixed, as his father had been, with firm ideas about how things should be done. Amy, as we know by now, feared nobody, listened rarely, and determined a path of her own, cast by her own volition and defined by limits that she and she alone set for herself.

The three weeks or so that led up to their wedding might have caused permanent and painful rupture to the engagement if it had not been for the erotic excitement of endless nights which always made up for the fractious rigmaroles of everyday reality.

Ralph's commands, issued at the breakfast table, as his father's had been before him, settled uneasily on the ear of the minx and did not find a path to sub-mission. Sometimes she would do as he suggested, sometimes she would not. He observed her activities, noticed her behaviour, and, at dinner every evening would outline her defects in no uncertain terms. This, not unnaturally, infuriated her; nobody likes criticism and especially not Miss Amy, who thought she was perfect.

Once or twice there were actual tears (hers not his); once or twice she actually admitted that he was right; once or twice she found herself over his knee, her skirts lifted over her head, her drawers pulled down and her bare bottom raised to receive a full hard spanking that, while making her desperate to receive him later that night, caused some difficulty sitting down to eat break-fast the next day.

The days of affiancement helped them discover each other's mettle; Amy found a handsome fuck that she could trust and who would give her the boundaries that her soul told her she needed if she was not to turn into an uncontrollable vixen with undisciplined passions and no personal stability; Ralph knew he had found an entertaining woman who would never bore him, who would always find something new to do in bed, and who would provide the sensible advice he needed in running the difficult business that was his wide-ranging inheritance.

And so, despite some smacked bums, some angry words, and a few slammed doors, the couple were deeply in love on the morning that the wedding day dawned.

Milly, of course, had hardly been to bed at all in three days, so intense was the schedule of her respon-sibilities. She was in charge of the wedding ensemble, a rich soufflé of ivory silk and gold embroidery whose effect was to enhance every physical advantage that the bride possessed; even teamed with a veil, the floating skirts and rich laces provided her with a wasp-waist and shameless cleavage that, even in its state of supposed virginal triumph, would serve to derange the psyche of any man who looked upon her.

Amy, too, was stressed, and often ordered Milly's fingers to massage her clit to take her mind off her worries. Milly willingly complied and provided these administrations with warm affection, knowing how her mistress liked to feel the gentle stroking of skilled fingertip on her wet lips and the forceful penetration of her hand in the sensual passages that wound to the inner womb. And so maid kissed mistress with fond mouth and massaged her mound with equal passion to the mutual satisfaction of both.

One afternoon, Ralph, who had just been hunting, walked into Amy's boudoir while they were doing this and, taken by surprise, was, at first, angry. He wished to pleasure his fiancée himself and resented a member of the lower orders taking this privilege. He pushed them both over the back of the chaise-longue, and gave them a good cropping with the whip that he usually used on his stallion.

Then he sent the maid out of the room and penetrated Amy with full sharp lusting lunges of his hard manhood. It was the closest they had ever been. Amy was quieter after this. She felt calmer and more relaxed. There was only 24 hours to go.

'Behave yourself, madam,' he instructed her, as Amy, hair dishevelled, lay sprawled on her bed. 'And please calm down.'

He leaned forward and kissed her on the lips, stroking her cheek and making her tingle as he always did

'And don't pout. I love you.'

'I love you,' she echoed, looking into his dark eyes

and feeling weak and knowing that, yes, she did love him.

They were married on a spring day and, yes, it was sunny. The only cloud was the face of the bishop's wife who was relegated to a seat behind a pillar and forced between some ignominious members of the village who smelled of the farm animals with whose activities they were closely related.

The bishop, meanwhile, who conducted the ceremony in the charming Church of St Mary and the Martyrs, derived much pleasure from the décolletage of the bride's dress and the flirtatious nature of her eyes. He worked his lectern as a man possessed with lust and suffered a severe erection that rubbed against his cassock during the entire proceedings and inspired a range of unchaste thoughts whose nature defied the lores of canonical code.

Everyone agreed that it was a lovely service and marched quickly to Lancaster Hall where a sumptuous 'breakfast' awaited them. Here long tables were laid out and ordained with white tablecloths; fiestas of greenhouse flowers sprayed from delicate Sevres vases, and the best china was paraded for every place. Four goblets were positioned at each table mat to boast the number of wines that were to be served, and the family's valuable antique silver (stolen from a Spanish galleon in the sixteenth century) was arrayed for the many courses that were to enhance the feast.

An army of liveried butlers wearing white gloves provided immaculate service for every reveller. No glass was left unfilled, no plate left empty. The result was an atmosphere of shouting exuberance and passionate bonhomie where inhibitions left the room as quickly as a burglar climbs out of a window with a sack of swag. New loves were made; old marriages dissolved and one woman, a countess who had sailed

253

in from Country Antrim, actually died which, as Trenton Dastard commented later, is always the sign of a good party.

Trenton Dastard, resplendent in a suit of deep purple shot silk with a glittering brooch that he had been left by an aunt in Henley-on-Thames, gave a deeply offensive and inappropriate speech which everyone enjoyed immensely.

Swept away by uncharacteristic and unfamiliar waves of sentiment, Dastard found himself in a garden gazebo with the maid Fanny Mutterton. Inspected by a tall stone statue of the god Mercury, the two engaged in relations of carnal adventure which impressed even Dastard with all his long experience of pagan debauchery.

Fanny Mutterton had large full breasts and large full lips and an expression of unparalleled wantonness. She was built on more generous lines than those to which Trenton was accustomed; his furrow had long been filled by London ladies of sylph-like proportions whose emotions were neurotic and whose affairs were well organised into the disciplined compartments dictated by extramarital romances. They only needed flattery and foreplay to display their shivering white thighs and to moan out their needy desires. It took little to persuade them that Dastard was the man of their dreams and this bored him.

Fanny, made of more earthy matter, was the daughter of a local tenant farmer and she knew a handy London dandy when she saw one, and she knew which side her bread was buttered. The result was that Trenton Dastard's arse was buttered. She spread him over her sturdy knee, pulled down the bespoke breeches, slathered the dairy gel over him, and buggered him mercilessly, first with her cruel fingers, and then with a carrot from the kitchen garden. The pleasure to his prostate and, indeed, to his whole body, was so intense that Dastard lost all sense of reality and thought he might die if he was forced to live the rest of his life without anal penetration.

The result was that something like true love sprouted in the shade of the gazebo and Fanny Mutterton made an engagement which in some circles is known as 'marrying up'.

Meanwhile, back at the house, tables a-litter with family heirlooms, candles burning down the silver candlesticks, trays full of cakes and fruits and rivers of liquors both sweet and mellow, all men and women sunk into a state of abandon where the body and mind thinks only of immediate gratification and where consequences are of no importance.

The feast went on into the late afternoon. Those who could not be bothered to leave the table slumped in their chairs and then woke up later to start again. Some passed out under the table and lay with the dogs; others crawled under the table in order to enjoy the scrum of an illicit fuck.

Bubb and the dowager found themselves as such. Bubb was deeply committed to the Church but the sacrament of commitment had yet to be made and the dowager, wily old hussy that she was, took advantage of this to persuade him that the Lord would not mind if he enjoyed one last taste of earthly paradise before surrendering his soul to the good of all mankind.

It was an act of love, she went on, and God believed in love, did he not? Bubb, exhausted by the emotions of the day, and very, very drunk, was swept away by the lusts of the moment. The dowager, so graceful and fine in aquamarine gown and strings of pearls, was a temptation that he could not resist. They rolled on to each other underneath the table, jolted only by the lumps that were the diner's boots. She pulled out his fabulous phallus from his fly, stroked it with the respect that it deserved, and slid it into her mouth where its proportion swelled to an ever greater size and would have caused her respiratory problems if she had not been experienced in the fine equation that is the line between oral sex and asphyxiation.

Bubb moaned loudly. He no longer cared about anything except the involuntary expulsion of pent-up juices. The dowager lay flat underneath him and he entered her smoothly and slowly, savouring every moment.

The dowager, wet, skirts asunder, appreciated him also. Her every nerve-ending was tuned by the thick girth; her insides filled up by the length. She too went to another place, and she would remember the young Bubb Fitzroy for many years to come.

Ralph remained relatively sober at his own wedding. He was a responsible person and he knew that somebody should remain sensible; the servants could not be relied upon to put a fire out should it start or cope with an accident should it happen.

Amy, suffering no such moral burdens, grew ever more flirtatious and tipsy. She would have initiated some quite serious trouble with Lorne Vermouth, the good-looking son of the Earl of Eden (and one of the Hacclesfield family's oldest friends) if Ralph had not quashed her mischief with a stern eye and a quiet threat whispered provocatively in her ear at around the same time that the wedding cake was wheeled in on a dog-drawn cart made of solid gold.

'I trust, Lady Hacclesfield,' he said, 'that you do not wish to suffer painful humiliation in front of Lorne Vermouth, or indeed any other guest who happens to be watching.'

Amy, knowing that he meant it, behaved herself and served around the sliced wedding cake with all the grace and hospitality that befitted the future chatelaine of the great house of Lancaster.

Then she sat happily beside her husband at the head of the table and contented herself with placing her hand underneath the white cloth and on top of his crotch, secretly stroking him and enjoying the feeling of its swell, as it rose and fell in her palm.

Her husband wanted her and her alone. She was a fortunate woman, and she knew it.

BLACK LACE NEW BOOKS

Published in July

SYMPHONY X
Jasmine Stone
£6.99

Katie is a viola player running away from her cheating husband. The tour of Symphony Xevertes not only takes her to Europe but also to the realm of deep sexual satisfaction. She is joined by a dominatrix diva and a bass singer whose voice is so low he's known as the Human Vibrator. After distractions like these, how will Katie be able to maintain her serious music career *and* allow herself to fall in love again?

Immensely funny journal of a sassy woman's sexual adventures.

ISBN 0 352 33629 3

OPENING ACTS
Suki Cunningham
£6.99

When London actress Holly Parker arrives in a remote Cornish village to begin rehearsing a new play, everyone there – from her landlord to her theatre director – seems to have an earthier attitude towards sex. Brought to a state of constant sexual arousal and confusion, Holly seeks guidance in the form of local therapist, Joshua Delaney. He is the one man who can't touch her – but he is the only one she truly desires. Will she be able to use her new-found sense of adventure to seduce him?

Wonderfully horny action in the Cornish countryside. Oooh arrgh!

ISBN 0 352 33630 7

THE SEVEN-YEAR LIST
Zoe le Verdier
£6.99

Julia is an ambitious young photographer who's about to marry her trustworthy but dull fiancé. Then an invitation to a college reunion arrives. Old rivalries, jealousies and flirtations are picked up where they were left off and sexual tensions run high. Soon Julia finds herself caught between two men but neither of them are her fiancé.

How will she explain herself to her friends? And what decisions will she make?

This is a Black Lace special reprint of a very popular title.

ISBN 0 352 33254 9

Published in August

MINX
Megan Blythe
£6.99

Spoilt Amy Pringle arrives at Lancaster Hall to pursue her engagement to Lord Fitzroy, eldest son of the Earl and heir to a fortune. The Earl is not impressed, and sets out to break her spirit. But the trouble for him is that she enjoys every one of his 'punishments' and creates havoc, provoking the stuffy Earl at every opportunity. The young Lord remains aloof, however, and, in order to win his affections, Amy sets about seducing his well-endowed but dim brother, Bubb. When she is discovered in bed with Bubb and a servant girl, how will father and son react?

**Immensely funny and well-written tale of lust among
decadent aristocrats.**

ISBN 0 352 33638 2

FULL STEAM AHEAD
Tabitha Flyte
£6.99

Sophie wants money, big money. After twelve years working as a croupier on the Caribbean cruise ships, she has devised a scheme that is her ticket to Freedomsville. But she can't do it alone; she has to encourage her colleagues to help her. Persuasion turns to seduction, which turns to blackmail. Then there are prying passengers, tropical storms and an angry, jealous girlfriend to contend with. And what happens when the lascivious Captain decides to stick his oar in, too?

**Full of gold-digging women, well-built men in uniform
and Machiavellian antics.**

ISBN 0 352 33637 4

A SECRET PLACE
Ella Broussard
£6.99

Maddie is a busy girl with a dream job: location scout for a film company. When she's double-booked to work on two features at once, she needs to manage her time very carefully. Luckily, there's no shortage of fit young men, in both film crews, who are willing to help. She also makes friends with the locals, including a horny young farmer and a particularly handy mechanic. The only person she's not getting on with is Hugh, the director of one of the movies. Is that because sexual tension between them has reached breaking point?

This story of lust during a long hot English summer is another Black Lace special reprint.

ISBN 0 352 33307 3

To be published in September

GAME FOR ANYTHING
Lyn Wood
£6.99

Fiona finds herself on a word-games holidays with her best pal. At first it seems like a boring way to spend a week away. Then she realises it's a treasure hunt with a difference. Solving the riddles embroils her in a series of erotic situations as the clues get ever more outrageous.

Another fun sexy story from the author of Intense Blue.

ISBN 0 352 33639 0

CHEAP TRICK
Astrid Fox
£6.99

Tesser Roget is a girl who takes no prisoners. An American slacker, living in London, she dresses in funky charity-shop clothes and wears blue fishnets. She looks hot and she knows it. She likes to have sex, and she frequently does. Life on the fringe is very good indeed, but when she meets artist Jamie Desmond things take a sudden swerve into the weird.

Hold on for one hot, horny, jet-propelled ride through contemporary London.

ISBN 0 352 33640 4

FORBIDDEN FRUIT
Susie Raymond
£6.99

When thirty-something divorcee Beth realises someone is spying on her in the work changing room, she is both shocked and excited. When she finds out it's sixteen-year-old shop assistant Jonathan she cannot believe her eyes. Try as she might, she cannot get the thought of his fit young body out of her mind. Although she knows she shouldn't encourage him, the temptation is irresistible.

This story of forbidden lusts is a Black Lace special reprint.

ISBN 0 352 33306 5

BLACK LACE BOOKLIST

Information is correct at time of printing. To avoid disappointment check availability before ordering. Go to www.blacklace-books.co.uk

All books are priced £5.99 unless another price is given.

Black Lace books with a contemporary setting

THE TOP OF HER GAME	Emma Holly ISBN 0 352 33337 5	☐
IN THE FLESH	Emma Holly ISBN 0 352 33498 3	☐
SHAMELESS	Stella Black ISBN 0 352 33485 1	☐
TONGUE IN CHEEK	Tabitha Flyte ISBN 0 352 33484 3	☐
SAUCE FOR THE GOOSE	Mary Rose Maxwell ISBN 0 352 33492 4	☐
INTENSE BLUE	Lyn Wood ISBN 0 352 33496 7	☐
THE NAKED TRUTH	Natasha Rostova ISBN 0 352 33497 5	☐
A SPORTING CHANCE	Susie Raymond ISBN 0 352 33501 7	☐
TAKING LIBERTIES	Susie Raymond ISBN 0 352 33357 X	☐
A SCANDALOUS AFFAIR	Holly Graham ISBN 0 352 33523 8	☐
THE NAKED FLAME	Crystalle Valentino ISBN 0 352 33528 9	☐
CRASH COURSE	Juliet Hastings ISBN 0 352 33018 X	☐
ON THE EDGE	Laura Hamilton ISBN 0 352 33534 3	☐
LURED BY LUST	Tania Picarda ISBN 0 352 33533 5	☐
LEARNING TO LOVE IT	Alison Tyler ISBN 0 352 33535 1	☐

Black Lace books with an historical setting

Black Lace anthologies

Black Lace non-fiction

---------✂---------------------------

Please send me the books I have ticked above.

Name   ....

Address ....

....

....

.... Post Code ....

Send to: **Cash Sales, Black Lace Books, Thames Wharf Studios, Rainville Road, London W6 9HA.**

US customers: for prices and details of how to order books for delivery by mail, call 1-800-805-1083.

Please enclose a cheque or postal order, made payable to **Virgin Publishing Ltd**, to the value of the books you have ordered plus postage and packing costs as follows:

UK and BFPO – £1.00 for the first book, 50p for each subsequent book.

Overseas (including Republic of Ireland) – £2.00 for the first book, £1.00 for each subsequent book.

If you would prefer to pay by VISA, ACCESS/MASTER-CARD, DINERS CLUB, AMEX or SWITCH, please write your card number and expiry date here:

....

Please allow up to 28 days for delivery.

Signature ....

---------✂---------------------------